The Comfort Letter

Novels by Arthur R.G. Solmssen

Rittenhouse Square (1968)
Alexander's Feast (1971)
The Comfort Letter (1975)
A Princess in Berlin (1980)
Takeover Time (1986)
The Wife of Shore (2002)

The Comfort Letter

By

Arthur R. G. Solmssen

Ross & Perry, Inc.
Washington, D.C.

Copyright 1975, Arthur R. G. Solmssen
Reprinted by Ross & Perry, Inc. 2002
© Ross & Perry, Inc. 2002 on new material. All rights reserved.

Printed in The United States of America

Ross & Perry, Inc. Publishers
216 G St., N.E.
Washington, D.C. 20002
Telephone (202) 675-8300
Facsimile (202) 675-8400
info@RossPerry.com

SAN 253-8555

Library of Congress Control Number: 2002114230
http://www.rossperry.com

ISBN 1-932109-40-4

Book Cover designed by Sapna. sapna@rossperry.com

⊗ The paper used in this publication meets the requirements for permanence
established by the American National Standard for Information Sciences
"Permanence of Paper for Printed Library Materials" (ANSI Z39.48-1984).

Library of Congress Cataloging in publication data for the 1975 edition

Solmssen, Arthur R   G
   The comfort letter.

   I. Title.
PZ4.S68824Co   [PS3569.058]   813'.5'4   74–34029
ISBN 0—316—80368—5

A Note for the 2002 edition
   Most of this story takes place in 1969. The problems and the issues have
not changed since then, but we have experienced considerable inflation.
When dollars are mentioned—and they frequently are—readers of this
edition should multiply by about 5 to get the right feel for those amounts.

Five years ago, in *Rittenhouse Square*, Benjamin Butler had this to report:

Ordway Smith is one of these men who has everything. He is young and handsome and rich and happily married to a beautiful girl from a famous family. He may not be a brilliant lawyer, but he is so frank and charming in his admiration for his intellectual superiors that they cheerfully do his paper work for him. In fact, like most successful lawyers, Ordway never seems to be doing any work. You will rarely find him trying a case or writing a brief or looking up a point of law. He spends his time seeing people or attending meetings or talking on the telephone. Philadelphia, Rittenhouse, Racquet, Merion Cricket, Radnor Hunt, Gulph Mills — you name the club, Ordway belongs to it. He is a director of the Ordway Chemical Company which was founded by his great-grandfather; he sits on the boards of the Greater Philadelphia Movement, the Committee of Seventy, the Art Museum, the Orchestra, and one of the fancy girls' schools. No Sunday society section is complete without a picture of Ordway in a white tie sipping champagne with the French Consul or welcoming Joan Sutherland to the Academy of Music. Ordway knows his job, and he does it well.

Book One

RAINMAKERS

1.

R.D. Chester Springs

"There are only two kinds of people I just can't *stand*," my mother used to say. "People who are sick all the time and people who never have any money."

I thought about that, one morning in my forty-sixth summer, awake before dawn, afflicted with insomnia, worrying about money. Did Ma ever worry about anything? If so, she never showed it.

No use lying in bed awake. I got dressed and drank a cup of coffee and saddled the mare. By then it was light enough to see, and by the time we had cantered all the way across the side hill the sun was up. The mare snorted as I reined her in. The mare's name is Minnie, as in Minnie Mouse. She used to belong to my sister, but now she's gotten fat enough to carry me.

It was cool and dark in the woods. I put my head down to avoid the branches. Dew dripped from the leaves. Ought to go through here with an axe again. We followed the path all the way up to the top, to the old stone wall and the new wire, and then I saw that some son-of-a-bitch had left the gate open again. Surveyors, probably. I had to dismount anyway, so I walked through the gate and down into the valley.

"Hyde-a-Way." Ridiculous name. He'll call it something else, of course. Something pretentious. At least it won't be torn down.

I've been looking at it all my life, but it still gives me a kick, every time I see it. The Hyde Place, we call it: exact copy of the Château de Montmort in the Île-de-France, a massive fairy-tale castle, all spires and turrets and chimneys, plonked down in our Chester County hills by Clarence Pickford Hyde, the traction king, in 1903. Formal gardens, vegetable gardens, orchard, swimming pool, tennis court . . . "a goddamned country club," my Old Man used to grumble, but he never went there.

I went there a lot. For a while I even lived there. That was when we were in law school. The Hydes had given up the place, too expensive even for them, couldn't sell it for some reason. (Leslie Patch at Conyers & Dean stubbed his toe on some zoning problem, I later found out.) The whole place going to rack and ruin, weeds growing through the cobblestones, frogs in the pool, windows broken by roaming urchins. . . . So a bunch of us got together, fixed it up and lived there. We cleaned it up and lived there and the Hyde Estate didn't charge us any rent. We had a lot of parties and a lot of fun, and most of us even managed to get through law school. No, that's not fair: some of them made Law Review, although I don't know how they did it.

I could have lived at home, of course, but Ma had died and the Old Man was getting more crusty. I don't mean he was disagreeable. He was always perfectly nice to me in a sort of abstracted way, but he wasn't easy to live with. Long silences, long monologues falling asleep over his Armagnac. One time I brought a girl to dinner and during dinner, without interrupting his lecture on the friendship of Lytton Strachey and John Maynard Keynes, the Old Man released a long honking fart.

The sun was higher now, glistening in a hundred win-

dows. I looked at my watch, then turned around and led the
mare back through the gate.

I shaved and showered, listening to the body count from
Vietnam, trying to remember what was on today, what suit
I should wear. Big meeting, work meeting to set up who
does what on Charlie Conroy's Debenture deal. Better try
to be on deck at nine. May have to play host, unless they
want sandwiches sent in. Blue suit? Going to be hot. Stink-
ing train. Drive? Air conditioning. No, too much traffic,
better be on deck on time, fly the flag, good example to the
troops. Seersucker then? Okay. Blue shirt? Too much blue.
Yellow shirt? No, Wall Street people. Play the country
squire? No, white shirt. Black shoes? Okay. Tie with Bulls
and Bears? No. Too cute. Plain navy blue tie. Okay. Wal-
let, wristwatch, pocket diary, pen and pencil, change.
What else? Cigarettes, lighter. Got to give it up. Think of
Ma, three packs a day. What else? Handkerchief. Okay.

The house is so quiet now that the kids are gone. Marion
had the breakfast laid out on the terrace, but she had finished hers and I saw with sinking heart that she had her
checkbook out. Paying bills at seven in the morning.

"Hi," I said. "Going to be hot as hell again."

No answer. Looking down through her glasses, writing
checks.

I ate my cantaloupe. "Something the matter?"

She looked up, took off her glasses. "Holding out on me
again, Ordway?"

"Holding out? What do you mean?"

"Why didn't you tell me that Charlie Conroy's bought the
Hyde Place?"

5

Oh Jesus. Already? "Didn't I tell you that? I told you that — "

"Come off it, Ordway! You certainly did *not* tell me, you coward."

"Well, I thought I did. . . ."

"John just told me, just now when he brought up the milk." John is the farmer.

I put some scrambled eggs on my plate and poured my coffee.

"Am I going to be expected to entertain his women?" asked Marion.

"What women? He hasn't got any women, he hasn't got time for women, we just got him his divorce. You know all that."

"Well, what did he buy the Hyde Place for? Is he going to live in there all by himself?"

"Damned if I know. Maybe he'll entertain visiting kings or something. Status symbol of some kind . . ."

"*Couldn't* be more poetic. The gardener's son who buys the manor house — "

"Poor old Conroy wasn't the Hydes' gardener, you know. He was ours. Hydes had a whole crew over there. Had a guy who did nothing but cut grass. When he finished at one end he started at the other."

"Just the same, it was the dream castle around here, wasn't it? Even for you?"

"Oh sure."

"An American Dream. Little Charlie Conroy, lord and master of Château Hyde-a-Way."

"He'll call it something else."

"Oh, I'm sure. How about Sans-Souci? Or Trianon? Or Belvedere? Or something more English, perhaps? Tredyffrin Park. I guess that would be Welsh. What we need is something Irish, with 'House' in it. Conroy House? Or just plain Conroy's House, but I guess that wouldn't be dignified enough. . . ."

"Okay, okay."

" — and think of the *convenience!* Your own lawyer right next door, where you can make him run over for meetings every hour of the day or night. You think Tredyffrin Park sounds too much like a housing development?"

"Would you rather *have* a housing development?" I was fed up now. "Because that's the choice, you know. The Hyde Estate can't sit on it any longer. It's either Charlie Conroy or it's three hundred ranch houses, plus roads, plus sewers, plus a school for their children. And maybe a couple of gas stations, and a shopping plaza — with E. J. ·Korvette and a Drive-In Theatre. Is that what you want?"

Marion was chewing the stem of her spectacles and regarding me thoughtfully. "You know what I think?"

"No, but what I think is I've got to make the train now — "

"I think this whole thing is *your* idea, I think you *sold* it to him, put the whole idea in his head! I'm right about that, aren't I? Look at me, Ordway! Anything to keep the fields open for riding, anything to keep your beloved monstrosity from being torn down. And the memory of all those tennis games, all those dances, all those nights by the pool, all those girls laid in every bedroom, not to mention the apple orchard by moonlight and the hay barn — "

"Well, you were one of them!"

"Yes, but isn't it funny how I don't have the same sentimental attachment to the dear old place. Being *one* of them and all!"

I stood up. "Okay, enough's enough."

"I thought you said Charlie was overextended already," said Marion. "How much are the Hydes — "

"I never said any such thing! Please don't go around . . . We're starting on the biggest deal of his life this morning, we have to raise a hundred million dollars so he can pay off the debts he made to buy Darby Turbine."

"Okay, but while you're raising a hundred million dollars, do you think you could put five thousand into my — "

"Five thousand? Marion, I just put — "

"That was for last month, dear heart. Want to see the bills? Here they are."

"No, I don't want to see the bills, but this is ridiculous! What I get from the firm, what I get from the Chemical dividends, what I get from the Old Man's trusts . . . it's ridiculous, we've got to be able to live on that. What do other people do?"

"What do other people do?" Marion put her glasses on again, folded her hands and looked up at me. "Well, for one thing other people don't pay taxes on three hundred acres of Chester County real estate. Other people don't keep a farmer — "

"He's sharecropping."

"Call it what you like, you paid him twelve thousand dollars last year."

"Oh, it can't have been that much."

"Want to see the books? . . . I didn't think so. What else don't other people do? Other people don't feel they have to contribute a couple of thousand a year to every institution they sit on the board of. Other people don't pay dues and house accounts at every club in Philadelphia and New York — "

I raised my hand. "Okay . . . I'll see what I can do. I've really got to go now, I've got to be on deck this morning. . . . So long, kiddo, I guess I'll be home for dinner."

"Ordway?"

I stopped, halfway down the steps.

"Why don't you sell some Chemical stock?"

That too this morning? "Marion, I've told you a thousand times, there's no market for our stock, it's closely held — "

"But you can take it public, can't you? Sally says people are doing this all the time, selling a private company's stock to the public through underwriters — "

"*Sally* said this?" Sally is her sister. What Sally knows about public companies or underwriters could be engraved on the head of a pin. But she is married to one of the young men in my office, and I could guess where all this had come from. "I think we'd better handle our affairs without advice from Sally and Ben, Marion. It's really none of their business."

Marion shrugged and bent to her checkbook.

2.

Working Group

$100,000,000
CONROY CONCEPTS CORPORATION
. . . % CONVERTIBLE SUBORDINATED DEBENTURES
DUE 1984

Issuer

Conroy Concepts Corporation 2300 Penn Center Plaza Philadelphia, Pennsylvania 19101 (215) L08-2300	Charles C. Conroy, Jr. President and Chief Executive Officer, Chairman of the Board Home Telephone: " Address :
	Jack C. Renfrew Executive Vice President and Chief Operating Officer Home Telephone: " Address :
	P. Lawrence Lenz Comptroller Home Telephone: " Address :
	Frank Fonseca Secretary Home Telephone: " Address :

Counsel for Issuer

Conyers & Dean
3100 Franklin Tower
Philadelphia,
  Pennsylvania 19102
(215) L03-5678

Ordway Smith, Esq.
Home Telephone:
  "   Address   :

Graham Anders, Esq.
Home Telephone:
  "   Address   :

Benjamin Butler, Esq.
Home Telephone:
  "   Address   :

Thomas W. Sharp, Jr.,
  Esq.
Home Telephone:
  "   Address   :

Managing Underwriter

First Hudson
  Corporation
60 Wall Street
New York, New York
  10005
(212) 770-6100

Paul B. Haliburton
Vice President
Home Telephone:
  "   Address   :

Counsel for
Underwriters

Iselin Bros. &
  Devereaux
One Chase
  Manhattan Plaza
New York, New York
  10005
(212) 770-1212

Harry Hatch, Esq.
Home Telephone:
  "   Address   :

Joseph A. Brown, Esq.
Home Telephone:
  "   Address   :

Andrew F. Smart, Esq.
Home Telephone:
  "   Address   :

Certified Public
  Accountants
_____

Pennypacker Poole & Co.   John K. Lundquist
1000 Franklin Tower   Home Telephone:
Philadelphia,   "   Address   :
  Pennsylvania 19102   Bertram E. Cooper
(215) PE5-9200   Home Telephone:
                            "   Address   :

Printer
_____

(To be supplied)

Indenture Trustee
_____

William Penn Trust   Angus MacDonald
  Company   Vice President
Broad & Chestnut
  Streets
Philadelphia,
  Pennsylvania 19101

TIMETABLE AND RESPONSIBILITY LIST

Date	Action Taken	Responsibility
July 1, 1969	Letter of Intent	Underwriters Issuer
July 7, 1969	First Planning Meeting (Philadelphia)	All Hands

Deals of this kind go on for months. I turned the pages,
running my eye down the long schedule of dates and
work to be done — fortunately not by me — and then
looked back to the first page of the memorandum.

Well, why shouldn't they put me up there as the head of our team? It's my client, after all. But everybody knows that Graham Anders will be running the show.

And Charlie Conroy? We'll be lucky if we can get him to read his own registration statement. What am I paying you guys for?

This first planning session is a tribal rite. The cast of characters assembles, not only to work out who has to do what and when, but also to give everybody a chance to look over everybody else and to allow a little dignified showing off one's efficiency and vast experience with every facet of corporation finance. When the cast of a new play meets for the first time, maybe the actors put on these little performances too. The home telephone numbers, for example, and the home addresses, which we are penciling in now. That's a Tommy Sharp touch: we work around the clock, may have to call you for a decision in the middle of the night, and the printer's messengers will have your proofs beside your Sunday morning orange juice! All true, of course, but still . . . And I wish they wouldn't write "Esq." after the name of every lawyer.

Debate about the timetable now. The underwriters as usual are pushing to have everything done faster (interest rates are going up, the market is acting funny) while Pennypacker Poole & Co., certified public accountants affectionately known as "PP," are as usual resisting (no *way* audited financials by July 15, down in Florida, the land companies, our people can only go *in* a couple of days before that because they won't even close their books until . . .)

John Lundquist, the PP partner in charge of this "engagement," is a boy genius. He looks like a college student — pink cheeks, huge horn-rimmed glasses — but I know from past experience that this is a very methodical and tough accountant, the guy who will have the last word about the presentation of CCC's financial statements.

I couldn't contribute to the discussion, so I sat back in my chair and looked at the others assembled around the table in our largest conference room. Charlie Conroy isn't here of course. He pays other people to draw up timetables. Jack Renfrew is a red-faced jittery chain-smoking operating man who has the job of actually trying to run the companies after Charlie has bought them and lost interest. (Charlie is mainly interested in companies he doesn't own yet.)

Larry Lenz is an accountant, a former manager for PP, hired by Charlie at my suggestion: crew cut, bifocals, short-sleeved shirts, a slide rule always within reach. I like him because he never gets excited and always comes up with the right numbers.

I don't like the Frenchman. Nobody likes the Frenchman. I don't think Charlie likes him but he couldn't ask for a more faithful dogrobber, gofer, fixer, watcher of other people. He is a former private detective, licensed to carry a pistol. He is supposed to be the corporate secretary of Conroy Concepts Corporation. His name is Frank Fonseca, which is Portuguese, and I've never inquired why they call him the Frenchman. He sits there in sunglasses, chewing gum, watching.

First Hudson is to manage the underwriting syndicate and the young men they've sent are appropriately gung-ho, which is more than can be said for their lawyer. Harry Hatch had smiled when he led his group into the room. "A great pleasure, Ordway. It'll be like old times. Always wanted to do a deal with you."

My law school classmate, fellow boarder at the Hyde Place, the little druggist's son from Lock Haven, Pennsylvania, metamorphosed into the epitome of icy Wall Street sophistication. Scholarships, Law Review, unremitting hard work, articles about things like antidilution clauses in convertible debentures, a big house in Greenwich, and the soul of an IBM 1260.

Harry Hatch may be smiling, but he doesn't like this deal any better than I do. The fact is that Conroy Concepts Corporation is finally in too deep. Charlie was determined to buy Darby Turbine — everybody advised against it but by God he had to have it. It meant something intangible to him, like the Hyde Place, his first blue-chip old-line acquisition, one of the best power plant builders in the country, maybe in the world.

Darby's management fought back tooth and nail. "Merge Conroy with *us?*" shouted their chairman in a private dining room upstairs at the Union League. "You don't merge shit with ice cream!" So Charlie had to pay cash for the Darby stock, a cash tender offer at twenty percent over the market price of Darby's stock. To get the cash he had to go to the banks for sixty-five million dollars of expensive short-term money, and the banks made him hock most of his own stock in Conroy Concepts. The loans come due this fall, so here we are forced to go to the market with a long-term debt issue in order to pay them, and the Dow Jones average has dropped a hundred points in three months!

Nevertheless, investment banking is built on optimism; the boys from First Hudson think Charlie Conroy is a genius, his stock is underpriced, and his convertible debentures can be sold if the interest rate is attractive enough, so Harry Hatch and *his* boys from Iselin Bros. & Devereaux move into the line of scrimmage to do their job.

(A cynic might feel that they have two jobs here. One is to make sure that First Hudson and the other underwriters do not incur one millimeter more legal exposure than the absolute minimum they can get away with. The other is to suggest — only by example, of course, and never, never in so many words — that it is a little quaint for a giant national organization like CCC to be represented by a Philadelphia firm instead of a Wall Street firm.)

I suddenly realized that Tommy Sharp was talking too much. Something about printers. The underwriters want the registration statement printed in New York, while Tommy wants to use his favorite printer here in Philadelphia. For a moment I listened to the young men fencing. Graham Anders and Harry Hatch were staying out of it too. Is this something we want to argue about?

I don't much care for Tommy Sharp. Why don't I? Because his eagerness makes me nervous? Because his father was a railroad conductor? Because he went to law school at night whi.e selling suits at Wanamaker's in the daytime? No. I don't much care for Tommy because he handles me with excessive deference — the deference you would show a much older man — and because he finds it necessary to explain things *very carefully* when he is explaining them to me.

"What difference does it make where we print?" I asked.

"Ordway, there's a substantial difference in cost," said Tommy. "As you know, this is going to be a monumental printing job. If we do it in New York it might cost between fifty and a hundred thousand dollars — "

"Oh no, it won't," snapped Larry Lenz. "We're not going to have all these last-minute changes, using linotypists as stenographers . . ."

Graham Anders and Harry Hatch glanced at each other, smiling bleakly. They had heard all this before. They glanced at each other, but not at me. Pat Forrester, the best corporation lawyer we ever had, used to talk about Workhorses and Rainmakers. When he'd had some drinks, which was every night. He is dead now. The Rainmakers bring in the work and the Workhorses do it. Perfectly proper division of labor. Not entirely true, of course. The real giants are both. Word gets around that some man is *the* expert in some field, everybody wants him, and of course he can't do it all so he has to get other people to help him. That's how all these firms began and how they grew to be so big.

The underwriters finally agreed to pay part of the printing cost if we would agree to print in New York for their convenience. Tommy Sharp looked at Graham Anders, who turned to the CCC officers. They nodded.

The time had come to fulfill my principal function.

"Gentlemen, if you want to go out for lunch I'd be glad to get us a room somewhere — "

A general looking at wristwatches. "Ordway, could we have sandwiches sent in?" asked Harry Hatch. "We're almost finished, and if we could keep going we might still catch the two o'clock. . . ."

An hour later, as the sandwich platter and the boxes of Coke and iced tea were being carried in, the telephone rang.

"Mr. Smith, Mr. Conroy calling. From his car."

"Hey, Ordway, can you hear me?"

"Yes, hi, Charlie, just a minute, we've got a big gang here, we'll put you in the squawk box. . . ." But I never understand how the goddamned thing works, there was the usual flurry as the operators had to put the call on another line and Tommy Sharp ran around the table to take the 'phone away from me and press the correct buttons, and then Charlie's voice came through the loudspeaker as from a rain barrel:

". . . want absolutely Category One Priority on this deal, is that clear? How many people are you putting on full time?"

"Charlie, we've got the fellows from First Hudson here, Paul Haliburton and — ah — Bill Tappan . . ."

"How are you, Mr. Conroy?"

"This deal has to be closed by the first of October, is that clear? And I don't want to hear a lot of double-talk about how long the SEC takes to process these things — " The voice in the rain barrel stopped abruptly.

"Lost radio contact," said Tommy Sharp. "Probably gone into a tunnel or something."

" — be in real trouble with the banks if we have to ask for another extension," continued Charlie without a stop. I could see him slouched in the back seat of the Coupe de Ville, white telephone receiver cradled against his head, the ashtray overflowing with cigarette butts. . . .

"Charlie, where are you?" I called into the machine.

"Expressway, going to the airport, have to be in Boston tonight, we're meeting with the Technolite crowd — "

"Mr. Conroy, this is Harry Hatch, Iselin Brothers. Maybe you'd rather talk to your people alone — "

"No, hell no, Mr. Hatch, we've got no secrets from our underwriters. Full disclosure! We're an open book, or do I mean an open Prospectus? Ordway, am I saying the right things?"

"You're doing very well, as usual."

"Hey, is Renfrew there?"

"Here I am, Charlie."

While the rest of us munched our sandwiches, Jack Renfrew submitted to a detailed cross-examination about a construction problem at Darby Turbine's West Virginia project. This ended abruptly when Charlie announced that he wanted to board his plane now.

"Hey, Ordway, can you come over to the Hyde Place tomorrow evening? I'm going to have the decorator out there, want you to see what he's planning to do. . . ."

"Sure thing, Charlie. Why don't you come for dinner?" Thinking of Marion's expression . . .

"Okay, thanks very much. Say, Ordway, is there any reason I couldn't come out in the chopper? We won't be back here till maybe five tomorrow, with all the traffic on the Expressway. . . . The chopper could have me out there in twenty minutes."

Well, I've lived there all my life. Is there an ordinance against landing helicopters in our hayfields? I took a chance on it: "No, Charlie, as far as I know there's no law against it. Why don't you use that field behind the Old Mill. I'll bring the jeep down. . . ."

My God, I thought, what will the neighbors say? And Marion. I'm never going to hear the end of this.

"Could we finish up this timetable?" asked Harry Hatch, looking at his watch.

3.

C & D

Marion says the office is my security blanket. Maybe she's right. When I go away from Philadelphia I'm just another Mr. Smith until I tell them I'm a partner in Conyers & Dean. When people think of Philadelphia law firms they think of C & D. It's old, but it's not a museum. We've brought in new clients, we've hired experts in the new fields — taxes, securities, labor relations — and most important of all, we've been able to maintain a balance: a few people like me, and a lot of hungry young tigers like Ben Butler and Tommy Sharp. Every morning when I get off the elevator and walk down the long oak-paneled hall, past the portraits, past the open doors where all the guys I've known so long are settling down to work . . . well, I confess it gives me a kick.

Maybe I feel that way because I almost didn't make the grade.

One of the portraits is of my Old Man. For a while they called it Conyers, Dean & Smith. Why? Because the Old Man was rich; they liked the cushion he put into the capital account. Helped to pay the rent in lean years, and there *were* lean years, even for Judge Conyers and the great Frederick Hamilton Dean. And the Old Man was on the board of Ordway Chemical (because Ma was one of the biggest stockholders) so he guaranteed that retainer, plus quite a few others; a surprising amount of business considering that he barely pretended to practice law.

The money came from real estate. My grandfather, also a lawyer, never went partners with anybody. He bought land, mostly up along the Wissahickon, beyond the Park, Chestnut Hill they call it now. Just farms then. He and his friends bought up the land cheap, lo and behold next year the Railroad built a branch, right from Broad Street Station to the top of Chestnut Hill. How did they know the Railroad was going to do that? Because they were on the board of directors, that's how they knew. Life was simpler then.

"Ordway, you're going to have to paddle your own canoe around here," the Old Man told me. "Times are changing. When I'm gone, they won't need somebody like me, and taxes being what they are, you'll have to make some money. You'll have to practice law in earnest, which means decent grades in law school — not outstanding, in your case — but *decent* grades. And then you've got to pay your keep here, which means either becoming an expert, an indispensable expert, or you've got to bring new business to the firm. Otherwise they won't have any use for you."

He was right. I got the decent grades in law school — barely decent — and they gave me a job, but I'll never forget the morning I had to go in to see the senior partner, who was old George Graham then.

Old George Graham was a prince. I'll never forget how he sat there behind his big plain table, in his shirt-sleeves and suspenders, rocking back and forth, his feet propped on the edge of his wastebasket, rocking himself back and forth and looking out at the statue of William Penn atop the tower of City Hall.

"Flunked the bar exam, eh?"

"Yes, sir."

"Badly?"

"No, sir. Sixty-eight, but a miss is as good as a mile. . . . They won't admit me to practice. . . ."

"You want to practice, Ordway?"

"Yes, I do, Mr. Graham."

"You sure? Isn't it just the line of least resistance, something to do because you can't think of anything better?"

"Mr. Graham, I'm absolutely sure I want to be a lawyer, and I want to be a lawyer in this firm. I've wanted that as long as I can remember."

For a long moment he looked at me in silence. Then he asked: "How old are you now?"

"I'm twenty-nine."

"How long were you in the navy?"

"Three years."

"Weren't in combat, were you?"

"No, sir. I spent the war in London and Pearl Harbor, on Admiral Breckinridge's staff."

"Had trouble getting back into the swing of things?"

"No, Mr. Graham, I can't blame the bar results on the war. I had an easy time, and I came back and finished college since then, and law school, I've gotten married. . . . There's really nothing wrong with me."

"Did you know your father failed the bar exam, first time he took it? Didn't ever tell you that, did he?" George Graham looked mildly amused. "I hear you've been doing good work in the office, whatever the examiners may think. Ames Mahoney says you were a real help in that Russell case, and he isn't the easiest guy to work for, I understand — "

"He's brilliant, Mr. Graham, he has a brilliant mind — "

"Yes, yes, he does." George Graham brought his chair down and leaned forward. "When do they give the bar exam again? In February? Better knock off in December and go back to cram school."

"Yes, I'm going to do that. . . . Ah, does that mean I can stay?"

"Yup — I mean, of course I have to consult the partners, but I think they'll agree to give you another chance. Brilliant minds aren't the only thing we need around here."

"Knock knock," said Graham Anders behind me, and I swiveled around.

"Sorry to disturb such intense cogitation."

"No cogitation, just thinking about your grandfather. Finest man who ever lived. I still miss him terribly. What's the matter, Graham, something wrong?"

There was a curious expression on his face, a mixture of amusement and embarrassment. He looked down at the sheets he was holding, a two-page opinion letter. "Ordway, I never thought of you as an expert in municipal bond issues."

"Never claimed to be any such thing."

"Well, did you sign this?" He put the letter in front of me, a formal printed opinion on Conyers & Dean letterhead *In re: Borough of Riverside Municipal Authority $3,500,000 Sewer Revenue Bonds, Series of 1969.* I turned to the second page and saw that I had signed for the firm.

"Sure, I signed this a couple of days ago, Graham. One of Sid's boys came in with it, all the bond partners were on the road, they had to get this signed to get ready for the closing. . . . What's the matter with it? Aren't these things all pretty much the same?"

"Take a look at paragraph eight."

(8) The Bonds are authorized investments for fiduciaries in the Commonwealth of Pennsylvania. "Well, aren't they?"

"No."

"They're not?" I felt my face flushing.

"Ordway, there's no reason you should know things like this, but they're only legal investments if they're backed by municipal lease rentals, unless the Authority has an earnings record. This Riverside sewer system is *not* being leased back to the Borough, so the bonds aren't backed by tax revenues, only by the sewer revenues the Authority collects, so they're not legal investments for trustees. Whatever kid prepared this forgot to cross out that paragraph when he marked up the opinion from the last deal. It isn't your fault."

"But you'd have caught it, wouldn't you? Good old Ordway, he'll sign anything you slide under his nose." I turned back to the first page and looked at the date on the opinion. "The closing's today?"

"Yeah, there's a three-ring circus going on over at the bank, so I thought I'd better warn you in case somebody says something. They had to withdraw the opinion, and Sid is more than a little pissed off. No real harm done, but you know how Sid is about his closings."

I know how Sid is about his closings.

"Oh, come on, Ordway, don't look like that, nobody expects you to know about sewer bonds. I really came in here to talk about a more serious matter, about Conroy's Debenture deal."

This time I knew what was coming: We couldn't spare so many people, experienced people, for one deal — no matter how big. Ben Butler was knee-deep in the Chemical Company tax litigation and was just about to start on a Schuylkill Steel acquisition with Lansing Merritt —

24

I was still smarting from the other thing. "How many hundred-million-dollar deals have we got around here?"

"That's not the point, Ordway. We have to balance the team. Tommy and I can do the Conroy deal with a couple of younger guys, and Lansing needs Ben for his — "

"I don't suppose I should ask why my brother-in-law works for Lansing while Tommy Sharp is assigned to *my* client."

"Now look, Ordway, this hasn't got anything to do with who is who's brother-in-law! The Steel Company people like Ben, he's really running deals by himself now, and Tommy's the right guy to work on this Conroy thing, he's really a very able lawyer and I wish you'd overcome your prejudices."

"What prejudices? I don't have any — "

"I know he comes on a little strong, he lacks polish — "

"It isn't that he lacks polish, it's that he treats me like I'm ninety years old and not quite bright."

"Nonsense, Ordway, that's your imagination. He's a first-class lawyer and he's the guy to work with Conroy and Conroy's people. You'll find I'm right about it. He's one of the best young men we have."

I gave up. "Okay. But with all due respect to Tommy's ability, you're going to stay close to this, aren't you? He's never done anything this big and I have a feeling it may get hairy. . . . If the market doesn't pick up, if Charlie keeps running off on tangents — "

"Yes, of course. I'm going to stay right on top of it." Graham stood up, clearly relieved that this interview was over. "Matter of fact, Tommy and I are meeting with Conroy's officers tomorrow morning to work out a travel schedule, we're taking the underwriters on the flower sniffing tour — "

"Flower sniffing?" Even standing in the doorway Ellsworth Boyle fills the room with his presence.

Graham smiled. "Not a very respectful term, is it? The underwriters are supposed to learn everything about the company, so they go out and look at the factories, talk to the operating officers, find out what they can — but how much can you find out by walking through a factory?"

Ellsworth Boyle nodded. "Something new every year. Securities work is like women's fashions. . . . What's all this about an opinion being withdrawn? Miss Leaming heard something in the girls' lounge . . ."

Graham jumped right in: "It's just a tempest in a teapot, Ellsworth — " but of course I had to interrupt and report what happened.

"Hmm," said Ellsworth Boyle.

Brief embarrassed silence.

"Who prepared the opinion?"

"Sid has already dealt with it," Graham assured him. "*More* than adequately. A couple of people were involved and they've been mightily chastised. Let's not add to the uproar. Did you want me for anything else? I'm late for a meeting."

Ellsworth let him by and he disappeared.

"I'm sorry, Ellsworth, I really stubbed my toe on that one."

"Yes, well, never mind, it's not your line of work, it's not something you're expected to know, and what's done is done so let's forget about it. I have a couple of other things."

He sat down heavily in one of the leather armchairs that came from my father's room. "Well, first of all, you know that Hammond Soap has brought in this man O'Connor from Chicago to be president and we want to get him into a club as soon as possible, and he's made it quite clear to me that he wants the Rittenhouse Club . . ."

I hate getting people into clubs. Ninety percent of the time it's all right, but once in a while there's some son-of-a-bitch with a grudge lying in ambush, and if you try to get somebody in and you fail, then that guy will hate you for the rest of his life.

It's my job, though. "Just off the plane from Chicago and it has to be the Rittenhouse Club? Won't the Racquet Club do for a start?"

"Apparently not."

I sighed. "All right, I'll see what I can do. When do you want me to meet him?"

Ellsworth took out his pocket diary. "I'm going out to eat with him at the plant on Friday. Can you come along?"

I nodded and made a note in my book.

"All right, the next thing: am I to understand there's some discussion of selling the Chemical Company?"

I paused a moment, trying to organize my thoughts. "Ellsworth, there's always some discussion about it, going public or merging with a listed company. The family's getting bigger and more restless, we've got dozens of estates and trusts and hungry grandchildren and great-grandchildren, everybody locked into a closely-held stock that they can't sell, every trust officer, every stockbroker son-in-law telling them they'd have ex-teen million dollars if we'd go public or merge with a public company. The family is growing faster than the dividends, and every time somebody dies his executors scream to me about the estate taxes. You know I'm resisting it as best I can, but the pressures are increasing all the time."

"I know all that," said Ellsworth. "I'm talking about a specific offer. From one of the conglomerates. I don't know which one."

"No, I haven't heard anything, but there's a board meeting this week and if something is cooking I should find out about it then."

"Hmm." Ellsworth turned to look out of the window. "They'd have a hard time going public in this market, but they'd make a nice morsel for somebody — somebody who might just strike without warning, make a tender offer the family can't resist. And if they're taken over by other people, what happens to C & D?" He regarded me with hard gray eyes.

"I'm aware of the problem, Ellsworth. I'm doing the best I can."

"Are you?" He rubbed his hand across his eyes, looking suddenly older and tired. How old is he now? "Saw your picture in the paper again on Sunday. Something about the Orchestra?"

"Yes, that was a reception for a woman who's written a book about Ormandy — "

"Yes, well . . . Ordway, do you think all of this stuff really brings us much business?"

"All of what stuff?"

"Oh, you know, all these boards, committees, civic functions, receptions, pictures in the Sunday papers — "

"I always understood you to say that a lawyer has a duty to the community, a lawyer should cheerfully accept civic responsibility — "

"Of course I've always said that, but I didn't mean it had to become a full-time occupation. . . . Now, your father was different, he could afford to go his own way, do pretty much what he liked, because he had the means and he was very firmly in control of these clients, certainly of Ordway Chemical, but times have changed."

I managed somehow to control myself. George Graham

is dead. Ellsworth Boyle runs the firm. "I'm well aware of the fact that times have changed," I said quietly.

"I mean except for the Chemical Company and Charlie Conroy and some estates — very nice estates, to be sure — there isn't much else, is there?"

"I can think of partners who supply less business than that. If you add up the fees from those sources — "

"Don't misunderstand me, Ordway, I'm not complaining, I consider you a great asset to this firm — " He stopped and turned his head because my secretary had appeared at the door.

"Mr. Boyle, there's a call from Mr. Rex in Chicago. Do you want it in here?"

"No, he wants to talk about the Hammond Soap consent decree." With a red-faced grunt Ellsworth stood up. "Have them find Mr. Atwater and ask him to come to my room, please. I'll be right there. . . . I guess we're finished, Ordway. I'm not criticizing, I'm just making the observation that you need a little more depth, perhaps more eggs but anyway more baskets. Don't you think so?"

4.

Conroy's House

The decorator is called MacDiarmid: black beard, paisley ascot, blue cotton blazer with silver buttons, khaki British military shorts, white knee socks, white tennis shoes. At one time or another, he's been a captain in the Argyll and Sutherland Highlanders, a salesman of Scotch whisky in New York and the manager of a beach club at Montego Bay, but he really found his niche right there, showing rich people how to spend money with a sense of theatre.

"What a magnificent pile! Absolutely splendid! Château de Montmort, bless my soul, it makes one's mouth water. . . . How's the plumbing? Plumbing function? No central heat in the original, even now, I'd lay a bet, but you've a boiler here, have you? . . . Hm, entrance hall, splendidly gloomy, actually *dank*, what this wants is some tapisserie, French hunting scenes, you know, seventeenth century, know just the fella who could help us. . . ."

(Don't ask me why a Scotsman has such an English accent. "He's just a perfect fraud, that's all," is Marion's explanation but if he were a fraud he'd have a Scottish accent, wouldn't he?)

Strolling ahead, hands in his pocket, obviously delighted. We followed him across the great hall, into the living room where twenty-foot windows looked out into the tangle of what had been a formal garden, then into the paneled library, bare dusty shelves to the ceiling — "Books, Conroy! We must get you lots and lots of books. Calfskin bindings! Shakespeare, Dickens, Sir Walter Scott, best thing will be to pick up the whole bloody lot at auction. . . ."

Charlie Conroy seemed unusually quiet. He wiped his face with his handkerchief, the Irish boxer's face, dark curly hair, the features according to Marion more Forrestal than Cagney. The miracle is he doesn't hate me. I danced to the music of Lester Lanin's orchestra in these rooms while he parked cars for the guests. They parked the cars in the meadow down by the township road. When you wanted to leave you would give your ticket to Mr. Alber at the door and he would call out the car number through some kind of loudspeaker down in the field and Charlie or one of the others would bring your car around. Later they used walkie-talkie radios. . . . He doesn't hate me. He likes being represented by Conyers & Dean, likes being in a position to send for me, to give me orders.

This present relationship began with a telephone call, in 1954 or 1955. I had passed the bar examination on the second try and was laboring deep in the bowels of Conyers & Dean, a dingy cubicle at the end of a corridor down on the twenty-ninth floor. "This is Charlie Conroy, Ordway. Remember me?" He sounded nervous, a little truculent, as if he had forced himself to call. He'd seen my picture in the paper. (At a horse show, as I recall it. Young lawyers have to advertise as best they can.)

I took him to the Racquet Club for lunch. That seemed to please him. People looked at us. Charlie had been fat as a boy; now he was enormous, tall *and* fat, the look of a construction worker, a pro football player gone to fat — but his eyes were cold and alert. He was expensively dressed, maybe a little too carefully The Rising Executive, collar stays and cufflinks, sincere necktie.

After the first awkward moments (his father stayed drunk the last two years of his life, his mother nursed him, my father's estate supported them, neither of us wanted to bring it up) he settled down to his story.

Harrison Peabody was dead. The legendary tyrant of International Bond & Share had made no provision for his own succession, and now his empire was torn by the struggles of competing factions. Charlie Conroy was too young to succeed to the presidency, and knew that whoever did succeed would get rid of the old man's special protégés anyway. Charlie had persuaded a couple of his best subordinates at the home office in New York to join him in a sophisticated job hunt, and now they were considering an offer from Philadelphia Sheet & Tube, or rather from two banks unhappily operating that company for various family trusts.

Why did they want a thirty-one-year-old president? Because he was trained by Harrison Peabody, because he was bringing along the core of a management team, and because they could get him cheap — or so they thought. The old Sheet & Tube Company had been running downhill for years. The trustees, perhaps worried by the possibility of surcharge claims, decided upon drastic measures.

Charlie said he wanted a lawyer his own age, someone he could trust, to handle the contract negotiations for him and the men he was bringing along. Would I like to represent them?

I had no illusions about it then and I don't have any now. Charlie Conroy didn't want me, he wanted to show up with Conyers & Dean in his corner. He'd been in New

York all those years, it must have been hard to come back to Philadelphia, it must have been hard to call me . . . but apparently I put on the expected performance. I spent the next days and nights reading everything I could find about employment agreements, restricted stock options, phantom stock plans, deferred compensation plans. I talked to our experts. I sat in on the negotiations.

Philadelphia Sheet & Tube and the banks were all represented by the Messrs. Openshaw, Prescott, Pennington and Lee, in the person of Mr. Frederick Lacey, a cantankerous old gentleman with bristling eyebrows who never understood how badly his clients wanted Charlie. Mr. Lacey fought like a tiger to keep Charlie's salary below $25,000, and we gave in on that. On the other hand, the salary was to go up in proportion to earnings and — what was infinitely more important in the long run — Charlie received options to buy large amounts of Sheet & Tube stock at the current very low price, plus loan guarantees which would provide him with cash to exercise these options if they became valuable.

We did a good job and Charlie knew it. After he had his men take charge, they began to consult me about other things: taxes, labor negotiations, antitrust questions involving their distributors. . . . Although I knew practically nothing about these subjects at first, I had all the facilities of Conyers & Dean at my disposal, and I ran back and forth between the questions and the answers fast enough to keep everybody happy. But the Openshaw firm, representing the trusts, continued on retainer as general counsel.

I had never seen anybody work the way Charlie worked. He was usually at his desk by seven o'clock reading production and sales reports — those of his own divisions, sometimes those of his competitors. Unless there was a business breakfast there would be a staff meeting at 8:30, and if you wanted to work for Charlie you had to be wide awake at these meetings. A good many of the old Sheet & Tube people couldn't adjust to the change of pace. They disappeared. To replace them, Charlie brought in tough hungry young men, usually lured away from competitors with promises of stock options and command responsibility. He spent his days receiving reports, making decisions, going on to the next thing, never looking back. After lunch he slept for fifteen minutes on a couch in his office, then worked until seven, had himself driven home to the apartment house on the Parkway, went through the motions of dinner with his wife, then back to his briefcase and the telephone. His people became accustomed to calls in the middle of the night: What if we switched to FIFO accounting for the copper tube inventory? How many cents per share could we gain? Why don't we try that? Let's get the accountants in to breakfast tomorrow, let's see if we can't hit the deck running on this one! Noting the turnaround in operating results the *Wall Street Journal* ran a story in which the term "workaholic" appeared. They meant it as a compliment.

After a few years of Charlie's reign things looked good enough to put out a public stock issue. At the same time somebody suggested that the name Philadelphia Sheet & Tube Company be changed to Conroy Concepts Corporation — so much more personal, so much more . . . contemporary? And so well suited to a beautiful new logotype using the initials of Charles C. Conroy, Jr., for the stationery, the trademarks, the advertising.

There are people who will tell you that Ordway Smith suggested this change, but if he did he's forgotten. It was probably somebody at First Hudson, or at N. W. Ayer. In any event, old Mr. Lacey was scandalized, genuinely angry and showing his anger with no thought of the consequences.

Philadelphia Sheet & Tube had been in business under that name for a hundred years, had established a reputation, had earned good will. . . . *Conroy Concepts?* What the hell was that supposed to mean? He talked to people at lunch, lobbied with the other directors and the banks. Of course Charlie heard about it. The Messrs. Conyers & Dean were asked to handle the public stock issue. By the time that deal was closed, we were general counsel to Conroy Concepts Corporation.

George Graham came downstairs to the twenty-ninth floor in his shirt-sleeves and walked all the way to the end of the corridor and stuck his head into my cubicle and said, "I was right, wasn't I?"

We followed MacDiarmid into the central tower, up the stone steps that circled the inside of the tower, then down the hall to the master bedroom. He talked about new wiring, air conditioning, white walls, paintings from the eighteenth century, and I wondered again what all this was going to cost, whether Charlie had any notion of what he was drifting into.

Marion was right, as usual: I had planted the idea in Charlie's head. I had not *sold* him the idea because we represent the Hyde Estate too, and the trustees have been trying to unload the place for years, but one day at lunch I just mentioned the thought, and he did the rest himself. But why did he? Why is he about to spend a great deal of cash that he hasn't even got, to establish himself — all alone — in what MacDiarmid is going to turn into a museum, a showplace to be photographed for *Vogue*: Mr. Charles C. Conroy, Jr., reviewing documents for another corporate acquisition at his Hepplewhite desk in the library of Conroy House in the hills of Chester County, Pennsylvania. Painting above the mantel one of the early works of Benjamin West. Three-thousand-volume library comes intact from the Estate of the late Earl of Cranmore. . . . I could see it all now.

It's what he wants, an image, tangible evidence of his success. And he deserves that, doesn't he? Not a penny to his name when he started. Maybe some mustering-out pay, some GI Bill when he got out of the army but no college degree, no nothing. Tried to sell bonds in the daytime, learned accounting at night school. What could that have been like, year after year, apartments in West Philadelphia row houses, trolleys, Horn & Hardart automats? How did he meet old Harrison Peabody? A giant, a robber baron from another day, denounced by Roosevelt, expropriated by Chile and Mexico, nitrates, oil, public utilities, steel . . . Charlie's apprenticeship was served in a pressure cooker. Old Peabody liked him, came up the same way, farm boy from the Berkshires, I think. The secret is work. Morning, evening, all the time.

The master bedroom still contained the canopied bed upon its dais, so big that nobody had thought it worth removing. Charlie stared at it glumly. MacDiarmid, always briefed as to domestic affairs of his clients, had ignored the bed, avoided any obvious jolly comment and headed straight for the little balcony, from which he was now loudly discovering the tiny outside stairs to the garden and the pool.

"Whatever became of Marie?" asked Charlie suddenly, still looking at the bed.

Of Marie? I was completely off balance. I'm thinking of Charlie's career, what this house will cost him, his divorce, and he is thinking about Marie?

"Marie's in New York, Charlie. She's married to Bill Westphal, the correspondent, you know. The guy who wrote the book about Orwell. She works for a publisher."

No comment. Charlie produced a cigarette, to which I applied my lighter. I thought he was going to ask another question about Marie, and I didn't want that. "Charlie, how did you ever meet Harrison Peabody?"

His expression changed. "Harrison Peabody? Didn't I ever tell you about that? My God, it changed my whole life. . . ."

"Hello up there!" MacDiarmid was shouting from the garden. "Look where I've got to!"

We walked out to the balcony and looked down at him.

"Well, I guess that this isn't the time and place," said Charlie. "Remind me to tell you about it some other time."

I wished he had not asked about Marie.

5.

Marie

There are people who will tell you that my Old Man brought
Alfred von Waldstein to Chester County to bask in reflected
glory, or even to get his hands on Waldstein's manuscripts.
For all I know they may be right. There is in fact a manuscript in the Collection, one of the last novels, with a handwritten note from the author.

My Old Man was a character, not easy to figure out. He
had inherited two houses, both very large. We lived at
1820 Delancey Place in the winter and out here in the summer. This same place I have now. The Old Man liked to
have breakfast in quiet. He'd smoke his first cigar and read
his paper. If anybody talked he would grumble about the
goddamned ceaseless chatter and clomp out, paper rust-
ling, cigar issuing blue smoke. If we were in town he'd walk
down to the office for a while. He had a beautiful room at
Conyers & Dean, piles of books and letters and files on all
the tables, but if he ever tried a case or wrote a will I never
heard about it; most of his correspondence had to do with
his real estate holdings all over the city, or the administra-
tion of the various trusts my grandfather had established
for the express purpose of keeping my father away from
those properties. Then he would go to lunch, usually to the
Franklin Inn, a small club supposedly for writers and artists. There are actually a few writers and artists, but the
bulk of the membership consists of museum directors, lit-

erary corporation lawyers, successful architects, rich men with collections, newspapermen (and their publishers) and a great many university professors. The Old Man apparently found this company congenial, because he ate there nearly every day — usually doing most of the talking. As the day wore on, he would become even more loquacious, and by the time he'd had his three martinis and his three glasses of Chablis he would be talking right through other people's conversation and my mother's voice was the only one he heard ("All right Walter, that's enough now. Don't be repetitive!")

There are people who will tell you that the Old Man was ineffectual, that he lived in the shadow of my Ma, a truly formidable person. But he wasn't ineffectual; he lived in his own world, tending his own garden, paddling his own canoe, quietly helping people who needed help. The biggest interest in his life was his Collection.

He started it as a young man and spent his whole life on it — adding things, trading some things for better things, attending auctions, reading catalogues, and locked in endless Byzantine negotiations with dealers in New York, London, Paris, Munich, Vienna, Florence, Rome — and most especially with Dr. A. S. W. Rosenbach at 1320 Walnut Street, with whom he carried on a ceaseless love-hate relationship spanning both their lives.

"Sixty-five thousand dollars! That's what that conniving Hebrew thinks we're going to pay for what the Brill Estate claims is Cotton Mather's psalmbook. I'm not that rich and I'm not that crazy! I'll be goddamned if I put up a cent over forty . . ." and the next day he and the conniving Hebrew would be chuckling over a private lunch at 1320 Walnut Street — terrapin stew and a light Moselle — rubbing their hands at how they were going to screw somebody at Parke-Bernet or Sotheby's.

In the spring of 1934 my parents went to Berlin. I don't know why. They didn't usually travel much, but when they did they went armed with introductions to the right people, especially people connected with the arts and music and newspapers. They were invited to parties, and at one of these parties they met the Waldsteins.

Alfred von Waldstein had won the Nobel Prize in 1930 and the Kleist Prize in 1931. The member of an immensely rich banking family, Jews who had become Christians and received a patent of nobility at the time of Bismarck, he had served as a cavalry officer in the First World War and had achieved tremendous fame and success for his stories and novels about the war, the revolution and the feverish life of Berlin in the 'twenties. Of course the Nazis burned his books but they had not done anything to him personally by the spring of 1934. He considered himself a German and had no intention of leaving his country. His wife, who came from a family of Prussian officers, told my father — later, when they invited my parents to their villa on the Wannsee — that she thought they would have to leave.

She was right. They came a year later. My Old Man and Waldstein's American publisher pressed the State Department to give them visas, and Ma had the Old Mill on our place redone for them. There was a picture in the New York *Times* when they landed, the family lined up on the deck of the *Bremen* — Waldstein in an English trench coat, looking grim and old; Frau von Waldstein, a smiling Valkyrie in mink; Marie, age fourteen, looking embarrassed.

She was the first girl I ever kissed — or tried to kiss. I was almost thirteen but tall for my age. Much taller than

Marie. That was in the tack room, after we had taken the saddles off the horses. She had the blackest eyes I'd ever seen. She hit me so hard that my ears rang.

"You think you have seignorial rights over me?"

I had to ask her what that meant.

"You are an idiot," she said and stomped out of the stable, the heels of her riding boots clicking on the cement.

I fell in love with her. I still am. She made me a different person than I otherwise would have been.

Her family played chamber music together. Professional musicians came to play with them. People from all over the world visited our Old Mill to talk with Alfred von Waldstein. Photographs and articles appeared in magazines. He made a rule that people could come on Tuesdays and Thursdays. Dorothy Thompson came on Wednesday and my parents had to put her up until Thursday. He was writing another book. On nice days he would sit on a chair in the apple orchard, wearing a linen suit and a straw hat, writing in his notebook with a fountain pen.

The Waldsteins had a Bohemian cook, ate wonderful meals, drank wine at lunch and dinner, listened to the Metropolitan Opera on Saturday afternoons. (At our house we ate roast beef and apple pie and listened to ball games on Saturday afternoons.) On Sundays Alfred von Waldstein went for walks with my Old Man, and Marie went riding with me. I was trying to become a steeplechaser then. I was skinny. Before I was old enough to drive Marie took me to race meets. She was there the first time I rode a real race; she was there the time I broke my collarbone; she was there the time I won the Hunt Cup.

Charlie Conroy must have been watching all this, but he was watching from a distance and I wasn't conscious of it.

In the winters my family moved back to town, but the Waldsteins stayed in the Old Mill and of course the Conroys, who took care of the place, remained in their house.

"Didn't Charlie Conroy ever ask you for a date?"

She laughed. "Ordway, you're not serious!" (This was years later, sitting in my car somewhere. Why were we talking about Charlie?) "My parents would not have allowed it anyway."

"That wouldn't have stopped you."

"Ordway, don't you remember how fat he was? And he never had a car, you know. Where could he have taken me? But anyway he never asked."

I think that was the only time we ever talked about him.

I was crazy about her, and I got her to do things most girls didn't do in those days. Not at that age, anyway. I guess that was one reason I was sent away to school next year, but I saw her during vacations. She had a lot of other people after her by that time, older guys from Princeton and Penn, even guys from law schools and medical schools. Then she got a scholarship to Radcliffe, and I was still in boarding school, playing football and hockey in New Hampshire.

We were able to be alone a couple of times, in New York. The first time it was an apartment on Park Avenue, her roommate's family had gone to Florida, Marie was visiting during Christmas vacation and the roommate had gone to a hockey game . . . and the next time we went to the Plaza. She made the reservations by telephone and we came in different taxis and took different rooms and I was scared but nobody ever found out.

She said: All right, I admit it. I'm very fond of you and I like you physically. Nice girls are not supposed to have these appetites, but they have them. You're very strong and very handsome and the best thing of all is that you don't tell people we do this. Most boys would boast about this, but you haven't.

— Marie, you love me.

— I *don't* love you, you're not a serious person, you're a very nice rich boy who knows nothing about life.

— Won't you please marry me?

— Ordway, you're still in *school!*

— Next year I'll be in college. . . .

But it was the same next year. She was going out with an assistant professor of English, author of a book on Housman. I was going to debutante parties. The war in Europe began. The assistant professor went off to join the Royal Canadian Air Force and a couple of months later he was killed in a training accident. Her father's brother was killed in Dachau concentration camp. Her mother's brother, a major in the German army, was killed in the storming of Fort Eben-Emael, in Belgium.

Even I could see that these events were moving her away from me.

"I can't tell if your world is the real world, or whether mine is," she said. "They can't both be."

She wouldn't even talk about marrying me. She spent most of her time in libraries, wrote an honors thesis on "The Stream of Consciousness in Schnitzler and Joyce," graduated magna cum laude in June of 1941, and got a job as a researcher at *Time.* She sublet a nice apartment in a brownstone in the East Eighties and she let me sleep there when I was in town. She took me to parties full of war correspondents and *Life* photographers and English officers. Some of them tried to be nice to me, but it was no good. She couldn't explain what she was doing with a sophomore who hadn't been anywhere and hadn't done anything. One night, at one of these parties, a very pretty and very drunk girl got mad at me and said: "You're a bridge and she's afraid to burn you!"

Her job at *Time* was to check the spelling and the facts in other people's copy. She soon tired of that, so when a bigshot on the *Herald Tribune* offered her a vaguely defined job as his assistant in their London Bureau, she went.

By then I was in the navy, two years of college in the V-12 program, commissioned, then quickly rescued from a submarine chaser by my Uncle Jack's friend Admiral Breckinridge, who claimed to need me on his staff in London.

When I got there, Marie was finished with the *Herald Tribune* and deeply involved with another professor. This one was an Oxford don by the name of Somerville. She married him. They lived in a small flat off the Marylebone Road. I went up there and had tea with them. He looked like an old man to me, and he must have been close to forty. He smoked a pipe and was an expert on Slavic languages. They told me he was on his sabbatical, working on a book at the British Museum. She must have known that wasn't true. He was in the SOE. One night they parachuted him into the mountains of Yugoslavia. By the time they told her he was never coming back, I had been transferred to Pearl Harbor.

When the war in Europe was ending, Marie signed up with a United Nations agency that was trying to care for the displaced persons — people who had been in concentration camps, people who had been forced to work in the German war plants, and the children who had lost their families. Once in a while I would get a postcard from Marseilles or Frankfurt or Munich, but I didn't see her again until she came home to bury her father.

6.

School Days

Do law students still work in "digesting groups"? I don't know, but that was the approved method in the winter of 1948, and we were doing it that Saturday afternoon in the dark empty library of the Hyde Place. Sam Stevens, Mo Patterson, Harry Hatch, a couple of others; our books and notes were spread across the big table under the single light bulb that dangled by an extension cord from the chandelier. A fire in the grate, cigarette smoke, pipe smoke, a pot of coffee, everybody in shirt-sleeves, Mo Patterson also in red firehouse suspenders. Rain hammered against the tall french windows.

"All right, fellows, let's go to this next one, Pennoyer versus Neff. Here's what I've got," said Harry Hatch, turning the page of his notebook.

("*Harry Hatch?*" Mo Patterson had been incredulous. "What the hell do we want him for? They wouldn't even take him into Sharswood."

"Mo, this isn't going to be an adjunct to a law club. We need six to pay the expenses, and he understands the work. We're going to need all the help we can get.")

So Harry Hatch told us about *Pennoyer v. Neff*: the facts, the holding, why did they put it into the casebook at this point? He was five feet five inches tall. He came from Penn State. He had a crew cut. He smoked a pipe bearing a fraternity crest. He wore a bow tie and a maroon corduroy jacket. He was hungry and observant. Once he brought his folks, from Lock Haven, Pa.; they seemed relieved to find a bridge game instead of the empty bottles, hunting dogs, naked women and whatever else they had apparently expected. By now we were used to Harry, and glad to have him.

We worked hard that first semester because we were scared. Too many people had returned from the war at the same time. The law schools had to take them, but they didn't have to keep them. The year before we got to Penn half the first-year class was busted out, so we worked under the gun. A lot of people spent the evenings in the library, but we usually drove out to our bachelor establishment, played a hand of bridge, cooked something in the echoing tiled kitchen, piled the dishes into the sink, and gathered around the library table.

The first weeks of the first year in law school are the worst because you have to learn a new language and a new way of thinking. Some learn it quickly, some learn it slowly, some never learn it at all. In class the professors don't lecture, they don't tell you "the law"; they call on you: Mr. Smith, Mr. O. Smith, what is the holding in Pennoyer and Neff? . . . Not the facts, I asked for the holding. . . . Mr. Stevens, is he right? . . . He *is*? Class? (A thundering chorus: *No!*) Why not? . . . Okay, over there . . .

No matter what you say, they take the other side and make you look stupid. Some people do a lot of talking but they don't know the answers either. Gradually a pattern emerges. You boil down the cases to a few lines, "digest" them down to basic essentials. It helps to talk, to see if others got the same points. The hours drag on. . . . "Come on, fellows, we've almost finished this chapter. . . ."

Of course we didn't work all the time. Even empty, the Hyde Place provided the setting for magnificent parties, and we gave some that people are still talking about. Marion Ellis came to one of them. She was a senior at Bryn Mawr, the roommate of Popsy Hyde, Mo Patterson's fiancée. She was somebody else's date but spent most of the evening talking with me. I knew who she was because I had seen her father at my parents' bigger parties, the parties they gave for Museum people. Mr. Ellis was a rare bird, a well-born yet extremely skillful portrait painter, a tiny very polite little man with white hair, a white moustache and a Legion of Honor ribbon in his lapel. He spent three months of every summer in Northeast Harbor painting rich people and three months of every winter in Palm Beach doing the same thing. His big picture of my mother in riding clothes makes her look even more regal than she was. My Old Man didn't like it and hung it on the fourth floor landing.

Mr. Ellis lived a pleasant life but never made much money. Certainly both of his daughters developed an intense interest in money and other practical matters. Sitting in the kitchen with Marion that first night, listening to people dancing in the dining room, I submitted to a thorough cross-examination: Did we pay rent to the Hyde Estate? Why not? Who washes the dishes? Who buys the groceries? Why wasn't I living at home? How long had I been in the navy? ("Have you ever seen such a pigpen?" shouted Popsy Hyde, coming into the kitchen for more whiskey.) Did anybody ever clean this place? Was I going into Conyers & Dean?

Popsy Hyde again, screaming: "Ordway, Marion, you've got to see this! Mo is riding a horse into the living room!" As it was my horse I had to rush out to deal with the situation, but the next day I drove over to Bryn Mawr and we walked to the Greek's for a cup of coffee and then I took her to a cocktail party, and one thing sort of led to another.

"Fellows, why don't we spend a little while on Agency now? I know it's an easy course, but it's the first exam. If we could really hit that hard — "

In the dining room the telephone rang.

"Let it ring," said Mo Patterson, but Stevens was having trouble with a girl so he went to answer it. A moment later he was back, looking impressed.

"Ordway, it's for you. I think it might be your Old Man."

That surprised me. He never used the telephone. My conscience hurt. He was all alone in the big house in town and I should have been there with him.

"Hello? Pa?"

"Ordway?" He sounded angry. "You'll have to go over to our place right away, to the Mill, I mean. You'll have to cope. . . . Do whatever they say, take care of things. I don't want to be involved in this kind of situation. . . ."

"What do you mean, Pa? What's wrong over there?"

"Alfred von Waldstein's dead. Apparently he killed himself."

Our farmer's wife came in to cook his lunch and dinner, but he only had coffee and a roll for breakfast and he fixed that for himself, so she came at one o'clock. When he wasn't downstairs by two she called, then went upstairs and found him. They had not moved him when I got there. He was in bed, dressed in pajamas, and his eyes were closed. On the bedside table, a glass of water and an empty pill vial. On the dresser, carefully propped against the silver-framed photographs, a sealed letter to Mrs. Marie Somerville, c/o International Refugee Organization, Children's Village, Bad Aibling, Bavaria.

I drove over to Idlewild to meet her flight. In those days they had to land at Shannon and Gander, the trip took fourteen hours and she had been up all night before on a train from Munich to Frankfurt. She wore some kind of uniform and they got her through customs and immigration quickly. She looked pale and exhausted. She kissed me, smelling of perfume and cigarettes.

"It's so good of you to meet me." I gave her the letter. She looked at it and put it in her purse. In the car she asked, "How long will it take to get home?"

"The memorial service is tomorrow, and it's here in New York. The publishers arranged it, and they thought . . . you know, most of the people who knew him are here, the people who read his books — "

She nodded. "Yes, it's the right thing. All the old German refugees . . . You know he hasn't published anything in ten years?"

"Well, I never saw him, but they said he was working all the time, you could hear the typewriter going — "

She shook her head. "Just articles for some magazines, in Germany and Switzerland. And letters. Endless endless letters, to friends, to General Marshall, to Adenauer, to Truman, to his publishers, to me . . . Oh Ordway, I should have been there with him, he was all alone since Mother died, an old man, forgotten and alone in a house in the country . . ." She bit her lip, pulled a handkerchief from her purse and blew her nose hard. "I'm sorry. Where are you taking me?"

"I've got you a room at the Plaza. Is that all right?"

"The Plaza! How sentimental of you." She blew her nose again, turned the mirror and began to repair her face.

When she finished she turned the mirror back and lighted a cigarette. We didn't say anything until I turned into 59th Street. She put her hand on my arm: "Ordway, it was wonderful of you to meet me, but I'm so tired and so *dirty* — "

"I'm not staying here, I've got a room at the Harvard Club. The service is at eleven o'clock so I'll pick you up for breakfast at nine-thirty. Okay?"

The little hall was packed. The speeches were in German, so I couldn't understand them. A string quartet played Haydn and I heard somebody crying, but Marie sat dry-eyed beside me. Old people came up afterwards, to speak to her. Outside in the winter sunshine she put her arm through mine: "Please take me somewhere and give me a drink."

When the taxi stopped she looked out the window: "No, I don't have the right clothes . . ." but I made her go in and they gave us a good table even though I didn't have a reservation. She drank two martinis and the color returned to her face. She looked around at the white linen and the glasses and the hovering waiters and the chattering people: "Forty-eight hours ago I was eating in a mess hall."

"Marie, what are you going to do?"

"I don't know. I'm tired. I'm tired of everything. I'm tired of mess halls and camps and quarreling people. I'm tired of the Germans, who all claim they didn't know anything, they didn't do anything, it was always somebody else. I'm tired of the Jews, who want everybody to feel so sorry for them all the time. I'm tired of the Americans, with their PX rations and their awful women — and most of all I'm tired of being in the middle, everybody pulling at me!"

She told me about her children's village at Bad Aibling in the Bavarian foothills, where they were taking care of the orphans, children of people the Nazis had killed, children from all over Europe for whom they were trying to find homes in Canada and Australia and the United States. She told me about other children the Nazis had taken from their families and given to German families, and how do you find them when the records have been falsified, and when you find them what do you do when a mother turns up after years in concentration camps but her children only know the German family that has raised them? What do you do when children run away from their own mother? Screaming. Do you take screaming children away from the only people they know and give them to a stranger?

She gazed at me across the rim of her glass, then shook her head and changed the subject. Did I know Bill Westphal, the correspondent? No, I didn't know him. Well, he was writing a book about these children and she was helping him with the research. He thought he could get her a job in book publishing when she was ready to come home.

We talked. We studied each other. We ate a splendid very expensive lunch and drank a bottle of Muscadet and then we took a taxi back to the Plaza and I lay on the bed and watched her take her clothes off, knowing that she was part of me, knowing that I would never ever get her out of my system.

She moved into the Old Mill, just for the time being, she said. The IRO had given her four weeks' leave, she wanted to organize and catalogue her father's books and papers. In the meantime the first couple of law examinations loomed ahead. At the Hyde Place we studied late into the nights and got on each other's nerves. Harry Hatch withdrew into his bedroom with his notes and closed the door. These were midyear exams, Agency and Property I, not enough to make or break anybody, but some indication of who had begun to penetrate the mysteries and who was still lost. I brought Marie for supper once — unlike other lady guests she did not offer to cook it for us — and the boys were impressed.

We took the exams. The results were no surprise, at least to me. Harry Hatch had one of the highest grades in the class. Sam Stevens and I passed with comfortable margins but no distinction. Mo Patterson failed. We decided it was time for a party.

Not Lester Lanin these days, just a group of Penn undergraduates in straw hats and colorful vests, blasting away on trombones and saxophones and a portable piano. The big hall of the Hyde Place was rocking, a sea of dinner jackets and evening dresses illuminated by Japanese lanterns swaying in the smoky air and tall candles flickering in wrought iron holders along the railing of the circular staircase. My generation — too young for the jitterbug and too old for the Twist — tends to a kind of jazzed-up foxtrot, always danced to show tunes played with an insistent beat. This year it was *South Pacific*.

I stood on the stairs, watching. I was watching Marion Ellis dancing with her date, a crew-cut Princeton clubmate of Mo Patterson's, indeed the same guy who had brought her here in the first place. This evening she had greeted me, one of the hosts, with a smile and a handshake and no hint that I had been unforgivably rude to her. I really liked her very much: I liked her matter-of-fact acceptance of life as it presented itself, I liked the way her gray range-finder eyes focused on people and problems, I liked the acerbic remarks that could suddenly dissolve a room full of people into laughter, I liked the cool professionalism with which she played bridge and tennis — and most of all I liked the fact that I excited her, that such a clever calculating cat could get so hot when properly stroked.

But I had done everything wrong. I had been with her two or three times a week through the whole semester, until that week Marie came home. Of course I should have taken Marion out a few times, or at least once, I should have explained . . . but I didn't have the sense to do that. I just let it go and put it off and didn't call Marion, and then so much time had passed that I was afraid to call her, so I didn't.

Way at the other end of the hall, Marie was dancing with Mo Patterson. She had not wanted to come, but I talked her into it. She bought a dress for the occasion, bare shoulders and black velvet. She looked terrific. People cut in all the time, I hardly had a chance to dance with her. . . .

I looked at Marion Ellis again and caught her looking up at me. There was no way out of it. I walked down the stairs, shouldered my way through the crowd, and cut in.

By three o'clock in the morning everybody had jammed into the enormous kitchen. People sat on the tables and the drainboards, talking and drinking. Harry Hatch and Sam Stevens were mixing another batch of Seabreezes in the silver punchbowl — equal parts of gin and grapefruit juice floating a cake of ice.

It's hard to reconstruct that moment — more than a moment, maybe a few minutes — in which the course of my life was changed. Squeezing into that crowded, brilliantly lighted kitchen behind Marion Ellis, cigarette smoke, faces, faces of friends and strangers, the sweet juniperberry perfume of the gin, the gin also in my blood, music welling in from behind — *"A kiss on the hand may be quite sentimental, but diamonds are a girl's best friend!"* — people talking, Mo Patterson drunk and sweatsoaked, his black tie askew, hollering about Alger Hiss, who had been convicted of perjury that morning: "The son-of-a-bitch, of course he was guilty, I hope they hang him up by his balls!" and some girl turning to Popsy Hyde: "I'm sorry Mo is having so much trouble with his exams," and Popsy's face, red, flushed with gin and anger, saying "Oh, it's so damn *unfair* making Mo and all these boys compete with those smart Jews in there!" and then Marie's face, I didn't even see her until that second, something changing behind her eyes, Marie sliding off the sink where she had been sitting between two men talking to her, pushing herself out of the kitchen.

"Hey, wait a minute!"

Chasing behind her up the stairs in candlelight, down the hall into the master bedroom where she began to sort through the pile of coats on the canopied bed, grabbing her hand: "Marie, for Christ's sake, she's so stupid she's funny!"

"Yes, that's why I'm laughing so hard!"

"Aw come on, do you think — "

"Do I think what?"

"Do you think a crack like that . . . you think that's something special here, that's something — uh, indigenous, for Philadelphia? People say things like that all over the world — "

"I'm quite aware of that, Ordway."

"Well, then, don't make such a stink about it."

"I'm not making any stink about anything."

"Marie, I love you, don't do this!"

"I'm not doing anything. It's three o'clock in the morning, I'm tired and I want to go. Will you take me home now?"

Later, in my car, parked by the Old Mill, the motor running, snowflakes blowing through the headlight beams: "You don't want me to come in tonight, do you?"

"No I don't, Ordway. Not tonight."

We sat there in silence for a moment.

"Marie . . . I'm sick of this life I'm leading, the beer cans and the card games and the grilled cheese sandwiches and living with men all the time. It's like school and college and the navy, living in dormitories all the time. You know what I mean?"

"Oh yes. You want to get married."

"That's right, I guess I'm about ready. And you know who I want to marry, don't you?"

She turned and put her arms around me. "Oh my dear, you've been so good to me for such a long time, but it won't work. I just can't stand this town, I guess I mean the people in this town."

"All on account of Popsy Hyde, that *moron?* Nobody pays any attention to those Hyde girls — "

She turned away and looked out the window at the flying snow.

"No, it isn't the Hyde girls, it isn't anything that anybody said, it's just the whole — I don't know, Ordway, the whole thing just came into focus that moment, all those people, all your friends . . . I grew up here too, you know, I went to school with those girls, I've known Mo Patterson longer than you have."

"Well, that's exactly what I mean, you fit in perfectly, tonight you were the belle of the ball."

"Oh sure, the belle of the ball. Ordway's exotic old girl-friend, back from her life of adventure . . . No, I'm sorry, dear, I'm really really sorry but I can't take it, I can't live here. . . . I can't see myself playing this role, the society lady, the Horse Show, the Dog Show, the Antiques Fair, the photographs in the newspapers — "

"You could ride with me."

"Yes, the riding . . . I loved the riding, riding alone with you would be so nice, but it wouldn't be like that, it wouldn't be like when we were children. . . . I've thought about it a lot, it would be the easy thing to stay here and marry you, but it won't work — "

"Well then, the hell with staying here! We won't stay here. Where do you want to live? New York? Soon as I'm through school we'll go to New York, I'll get a job in Wall Street. I've got a cousin at Cravath, he's written me, I'll bet you they'd give me a job — "

"Ordway, don't talk such nonsense."

"It isn't nonsense, I don't have to stay here — "

"Yes, you certainly *do* have to stay here. You have to stay here and go into Conyers & Dean, you are the only son, you have to take care of the properties, you have to take care of your father and your sister, you have to go on all those boards of directors, the Museum, the Chemical Company, all those things your mother and your father did — "

"I don't have to do that, I don't have to do anything — "

"Oh yes you do, and you want to, too! You want to take your place, to do what's expected of you, and if you ran away from it, to New York or to any other place just to follow me, then in the end you'd hate me for it . . . No please, Ordway, don't do that, it isn't easy for me, I'm all alone, but they need me at Bad Aibling, they still have all these children, we've got to find homes for them, so I'm going back and you're going to stay here and marry a younger girl who likes to do the things your wife will have to do. And you'll live happily ever after." She kissed me and ran into the Old Mill, and I drove back to the Hyde Place.

7.

Living Happily Ever After

5:45   Alarm clock. Dress, saddle mare, ride. Broken window in Old Mill still not fixed.

6:30   Unsaddle mare, put mare in pasture, shave, shower, dress.

7:00   Breakfast. Marion. Window not fixed because can't call Mr. Shoemaker till pay him for job on barn. April. $465? Drive to Paoli.

8:00   Train. Can't read paper, Mo Patterson talks growth stocks.

8:50   Office. Mail. Bills. Four announcements for law seminars, New York, Las Vegas, San Francisco. Secretary of school class, send money. Harvard Divinity School (?) send money. Childrens Hospital, ditto. Also try to write it into your clients' wills. Lawyers' Committee to Elect Arlen Specter District Attorney, name on letterhead? Also send money. Dinner Meeting, Bar Association Committee on Corporation Banking and Business Law. Please mark your calendar. Aunt Philippa (Ordway) Tench, Dunromin Ranch, Jackson Hole, Wyoming: Why is William Penn Trust taking so *incredibly* long to complete distribution of Mother's estate?? Are they not being *complete stinkers* in refusing a (fourth) advance? And Mr. Tench, retired stockbroker, wonders if this not right time to "go public" with Ordway Chemical or merge with public company? Brochure explaining services of his former firm in these areas enclosed, just in case it may be of interest. Bottom of pile blue envelope marked "Personal" from MvWW 65 E. 79 NY NY 10021.

9:15   Interview with B. Butler, Esq.: B. Butler, Esq. to refrain from financial advice re: status of Ordway Chemical Co. which reports operating results to Internal Revenue Service, *not* to public; information in tax returns not to be discussed outside office; this not Smith money, not Rochester money, this *Ordway* money, clear? Sally Ellis Rochester Butler & Marion Ellis Smith long way from poorhouse so let us leave affairs of Chemical Co. to its management, okay? B. Butler, Esq. crestfallen, Gee Ordway, didn't mean . . . only trying to help . . . Okay, let's forget it, want to play squash 5:30?

9:30   Conference Room B. Hiring Committee. O. Smith, senior figurehead, suave impressive interviewer of law students, walks in late. Conversation about huge salaries being paid to law school graduates, but the faces turn: We've been saving this file for you, Ordway. Knowing of your interest in broadening the social groups in the office. The file comes sliding. Ms. Myra Rosenstern. Married to medical student. O. Smith flips through the folders, puzzled. Night law school? Not Law Review? Middle of the class? Name bother you, Ordway? Certainly not! And you want us to get some girls in here, don't you? Yeah, but you must have girls with better credentials than these. . . . What is she, a Playboy bunny? Have you got a picture? And now the picture comes across the table: Ms. Rosenstern is indeed very pretty — and very black, and four young partners are roaring, laughing so hard that Ames Mahoney puts his head in the door: What the hell is going on in here?

Hey Ordway, you should see your expression!
Hey Ordway, how's that for touching all bases? Tokenwise.
Hey Ordway, think we could get her for twenty a year?

O. Smith rises with dignity: I've got a Committee of Censors meeting. I'll leave you gentlemen to your deliberations. Go ahead and take the picture with you, Ordway. But Ames Mahoney is studying it now.

10:00 Philadelphia Bar Association Committee of Censors. Solemn faces. Cigar smoke. Committee Secretary reads report from hearing panel. Lawyer took $750 from a widow's insurance proceeds. First said it was fee. Then said it was mistake. Made restitution. Shall we ask the court to disbar him? His lawyer writes: old man, serious heart condition, federal tax liens, wife has cancer, already punished enough, etc. But he's done it before. Sighs. Speeches. Angry faces. Easy enough for you fellows to talk, big banks, big corporations, what do you think it feels like . . . Dignity of the profession, officer of the court, what will the public think? Deprive a man of his livelihood? Sick wife. Starve to death? Plenty of things he can do. Man of seventy? Must be joking. Disagree with you.

Temper justice with mercy. Stole money from his *client!* Take a vote. Ready to vote? Question! Four for disbarment, two against. Up to the court, after all.

12:30 Lunch. Midday Club, private room. Board of Governors, Greater Philadelphia Movement. Three bank presidents, half a dozen company presidents, eight lawyers, one federal judge, one labor leader, one university president. Two Negroes, five Jews, four Catholics (one Italian, three Irish), one professional Quaker, four members of Philadelphia Club. Everybody smiling. Snapper soup, club sandwiches, iced tea or iced coffee. Student riots, moon landing, Vietnam, stock market.

We happy few, trying to revive gritty decaying old town, conscious of power around table but really only representing power blocs, cross section of community. Eight lawyers? Not counting federal judge. Eight flags flying, the biggest firms . . .

"Gentlemen, if you're ready, we're going to consider this report on black business." Must develop larger class of black businessmen, storekeepers, garage operators, contractors, a black bank . . . minimum capital, state authorizations, etc.

O. Smith not listening. What's really wrong? Look at Boston. Look at San Francisco. What's the matter with us? Curtis going broke, Pennsylvania Railroad going broke, Reading going broke, Philco sold to Ford . . . Are we stagnant? 8:20 from Haverford, read *Inquirer*, walk to office, work at desk. 12:30 walk to Club, same guys at same table. 2:00 walk back to office, work at desk or go to meeting, walk to station, buy *Bulletin* from same man, ride 6:10 reading *Bulletin* among same people also reading *Bulletin*, get off at Haverford, walk in formation to parking lot at Club, get in car, drive home, kiss wife, mix pitcher of martinis, turn on TV.

Is that wrong? Probably no more corrupt than any other place, maybe more contented? Boston and San Francisco don't have New York next door. Do we want to compete with New York, where they all work like Charlie Conroy?

A black bank? If we thought a black bank would offer real competition would we be so hot to start one? Anybody want to start a Jewish bank?

"What's so funny, Ordway?" asks the Chairman of the William Penn Trust Company.

2:15 Telephone messages: Mr. Patterson, First Hudson, sending over materials on growth stocks discussed on train this morning. Mr. Hatch, Iselin Bros. & Devereaux, transferred to Mr. Anders. Mr. Chew, please call re Federal Estate Tax return, Mrs. R. W. Ordway. Miss Ridgeway, Phila Museum of Art, is Mrs. Smith coming to the dinner tonight, or not? Seating arrangements! Please call . . .

2:35 Tommy Sharp reports, constantly glancing at wristwatch. Progress of CCC Underwriting. Just back from first trip. Problems. How check out Darby Turbine, twenty construction projects all over the world? How check out forty or fifty land development deals, Florida and Texas? Can't do it. Have to do it! *Escott v. BarChris Construction Corp.* 283 F. Supp. 643 (S.D.N.Y. 1968) Biggest local deals can be covered by opinions from local lawyers. Spot checks. In-depth interviews with operating people at local level. Keep memos showing what we've done. Need more men for spadework. Talk to Boyle.

3:30 Meeting of the Board of Directors, Ordway Chemical Company. Ted Canby, bright young president, reports fairly good second-quarter results. Other news: another feeler for merger. ABC Industries, you've all heard of it, formerly Allied Bolt, Pericles Pappas, a very well run conglomerate. Called me himself. Are we interested in talking? Says he doesn't like takeovers, wants our management, wants to use us as base for wider entrance into specialized chemical industry.

What price? asks man from William Penn Trust, mouth watering. Didn't really talk price, but he made a damn close guess at our last year's earnings and he didn't think forty times would be out of line. Silence. Everybody putting that into dollars, and the dollars into his particular basket of problems.

Cash or Chinese money? asks O. Smith.

Well, I'm sure he's thinking of securities, to avoid tax problems for our shareholders —

And he hasn't got that kind of cash.

We could sell his securities, couldn't we? Those who want to?

Long discussion. Not the first time this has come up. William Penn Trust, besieged by beneficiaries and tax lawyers, wants to sell out. So does icy London merchant banker, representative of O. Smith's sister — more accurately representative of her husband's family. (O. Smith's sister gamely trying to support unemployed 11th baronet, plus their five children, plus town house in Eaton Square, plus small 16th-century manor in Somersetshire, on her income.) Ted Canby doesn't want to be merged out of good job, but at forty times last year's earnings he would be a millionaire, at least on paper, and they will surely offer him an employment contract — if they haven't already.

O. Smith delivers speech: This family business. Well run, makes money, supported family all these years. Good dividends, getting more valuable all the time. Inflation. Only answer to inflation is owning business, money machine. If sell out, what do with money? Spend capital? Just have to invest in something else. What? Somebody's else's company, something we don't know anything about? AT&T? IBM? Xerox? Municipal bonds? Some go up, some go down. Who knows? Certainly not the brokers. This company gone up steadily in value, if you start in 1878.

And do we really want to work for somebody named Pericles Pappas, former junkman from Jersey City? Pericles *who*? asks Uncle Jack, windburned yachtsman, racer of other people's 12-meter sloops, youngest brother of O. Smith's mother.

Can't hurt to talk to him, says William Penn Trust's director, who has heard O. Smith's speech before. O. Smith can hardly object to that. Do we want a committee? No, let Ted find out exactly what he has in mind.

Who is Pericles Pappas? asks Uncle Jack.

5:20 Taxi. Blue Envelope. Blue Letter Paper. Blue difficult handwriting.

64

. . . Do you think that's selfish of me? Not to want to exile myself, not to want to sit amidst a bunch of desperately unhappy American writers and movie people, all feeling sorry for themselves, all "into" drugs and psychoanalysis and wife-swapping? I hate this war as much as Bill does, but I can't see what good it does to run away from your country. Maybe I feel that way because I know how it is to be without a country, and none of these people know that. And I really like my job, I am working with two of our most important writers now, I have brought in several new writers of my own, and if I follow him to London I'll have to throw all that away. (He talks of getting me a job with his English publishers but I know what that will mean — reading slush at home, for less than the charlady gets!) So I've just about made up my mind to stay. He says he will switch back and forth this year, to test the water and apparently the magazine is willing to fly him back for meetings frequently. But what it means in the long run — it's too soon to know.

Yes, go ahead and tell Parke-Bernet they can put all the 1914–1918 letters in their fall catalogue. I think they are right; the time has come to sell a few of the earlier things. You will tell me if there's anything you want for the Collection, won't you?

That's all for tonight. Love, M.

5:46 Racquet Club. (Running late) Mr. Butler is warming up while waiting for you, Mr. Smith. Change. Just fast game tonight, running late. Ben getting fat? Ordway getting old? Good shot, not so old yet. Thunk. No, let it go. Good shot, Ben. Last year would have gone for it. Sweating too much. Thunk. *Shit!* No, it's okay, only hurt for a second. . . . All right, careful . . . good. More like it. Still hurts. Forget it. Might swell up a little. Okay, all for today. Sorry, late. Could you have them send up a martini? Double, no, on rocks. Shower. Hot. Not swelling yet. Cold. Okay. Ten minutes? Clean shirt. No cummerbund? No vest? Black tie. Ambassador mean white tie? No, not in summer. Where's drink? Hurry up. Running late. Beefeater? Taxi.

6:30 Great Hall, Philadelphia Museum of Art, opening of Goya exhibition. Marion? Faces. Evening, nice to see you. O. Smith kisses old women. Tray of champagne. Yes. Spanish Ambassador. How do you do, sir? Good of you to come, etc. Musicians playing. Faces. Good evening, nice to see you. Faces. Behind each face a story. O. Smith knows too many faces, too many stories, sees only one Goya, Don Manuel Osorio de Zúñiga according to his sign, a little boy in red velvet suit, two cats + birdcage. Faces, kisses, another glass of champagne. Ordway, can I see you a minute? Friends of Museum collected $84,000 already, if we could double that we could have a crack at the Garnet Matisse that's coming up for sale in the fall. Is there any chance we could sell more junk from the Wilstach Collection? Would we have to auction it? If I send you the instruments tomorrow could you have somebody look at them? (O. Smith not qualified to look at them himself?) Marion, in black: Sorry, traffic. You limping? They want you to sit over there. Spanish Ambassadress. Good evening, so nice to have you here, is this your first visit? Enormous emeralds surrounded with diamonds. Suntan, nice black eyes, Balenciaga? Vichyssoise. Student riots, Harvard, very disturbing, young people never realize, etc. Sangría in Philadelphia, ha ha. In your honor, I suppose. Coq au Vin. Talk, talk, talk. Sherbet, coffee, O. Smith on his feet: Your Excellency, Marquesa, ladies & gentlemen, great honor & pleasure, etc. O. Smith has done it before, doesn't need notes.

10:35   Cars coming up. Good night, good night, so nice to see you, etc.

Do you want me to drive, Ordway?

Expressway. Traffic.

Silence. Cigarettes. Tell me what you did today.

Oh Christ, I can't remember.

Blue envelope. Where? Okay, in desk drawer. Ankle aches.

11:00   How did you get here?

What?

Old story: Supreme Court of the United States. Lawyer begins to argue his case. Mr. Justice Holmes asks, Counsel, how did you get here? Lawyer replies, May it please the Court, on the Baltimore & Ohio Railroad.

Ordway, I don't know what you're talking about!

I don't either. Sorry.

Book Two

WORKHORSES

8.

The Cadillac of Washing Machines

In the darkness the telephone rings.

"My God, Ordway, who is it?"

At two o'clock in the morning who else could it be?

Ordway? Did I wake you up? Listen, we've been playing back this Hydroflo situation all evening, there's nothing for it, we've got to go down there in the morning and I want you along. Tell you about it on the plane. No, you won't need any papers, we've got all the papers, but I want to be down there for lunch, that means wheels up out of Atlantic Aviation before seven because we've got to pick up Larry Lenz in Memphis, he's with your gang on the Debentures but I want him with us at Hydroflo. Okay if I send the chopper for you? If there's ground fog in the valley he may not get in, but light your flares, let's try it. Save all that driving. I'll see you on the plane.

"He's going to send a helicopter here at dawn?" asked Marion. "Colonel Pickering says he's going to see the township supervisors, going to ask them to pass an ordinance . . . he says it's an outrage and he's right, Ordway!"

Sure he's right, but what can I do about it? I packed my overnight bag, set the alarm for five o'clock, and tried to go back to sleep.

Hydroflo? One of Charlie's earliest acquisitions, one of the brightest jewels in the CCC crown. Best washing machine in the world. Also the most expensive. The Schwenk family of Schwenkstown, Arkansas, where everybody works for Hydroflo. Sixty-one? Sixty-two? Didn't have our own plane then, flew to Fort Smith, was it? They met us in *their* plane, brought us into Schwenkstown, cottonwood trees along a muddy river, brick houses, clean new factories, a country club with a white-pillared portico, mint juleps and blonde girls playing tennis, old man Schwenk, son of the founder but he didn't have sons of his own, wasn't that it? Got a high price, a lot of CCC stock, employment agreements . . . the old man wanted to retire, but there was a good president — what was his name? Big heavy man. Wanted an employment agreement for their president.

No ground fog, but I lighted some flares so the pilot would know which pasture to use. The helicopter made an ungodly racket, and I knew Marion was getting telephone calls as we rose clattering over the treetops, over the Hyde Place — still empty — and flew toward the Schuylkill, directly into the rising sun. I didn't try to talk to the pilot. At Conshohocken we hung over the river for a moment, then followed it, followed our shadow all the way down, the sky changing from pink to washed blue, the Park . . . the Expressway was empty, I could easily have driven but it gives him a kick to send for me this way . . . the city curiously beautiful. Long shadows in the slanted light, factories, row houses, railroad tracks, the refineries still glittering with lights, flowers of flame pulsing from the stacks, the Penrose Ferry Bridge . . . we made a curve over the broad rippled Delaware, glanced back to see if the approach was really clear, then swept across the reedy swamplands, the military hangars, and settled in front of the private aviation buildings, right next to the needlenosed navy blue Learjet with the white CCC logo on the tail.

As soon as we were airborne they began to pass orange juice, coffee, Danish pastries around the cramped cabin. Shirt-sleeves, sunglasses, open dispatch cases, cigarette smoke. While Charlie retreated behind his *Wall Street Journal* — where had they found him one so early? — Jack Renfrew and the Frenchman briefed me: Screwing up the detail down there. Look at these numbers. Profit center budget. Thirty-five percent shortfall, first half. Twenty-two percent last year . . . Does that mean their profit is down? No, profit is flat.

So, it's the rate of *increase* that's down?

Right. Shortfall in profit center projections.

I did not ask who had made these projections.

More columns of figures. We were counting on Hydroflo to jazz up the whole consolidated picture. That was Charlie's game plan. And now look at this mess. Unless we can pool in another couple of acquisitions before the end of the year we might not make the *Fortune* 500 next June. And they'd have to be manufacturing, because at the rate we're going we're not going to have 50 percent of revenues contributed by manufacturing, and that would knock us off the list. The cable TV and the loan companies and the real estate deals are getting to be a damn big proportion. Not manufacturing.

Well, what about Darby Turbine?

Jesus! Eyes rolled to the ceiling. Let's not get started on *that* can of worms.

Charlie folded his *Journal* and stood up: Let him look at the contracts. Then he made his way to the empty starboard inward-facing seat, which covers the toilet. He fumbled with the curtain, stepped through and closed himself off. The two big status symbols in corporate aircraft are jet engines and private toilets. We've got the one but not the

73

other yet. We almost got a big comfortable secondhand Gulfstream I, but that was a turboprop which cruises at 300 as opposed to 500 for the Learjet. So the Chairman of the Board squats behind a curtain until we can turn CCC around sufficiently to warrant both jets *and* a private shithouse. The rest of us can wait until we land.

The Frenchman dug into his briefcase and came up with the bound volume containing all the documents for the Hydroflo acquisition. This Plan and Agreement of Reorganization by and among Conroy Concepts Corporation, a Pennsylvania corporation and Hydroflo Washing Machine Company, Inc. a Delaware corporation, witnesseth: . . . Turning the pages I saw right away that Pat Forrester had drawn this, one of the last jobs he did with me before he died. The agreements were works of art if you know how to appreciate this kind of art, crisp, concise, easy to comprehend, everything in logical order and in place like the works of a fine watch. All the Hydroflo stock had been owned by the Schwenks and a few of their employees. We exchanged all of their stock for a block of CCC Convertible Preferred, plus more in each of the next three years depending on how much Hydroflo's earnings increased in those three years. Complicated formulae for computing the earnings. One employment agreement with Hydroflo's president, George Morehouse.

I remembered him clearly now. A tall heavy man, native of the region, a lifetime in the service of Hydroflo and the Schwenk family. Knew every Hydroflo distributor in the country, seemed to know most of the workmen in the factories he showed us. Drank bourbon, talked about poker and duck hunting. And washing machines. The Schwenks had wanted a ten-year employment agreement for him. *No way,* Charlie had said. We don't make ten-year employment agreements with anybody. People can change too much in ten years. George will be indispensable five years from now, we couldn't run Hydroflo without him. So they agreed. George Morehouse got a contract for five years, big bonuses for increases in Hydroflo results, options to buy CCC stock, the usual perquisites. But the five years had ended two years ago.

I looked over at the Frenchman: "Was Morehouse's contract ever renewed?"

"No way."

It was raining in Memphis. When they opened the cabin door damp steamy air came in, and with it came Larry Lenz, CCC's comptroller, in a plastic raincoat, dripping, loaded with briefcases and bulging file envelopes.

"Oh man, have we been working. . . ." He stripped to his shirt and settled back.

"Give him a Coke," ordered Charlie.

One of the pilots put his head in. "We have to take on fuel, Mr. Conroy. They don't have any in Schwenkstown."

"Well, pop to it, we're due there for lunch."

The fueling took only a few minutes, but then they made us wait in the rain behind a couple of Delta 727s. Larry Lenz sipped his Coke and described his week with Graham Anders and Tommy Sharp and the team from First Hudson. They had been looking into the cable television companies and the Florida land developments.

"Those guys are gung-ho, Ordway. Read all the cable franchises, looked at the microwave towers, interviewed every last system manager. . . . In Florida they drove out and looked at the sites, talked to the county solicitor. . . . They're going to need local title opinions, by the way. . . ."

This was just a year after *Escott v. BarChris Construction*

Corp. came down, a case that really frightened the people who make their living issuing securities — investment bankers, accountants, lawyers. Not because it announced any new principle of law, but because everybody who read the opinion — every securities lawyer in the United States had read it within a week of its publication — thought: There but for the grace of God go I.

The BarChris Construction Corporation was building bowling alleys at the height of the bowling craze. At the height of another craze — the new issue craze of the early 'sixties — BarChris put out an issue of convertible debentures through a syndicate organized by one of the oldest investment firms in the United States. Not long afterwards BarChris went bankrupt, and the people who had bought the debentures sued everybody in sight — officers, directors, accountants, investment bankers and lawyers — under the Securities Act of 1933.

In a brilliant opinion, Judge McLean of the Federal District Court for the Southern District of New York found the BarChris Prospectus to be materially misleading. Point by point, item by item, line by line, he broke down the narrative and the financial statements, not only how the testimony showed the Prospectus to be wrong, but what it would have said if it had been right. For example, the Prospectus should have disclosed that after the bowling craze ended BarChris could not get paid in cash for the bowling alleys it had built, therefore had taken back "paper" — notes and mortgages issued by the bowling alley operators — and when the operators defaulted on their "paper" BarChris had to take the alleys and operate them. At a loss, of course. So BarChris wasn't really a construction company any more; it had become a bowling alley operator, at a time when bowling alleys were a drug on the market. Since none of this was in the Prospectus, the people who had issued the Prospectus to sell the Debentures had to pay colossal damages. (The case was finally settled so nobody on the outside knows exactly how much was paid.)

How could something like that happen? Perhaps some of the insiders really knew the whole story, knew every last detail of BarChris's business and deliberately concealed the facts from everybody else. What about the underwriters, their lawyers, the independent accountants? Why didn't *they* know the full story?

Why indeed. With 20-20 hindsight it is easy enough to say: "They didn't do their homework" — and many people said it. On the other hand, how far can any outsider go to prove out detailed information about the affairs of somebody else's company? You are supposed to exercise "due diligence," says the Securities Act of 1933. What is "due diligence"? Are you allowed to believe what people tell you, when you ask them specific questions? Are you supposed to go through the president's desk drawers, to read his correspondence files? Are you supposed to tap his telephone, or engage private detectives to investigate his past?

The case frightened people. At the rate issues were being ground out and sold to the public, it was physically and economically impossible to make the kind of investigation Judge McLean's decision seemed to require — and yet you couldn't argue with the basic philosophy: if you are taking people's money in exchange for securities, you've got to tell them the full story, and the lawyers and accountants who are paid to tell it have got to work harder and be more aggressive in digging out the facts.

And so the verb "bar-chrissing" crept into the English language. Graham Anders and Tommy Sharp and the people from First Hudson are traveling up and down the country bar-chrissing Charlie Conroy's companies, so that the facts in the Debenture Prospectus will be correct. We hope.

I had explained it all before, and they heard it all before so they just nodded, knowing it was going to cost a hell of a lot of money but that they didn't have much choice. Up on the flight deck the radio squawked, the pilot put his hand on the throttle, the copilot put his hand on top of the pilot's, their hands moved forward, the engines roared, we flew down the rainslicked runway, angled sharply to the left and crossed the wide brown Mississippi. Charlie Conroy slouched back in his chair, brooding out of the window, the Hydroflo budgets lying in his lap.

In less than an hour we landed again. There the sky was deep blue, and a hot dry wind blew what looked like tumbleweed across the runway. A painted cinderblock airport building. "Welcome to Schwenkstown Ark   Pop. 12,400 Home of Hydroflo, the Cadillac of Washing Machines." The big black limousine drove right up to the plane and George Morehouse climbed out. He looked considerably older than I remembered him, unhealthily fat, dressed in a rumpled tropical suit and a straw hat. He smiled, shook hands with an enormous paw and introduced a carefully dressed young man by the name of Bill Billington. No further explanation. The car was big enough to hold us all, and young Mr. Billington drove us to the Schwenkstown Country Club, a white colonnaded plantation perhaps inspired by *Gone With the Wind*. The huge building was cool and empty. We washed in a gleaming tiled bathroom and then moved into a private dining room. Hydroflo's Vice President–Sales and Hydroflo's Executive Vice President, both wearing sport jackets, both claiming to be awful happy to see us. Windows to the terrace and a vast expanse of golf course, over which sprinklers whipped lazy silver arcs. Two silent black waiters served lunch. Charlie ordered a Bloody Mary, so the rest of us, except Billington, ordered the same. Billington wanted dry sherry. Charlie looked across the table at him.

"What do you do at Hydroflo, Bill?"

Before he could answer, George Morehouse said: "Bill's bringing a little Harvard Business School class to us country boys, Charlie. He's married to one of Herman Schwenk's granddaughters, and he claims he wants to learn the washing machine business. We're doing what we can to teach him."

It was not a particularly pleasant lunch. We talked about the weather, the landing on the moon, the problems of the Phillies . . . everything except the matter at hand. Actually Billington and Larry Lenz and I did most of the talking. The others ate their steaks methodically, making little effort at conversation. Charlie did not want dessert, so nobody wanted dessert. "Just coffee." The waiters cleared the table. George Morehouse looked at his watch.

"Well, gentlemen, you want to run over to the plant now?"

Charlie lighted a cigarette. "George, as far as I'm concerned we can stay right here. These boys have brought their papers, and I guess they just want to ask some questions."

There was a bustle of opening briefcases, people shifting their chairs, an unconscious collective sigh. The waiters withdrew and closed the door.

— Hello?
— Ordway! Where are you?
— Schwenkstown, Arkansas.

— What? Where?

— Schwenkstown, Arkansas. You've never heard of Schwenkstown, Arkansas?

— Ordway? You sound a little drunk.

— I am a little drunk.

— What are you doing . . . where? In Arkansas?

— Taking part in an execution.

— An execution? Oh, is this something for Charlie Conroy?

— Yes. We flew down this morning, held a little trial, convicted the defendants, then Charlie and his court flew off to California and left me down here to carry out the sentence. . . . Hey, I got your letter.

— Carry out what sentence, Ordway?

— Hey, your friend isn't home, is he?

— What friend? You mean my husband? No, I told you, he's in London for the time being.

— What are you doing?

— What am I ever doing? Reading manuscripts.

— I feel like talking. Can I talk to you?

— Yes. . . . Just a minute. . . . All right, now go ahead.

— You know the trouble with Charlie, the trouble with Charlie is that he's become more interested in buying companies than in running companies. He's off on another deal right now, hoping to buy a company that will make his earnings look better, spending all his time and his energy wheeling and dealing, trying to buy something he hasn't got when what he *has* got isn't doing well, what he has got is in trouble. . . . Can you follow any of this?

— Yes, sure. Go ahead.

— Oh what the hell, Marie! What am I doing in the Riverview Motel in Schwenkstown, Arkansas, telling you Charlie Conroy's troubles?

— Would you rather tell me your own troubles?

— Well, they're mostly the same thing these days. . . . Marie, you're sorry, aren't you?

— About what?

— About Bill Westphal. About not marrying me. All that about not wanting to live in Philadelphia, not wanting to officiate at antique shows and museum openings . . . All those things you told me —

— What *is* going on down there, Ordway?

— Listen, I'm asking you a question, will you answer my question?

— No, dear.

— Because you know I've loved you every ——

— What's wrong down there, Ordway?

— Oh, we bought this company, they make washing machines, really a *very* good company, and the idea was we'd let them alone, that's Conroy's Concept, right? *Right?* Now they've got *me* saying it! His concept . . . buy good management and let them run their own show. And that's the way it was. He'd buy these companies and leave them alone and they did all right. Decentralization. It worked, didn't it?

— Yes.

— Well, why didn't he stick to it?

— Didn't he?

— No, I'm beginning to see he *didn't*. I've just spent a whole evening drinking with a man called Morehouse, a damn impressive guy. He gave me an earful. . . . Are you really interested in all this?

— Yes.

— He is — was — the head of this company down here. They make washing machines, good ones, sell them all over the country. We paid forty million in CCC stock to get them and then we — I mean Charlie's people — *didn't* leave them alone, last couple of years we tried to tell them how to run their business, we put them under some asshole of a group vice president — since departed, incidentally — but this guy, this group vice president pushed them so hard to increase production that the quality suffered, the machines couldn't be inspected properly, they sent defective machines to their dealers, then the machines broke down after people bought them and the dealers had to repair them, or replace them. Hydroflo has this policy, old old policy, they'll repair any machine anywhere *the same day* it breaks down. Some housewife with a busted machine in Keokuk, Iowa, or out on a ranch in Arizona, if her Hydroflo breaks down she knows the dealer will fix it the same day or he'll lend her a new one.

— Sounds like a good policy.

— It was a terrific policy, but it required in the first place good machines that didn't break down much, and in the second place it required profitable dealerships so the dealers could provide all this service, keep all those repair men riding around in cars with two-way radios. And this group vice president of Charlie's apparently tried to chisel down the dealers on their discounts, in other words their profit margins, at the same time he was speeding up the production schedules, so Hydroflo began letting out malfunctioning machines at the same time the dealerships had to cut down on their service costs.

— That sounds ridiculous.

— It was ridiculous, and Morehouse says he's written reports about it — he even showed me copies — and he tried to get through to Charlie, they have these quarterly managers' meetings, supposedly to report and tell their problems, but Morehouse claims he could never get through to Charlie, this group v.p. had convinced Charlie that Hydroflo was running an old-fashioned operation, paternalism, nepotism, trying to run Hydroflo just the way the Schwenks had always run it, Morehouse was just an old fogy who got his business training on the job, just a hick from Arkansas, you see, which is what he looks like.

— But you believe his story, Ordway?

— Yes, I do, because it sounds true and because they were doing fine when we bought them, they were doing fine when we left them alone, they only got into trouble when we began to mess with them, establish growth targets, all this B. School crap about profit centers, profit center growth projections, *game plans* ——

— But Charlie Conroy didn't go to business school either.

— That's the point, he's self-conscious about that, he's impressed with all these guys with slide rules and what looks to him like an intellectual approach to business. He wants to convey that impression, the efficient growth machine, staffed by experts ——

— And he won't listen to people who tell him what's going wrong?

— He won't listen to what he doesn't want to hear, that's what worries me so much. Because that's new, he didn't used to be that way. He was always a tough guy, but he was tough with himself too, didn't kid himself or let other people kid him. Now he listens to people who tell him what he wants to hear.

— Does he listen to you?

— Yeah. Some of the time. He asked me should he buy a double-breasted suit and I told him "No" and he didn't buy one.

— Oh, Ordway!

— Shows me photographs of English furniture MacDiarmid wants him to buy. Five thousand dollars for a chair, a George III cockfighting chair.

— But he brought you along on the trip. He needed you down there in Arkansas.

— Window dressing. The great man with his retinue, his Philadelphia lawyer. You should hear how he talks these days: *our* attorneys, *our* investment bankers, *our* pilots, *our* people . . . speaking of investment bankers, that working team for the debentures is due here next week, you can imagine what the boys from First Hudson are going to think of all this, not to mention Harry Hatch's lawyers. They come down here to check out what is supposed to be one of CCC's best operations and look at the mess we've got to show them!

— Charlie fired this man, this man who was in charge?

— Not in so many words, but that's what it amounts to. We had this meeting, more like a trial, really, but it wasn't a trial either because our people had made up their minds before it started, everything the Hydroflo people said just sounded like excuses, trying to put the blame on this guy who isn't around any more, and finally Charlie said, "Well, I guess we're going to have to make some changes down here, George, and I'll leave Ordway with you for a couple of days to work out the details." What he means is I'm to take my instructions from him by telephone and work out some kind of a deal where Morehouse submits his resignation to devote his time to personal affairs or some such face-saving statement for the papers, but that's all baloney, Morehouse is the president of the biggest employer here, practically the only industry in town, and what's it going to look like? And what is Morehouse going to do? Fifty-seven years old. Is he going to pull up stakes and move to Detroit or St. Louis or someplace? His whole family is here in Schwenkstown, he was born here, lived here all his life. And what are we going to tell the stockholders? You know, a couple of years ago Charlie got this brainstorm, he copied what Jim Ling did with his company, which was to sell the stock of some subsidiaries to the public so that the value of the stock we *kept* could be hocked to borrow more money from the banks . . . Oh hell, it's too complicated to explain, but about 30 percent of Hydroflo's stock is owned by the public now, we have to publish reports, what are we going to say about all this?

— I don't know, Ordway, but Charlie must have considered that.

— I reminded him but he doesn't seem to care, he's so busy figuring out a way to buy that company in San Francisco, I just can't get through to him about Hydroflo and that's why I'm so damned worried. He doesn't see this as a challenge, he doesn't see it as a danger, he doesn't see it *at all.* Doesn't want to see it. Averts his eyes. . . . I'm sorry, Marie, I'm raving. . . . Hey, I'm going to be in New York next week. Will you have dinner with me?

— You think that's a good idea?

— Yes.

— Mmm. I'll think about it. When are you going to be here?

— I'm not sure. I'll call you, okay?

— Okay.

— Go back to your manuscript now.

— No, it's too late, it's an hour later here, you know. . . . Ordway?

— Yeah?

. . .

— What's the matter? Marie?

— I'll tell you when I see you. Good night.

9.

O'Hare

Who's News

Management—
Personnel Notes

* * *

* * *

HYDROFLO PRESIDENT QUITS IN SURPRISE MOVE

Personal Reasons Cited for Management Switch

By a WALL STREET JOURNAL *Staff Reporter*

SCHWENKSTOWN, Ark. — Hydroflo Washing Machine Co. a subsidiary of Conroy Concepts Corporation, announced the resignation of George F. Morehouse, Hydroflo President for over fifteen years, one of the best-known figures in the home appliance industry. A spokesman indicated that Mr. Morehouse, 57, wished to devote more time to his family and his personal affairs. Oren F. Sneed, executive vice president, will act as chief operating officer, it was announced.

Neither Mr. Morehouse nor Charles C. Conroy Jr., Chairman of Conroy Concepts, could be reached for comment. In Philadelphia Frank Fonseca, Conroy's corporate secretary, indicated that any further announcements would come directly from Hydroflo. "We are a decentralized operation," he said. "They run their own show down there, and we don't try to second-guess them."

I read the story while having my shoes shined in Chicago. O'Hare is a truly "international" airport now; Aeronaves and KLM and Lufthansa planes wing to wing with United and Ozark and North Central; passengers from Frankfurt and Mexico City and Minneapolis stride through the endless hallways, visit the toilets, browse among paperback books, each traveler alone, not really in Chicago but in limbo, suspended for a few minutes or a few hours between where he was and where he will be, between past and future.

I had done the best I could in Schwenkstown. Although I was still angry at Charlie for leaving me alone in the enemy camp — especially after it appeared that the enemy was right and we were wrong — the whole thing had not been as unpleasant as I feared.

I did not see Morehouse after we consumed the bottle of Virginia Gentleman he brought to my motel room. In the Hydroflo executive suite they put me into an empty office and kept out of my way. Billington was my liaison with the washing machine people. He was polite and efficient and kept his feelings to himself, conveying the impression that he realized I didn't like my assignment. We worked out the bare-bones press release and a reasonably generous early retirement deal for Morehouse. Oren F. Sneed, executive vice president, mopped his brow and sweated through his nylon shirt and couldn't understand what was happening atall, not atall, Mr. Smith, and after all these years under George Morehouse he certainly never expected to take over the whole show, why he was only a year younger . . . I assured him it was just a holding operation. According to the Frenchman, the headhunters in New York had already found some dissatisfied hotshot at General Electric, but Charlie wanted to talk to him and Charlie was busy in San Francisco so I would have to find somebody to hold the fort for maybe a couple of weeks, so I did.

There was one disturbing incident. From Little Rock Airport, on my way home, I called the local law firm Hydroflo uses for routine work. I spoke with one of the partners and told him in general terms what kind of an agreement we wanted with Morehouse and would he please have it prepared?

Long pause. Then: "Well . . . Mr. Smith, I think maybe we might have a little problem here. Maybe you'd like to have your own people draw up such an agreement, if you don't mind."

"What kind of a problem?"

"Well you see . . . our firm has always represented the Schwenk family, the Schwenk Estate — you're well aware of that, of course."

"Sure I'm aware of it. But you've represented Hydroflo since the Schwenks sold it to us, haven't you?"

"Yes sir, that's correct."

"Never any problem about that?"

"There has not been any, no, sir."

"But now you see a problem?"

"I hope there is *no* problem, Mr. Smith. But I would hate to see any complication — "

"Are you suggesting you see a conflict of interest here?"

"I sincerely hope there is none, but — "

"Where's the conflict of interest between Hydroflo and the Schwenks?"

"There is no conflict of interest between Hydroflo, as such, and the Schwenks."

"What do you mean, as such?"

"Mr. Smith, I hope you won't consider me discourteous if I merely repeat that our firm will not be in a position to prepare the agreement you have in mind — "

"Or to represent Hydroflo from here on in?"

"Oh no, Mr. Smith, that's not my position at all."

"Then I'm confused."

"I didn't think Philadelphia lawyers got confused, Mr. Smith."

"Just one more question, please. Do you by any chance represent Bill Billington?"

Another pause, a short one. "I beg your pardon, had to think a moment. I don't believe we have represented Bill in any substantial matter. We may have drawn a will or helped with the purchase of his home. But I'm sure you know that Clara — Mrs. Billington — is — "

" — a granddaughter of Herman Schwenk. Yes, I've been told."

"We're just country boys down here, Mr. Smith. Just country boys trying to get along."

"Did you ever hear what Harold Ickes called Wendell Willkie, back in 1940?"

"I don't believe I had that pleasure, Mr. Smith. What did Harold Ickes call Wendell Willkie, back in 1940?"

"He said 'Wendell Willkie is a simple barefoot Wall Street lawyer.' "

"Ha ha ha, that's a good one, Mr. Smith, I'll have to tell that to my partners. Now have a good trip home, we hope to see you the next time you're down this way!"

I paid for the shoeshine, put the *Journal* into my dispatch case, and made my way through one of the long hallways to the gate where United 342 was boarding passengers for Philadelphia and Baltimore. I checked in, moved into the crowded lounge, and came face to face with Tommy Sharp.

"Ordway! Jesus, am I glad to see *you!*" To my astonishment, he obviously meant it. He was carrying two dispatch cases and a bulging Conyers & Dean accordion file.

"Here, give me some of that stuff," I said. "What's going on? I thought you were in Memphis, checking out the cable companies."

"No, we finished there, Ordway. We've been out to St. Paul, looking at Baxter Instruments, the Wall Street guys just went home for the weekend — "

"Well, where's Graham Anders? Isn't he with you?"

Tommy looked down at the floor, then back into my eyes. "Graham got sick, Ordway. He can't walk. Mr. Conroy sent the Learjet out to bring him home. We tried to reach you, but — "

"He can't *walk?* What the hell are you talking about?" But we were boarding now and I had to fuss with the ticket agent and the stewardesses so that Tommy could sit beside me, and it wasn't until we got all the bags stowed away and our seat belts fastened that I heard the story.

"He'd been sort of quiet for a couple of days, but I didn't notice anything, in the evenings he drank a lot but he always does that, doesn't show it much, but then I noticed he was limping and I asked what was the matter and he said his feet hurt, and one knee was swollen so he could hardly bend it. Said his knee felt like it was stuffed with cotton, he could hardly bend it to put his shoe on in the morning."

"When was all this?"

"It began in Memphis, and then in St. Paul it seemed to get worse and yesterday morning when he tried to get out of bed it hurt him so much he couldn't stand on his feet at all. We were in a motel and he called me on the phone and I came to his room and tried to help him. He was mad as hell about it, but I was scared. He didn't want to go to a doctor, but the Baxter people called one and we drove him over there and the doctor examined him and said it might be arthritis."

"Arthritis?" I didn't even know exactly what arthritis was — something old ladies get that makes their knuckles swell?

"This doctor in St. Paul said arthritis is any kind of a joint disease, there are all different kinds, the first thing is to find out what kind you've got, some of them respond to drugs — "

"*Some* of them respond to drugs?"

By now we were in the air, the girls had finished the routine about the oxygen masks and were serving drinks. It was only midafternoon but I badly needed the two little bottles of bourbon that were placed in front of me.

"What did the doctor do?" I asked.

"He gave him a whole bunch of aspirin."

"*Aspirin?*"

"And he told me to get him home and to his own doctor as soon as possible. And to keep him off his feet. I was really scared, Ordway. I didn't know what to do, and Graham kept saying he'd be all right, he'd just stay off his feet and come home with the rest of us. So I called Mr. Boyle — I couldn't reach you — and I guess he called Mr. Conroy and the plane was out in Minneapolis–St. Paul the same afternoon. And Graham would only go home if the rest of us stayed to finish up with Baxter, so we did."

I drank my bourbon and looked out across the ocean of

clouds. I was scared too, but for different reasons. If Graham was really out of commission — and this sounded as if he was — then who would be in charge of the CCC Debenture deal? We have almost a hundred lawyers — I'm never sure exactly how many we have — but they're either too inexperienced or too busy for something like this. Phil Rieger? He could do it all right, but he's in London, negotiating North Sea drilling rights for the Eastern Oil group. Lansing Merritt? No, Charlie can't stand him. Ellsworth Boyle himself? Obviously not. Might be flattered to be asked. No, that's ridiculous, much too old for the traveling and the night work and he's been out of it too long.

Relieved of his burden, Tommy Sharp chattered away about the cable companies and Baxter Instruments and the hard time the lawyers from Iselin Bros. & Devereaux were giving everybody, but I wasn't listening.

You're going to have to do this one yourself, sport.

Oh the hell I am!

The hell you're not. It's your client and there's nobody else to do it.

I don't know how to do something like this. A deal like this is for experts.

Never too late to learn. A good lawyer can learn anything fast.

I'm not that good a lawyer. And Harry Hatch will be right there to make me look like I don't know what I'm doing.

That's your problem. You'll work it out, you always have.

How in God's name can a guy suddenly catch arthritis?

The flight takes an hour. As soon as we landed I called Caroline Anders. She sounded pretty cool and collected, but she always does. She told me Graham was in the University

93

Hospital, they were still giving him tests. Sure, he'd be happy to see me. Ravdin 942. I sent Tommy home and took a taxi to the hospital and marched right into Graham's room. That was a mistake.

10.

Ravdin 942

Graham Anders is five years younger than I am, and he gets away with murder. He is the grandson of the sainted George Graham, who didn't kick me out of the firm when I flunked the bar exam — and the husband of Caroline Boatwright, who is very rich and who loves him so much that she puts up with his hobbies: listening to opera records, drinking, quietly screwing other people's wives. He is one of the best corporation lawyers in a town that is full of very good ones — and my best friend in the firm.

Now that he's passed forty he has settled down a little, gaining weight and losing hair like everybody else, but as I burst through the door of Room 942 of the Ravdin Pavilion I saw that one thing hadn't changed, because Laura Cunningham was sitting on his bed, and Laura Cunningham was crying.

We don't like this kind of thing at Conyers & Dean; in fact we have dropped the occasional young man who can't leave the secretaries alone, but in this as in everything else Graham Anders is a special case.

Laura must have been very young when she started with us, as Patrick Forrester's secretary, the most beautiful girl you ever saw in your life. She must have been crazy too. She threw herself at Graham Anders, which was all right, I guess, but then she fell in love with him, which wasn't. She quit and tried college, didn't like it, came back as

Graham's own secretary. Still is. They are discreet, no funny business in the office, she has an apartment somewhere. Everybody knows about it, by now everybody is used to it — even Caroline, I suppose. Laura is still beautiful, but she isn't getting any younger and here she is jumping off Graham's high hospital bed, tucking her blouse into her skirt, red-eyed, mascara running down her cheeks.

"Oh hello, Mr. Smith . . ." grabbing a Kleenex to blow her nose ". . . I just brought over some papers — "

"Greetings, Ordway," said Graham, cool as he could be. "Just read the dispatch from Schwenkstown." He wore blue pajamas and lay neatly under his blanket. He turned to roll a bottle out of the bedside drawer. "Sit down, sit down, pass me that glass over there."

Laura Cunningham reached for her purse and slammed into the bathroom.

"Sorry about that," I said lamely, settling into the visitor's chair, watching him pour Scotch into our glasses.

Graham shrugged. "What's new? Here, I think there's still some ice left in that thing — there you are. Cheers."

"Cheers. What's all this about arthritis?"

"Yeah, well. They don't seem to know what causes it, they give me blood tests, x-rays, they stick a hollow needle into my knee and draw out something that looks like whiskey. . . ."

The toilet flushed and Laura came out of the bathroom smiling, her face restored. "Well, I guess I'll go home now, good night, Mr. Smith."

"Don't go, Laura, I'm only going to stay a minute."

"No, that's all right, I have some errands, be back tomorrow. . . ." The door closed behind her.

We sipped our drinks in silence for a moment. Then I asked: "Any idea how long?"

Graham shook his head. "Few weeks? Maybe more. They just don't know, Ordway. Sometimes it goes away. Sometimes it doesn't. I've been upstairs where they put you into a tank and give you whirlpool treatments, and some of the other people there, their feet and their hands don't look so good. . . . Well anyway, I'm sorry about the Conroy Debentures, but Tommy's a good boy, he'll be able to handle it."

"Not by himself."

"Oh no, they'll have to change the team a little, give you one of the younger boys, maybe a couple of them, and Phil Rieger can take over — "

"Phil is in England."

"Right, so he is. Well — "

"I guess I can always call you if I have any questions."

"Sure you can. I'll be here."

An awkward silence.

"Graham, you've been working on this deal for weeks. What do you think of it? What's your impression of Charlie's empire?"

He lit a cigarette, leaned back into his pillows and blew smoke toward the ceiling. Too close to it for an overall picture, he said. Too many details, too many meetings with too many people in too many different cities — maybe it was a good idea that he could just lie around and think for a few weeks, because nobody ever has the time on these deals, these deals are always put together in such a sweat, whole gangs of people working their asses off to describe every nuance, every detail, against deadlines so that they don't see the whole picture.

"You must have *some* impression by now."

Graham took another drag from his cigarette. Well . . . the main problem, maybe he's grown too fast, the thing seems to have gotten away from him a little. Too big. He's trying to keep it all in his head, but he can't do it any more. Decentralization sounds nice, but what does it mean? It means you've got all these separate little kingdoms — some of them not so little, either — and each kingdom has its own history, its own problems, its own palace intrigues — how can one man expect to keep his eyes on all these separate poker games?

Group vice presidents?

Oh Jesus, group vice presidents!

Well, if he could find some good ones, wouldn't that be the answer, consolidate everything into four or five groups —

"I don't know, maybe, but in the meantime he's got some real problems — "

"Hydroflo?"

"No. I mean I heard about some shakeup down there, and I read the *Journal* squib, but we haven't even looked at Hydroflo. I'm talking about Darby Turbine."

"What's the matter at Darby Turbine?"

"Nothing special the matter, it's just so damn *big!* You realize that Darby Turbine is bigger than the rest of CCC put together? Talk about the tail wagging the dog . . . if Charlie Conroy worked twenty-four hours, seven days a week just on Darby Turbine matters — not any special crisis, just running a company that size, atomic generator projects all over the world, they've got this coal-burning electric plant down in West Virginia, almost finished but not paid for — "

"But they've got their own management — "

"They *had* their own management, men who'd been with them twenty, thirty years, they weren't gung-ho enough for Charlie, he went out and hired new people, people who want to do everything the way it's done at Westinghouse or GE, he changed the accounting methods to hypo the earnings — "

"Didn't leave them alone to run their own show?"

Graham Anders shook his head, reached out to extinguish the cigarette, sank back into the pillows. "Well, you asked me. But what the hell, is this our job? Are we financial analysts? Are we management consultants? We're his lawyers. We give legal advice, we help prepare the registration statement. Let Charlie run his companies . . ."

"When are you going to file the registration statement with the SEC?"

"Have to file this month, or the financials will be stale. They've got a draft at the printers, the first proof should be distributed tomorrow, I guess we'll get a day to read it and then a work session the following day — is that Thursday? I've lost track of time."

"How long will it sit at the SEC?"

"Few weeks? Shouldn't be too long because there aren't many issues coming in this lousy market. . . . Ordway, you think First Hudson can do it?"

"Do what?"

"Sell these CCC Debentures."

"You mean they'd let us do all this work, months and months of work, lawyers, accountants, printers, teams of people flying around in airplanes — and then they won't do the deal?"

"Ordway, the underwriters are not on the hook until they sign the Underwriting Agreement, which they do on the morning the registration statement becomes effective — when the SEC has cleared everything and all the work's been done — that's when you sign with the underwriters."

"Yes, I know that."

"And if they haven't sold enough bonds — okay, theoretically they're not allowed to 'sell' them until the registration is effective — if they haven't got enough of what they call 'indications of interest,' if they don't think they can move the bonds, well . . ."

"First Hudson would walk away from the deal?"

"Been known to happen."

"A deal this size? A firm like First Hudson?"

"Not yet, but the times aren't good, Ordway. This bear market has been killing the brokers. Last year they spent fortunes to cope with their back office problems, hired people to deal with the volume of business, installed computers to handle the bookkeeping, this year they've got to pay for all that but now the volume's dried up, no trading commissions and damned little underwriting. So their expenses are way up and their income is way down — "

"My God, they must be rubbing their hands at the thought of a hundred-million-dollar bond issue."

"Sure. If they can sell it. But what happens if they get stuck with it? Remember they've got to borrow the money to carry the issue while they're on the hook for it. If they get stuck with something this big, and it doesn't move . . . well, it might choke them. And they know it."

A pause while we contemplated the future. Sounds of television from the next room.

I stood up. "Well, as you say, that's not our department. All we can do for Charlie is tell him what the law is and provide faultless paperwork."

"Agreed. How about another drink?"

"No thanks, I came right from the airport, better head for home. So long, hotshot, I'll call you. . . . How the hell could you catch arthritis, of all the crazy things?"

"Damned if I know, maybe these horse doctors will figure

it out. . . . Call themselves rheumatologists, did you know that?"

He lay there in his blue pajamas and looked at me in a funny way, and then I said something I shouldn't have. I said: "You're really *all right*, aren't you?"

He looked at me. "You're thinking about Pat Forrester."

I nodded.

"Well, I'm not like Pat. I'm not driving my car into any turnpike abutment. I've got my problems, but I can handle them."

"Glad to hear that."

"And you can handle yours."

"What's that supposed to mean?"

"Don't sell yourself short, Ordway. You're a good lawyer. You've got it in your head that you're some kind of . . . I don't know, lightweight, bullshitter, front man, party boy. But you're not. Not any more. You're a good lawyer and you can run this deal of yours just as well as I can, but you've got to believe it yourself."

"It's nice to hear you say that, but I'm not sure the world agrees with you."

"Never mind about the world. It's what you think of yourself that counts. . . . Tell that redhead at the desk I need more ice." He waved goodbye and I closed the door.

11.

Manhattan

Article IV. The obligations of the Underwriters here-
under are subject to the accuracy of and compliance with
the representations, warranties and agreements of the com-
pany herein contained and to the satisfaction, on or prior
to the Closing Date, of the following additional terms and
conditions:
   (a) The Registration Statement shall have become effec-
tive not later than 5:30 o'clock P.M. New York City time on
the date of this Agreement, or . . .

Boilerplate is what we call these provisions. Locked into
type, the same words for every deal.

   (b) No stop order suspending the effectiveness of the
Registrations Statement shall be in effect.

More boilerplate. My eye skipped down to see what we
would be on the hook for.

   (d) The Underwriters shall have received, on the Closing
Date, a favorable opinion (in form satisfactory to Messrs.
Iselin Bros. & Devereaux, counsel for the Underwriters)
dated the Closing Date, of Messrs. Conyers & Dean, coun-
sel for the Company, to the effect that:
   (1) The Company has full right and power to enter
into this Agreement and to issue, sell and deliver the
Debentures being sold by it . . .

Okay.

(2) *The Indenture has been duly qualified under the Trust Indenture Act of 1939* . . .

Okay. My eye skipped down the lines of type.

(4) *The Debentures will (when duly executed, authenticated and paid-for) constitute valid and legally binding obligations of the Company in accordance with their terms* . . .

This is the Underwriting Agreement, the contract between Conroy Concepts Corporation and First Hudson as representative of a syndicate of underwriters. It won't be signed until the very last minute, when the deal has cleared the SEC and is all set to go, but then of course there won't be time to negotiate anything but the interest rate of the Debentures and the price at which they can be converted into stock, so the form of the agreement has to be filed with the SEC now and shown to all the underwriting firms. Graham Anders and Tommy Sharp had already reviewed the proof, Harry Hatch had agreed to a few changes, and now I was supposed to approve these.

As I said, these agreements are supposed to be standard, the same for every deal, but the people who work with them all the time expect a certain amount of ritual — little gavottes danced by the lawyers to demonstrate their skills. Counsel for the company must deliver a broad opinion as to the legality of the securities being sold and the accuracy of the offering Prospectus, and the independent accountants hired by the company have to supply what is called a "comfort letter" saying, in effect, that the financial statements they have certified are correct, and that since the date of the last audit nothing terrible has happened to the company — so far as they know. Of course the underwriters want as much protection as they can get, while the accountants know that these letters put their reputations and their personal fortunes on the line, so they are very, very careful what they agree to say, and sometimes the comfort they give carries a chill.

(7) *The Company and each Significant Subsidiary has been duly incorporated and is a validly existing corporation . . .*

Boilerplate.

(8) *The Registration statement and Prospectus* [Here was where Harry Hatch apparently made a change that Graham Anders asked for] *comply as the form in all material respects with the Securities Act of 1933 and the Trust Indenture Act of 1939 and the rules and regulations of the Securities and Exchange Commission relating to registration statements and prospectuses . . . such counsel know of no facts that lead them to believe that the Registration Statement contains any untrue statement of a material fact or omits to state a material fact required to be stated therein or necessary in order to make the statements therein, in the light of the circumstances under which they were made, not misleading . . .*

Contains no untrue statement of a material fact nor omits to state a material fact necessary in order to make the statements — in the light of the circumstances under which they were made — not misleading . . . exquisite convolutions of thought, the magic words of federal securities law, familiar even to me. We don't of course cover the financial statements with our opinion, and Graham had insisted that this exception be expanded: Conyers & Dean was also giving no opinion as to the statistical information under the caption "Business" in the Prospectus, because there is no way for us to check what proportion of CCC's business is represented by Darby Turbine, by Hydroflo, by the cable TV companies, or by any of the other subsidiaries.

(12) *There are no claims, actions, suits or proceedings known to such counsel threatened or pending against the Company or a Significant Subsidiary in any court or before any government body, which might materially affect the business of the Company or any of the Significant Subsidiaries, or their financial condition on a consolidated basis, which are not adequately disclosed in the Registration Statement and Prospectus . . .*

Boilerplate. We have to give them that.

"Okay, Harry, I think we can live with this."

"Call the printer," he said, not even looking up ·from the proof of the Prospectus, and one of his young lawyers reached for the telephone.

A dozen people worked around the big table. Behind us, a fantastic view of lower Manhattan, the East River, the Brooklyn Bridge, the whole city spread out in the blazing afternoon. Like many "Wall Street" firms, the Messrs. Iselin Bros. & Devereaux had abandoned their gloomy old quarters between the graveyard and the river. One block north and five hundred feet higher, they now occupy several floors of beige carpets, Danish furniture and sunlight.

Every registration statement consists of three parts. Part I is the Prospectus, the only thing the investor ever sees and therefore the crucial element; Part II contains some additional information and supporting financial schedules. The third part consists of exhibits, huge piles of documents such as the corporate charter, the trust indenture, all material contracts — and the underwriting agreements. Since I had given clearance on these, the exhibit package could now be assembled.

The others were going over the Prospectus line by line. Having worked on it for six weeks, they seemed to know it by heart. The boys from First Hudson were still asking for changes: could we say Baxter "manufactures" electric pressure valves?

"What's the matter with 'makes'?" I asked.

" 'Manufactures' is what you usually see . . .," sliding two other Prospectuses across the table . . .

We had been at it since ten o'clock in the morning. Paper cups and uneaten pickles, the remains of our sandwich lunch, were heaped into a cardboard box on the floor. At one end of the room Tommy Sharp cradled a telephone against his ear, the proof on the table before him; copies had been delivered to CCC's subsidiaries all over the country, and now Tommy was calling the responsible officers to pick up last-minute corrections.

"Fellows, I think we'd better lay off these cosmetic changes now," said Harry Hatch. "If this thing doesn't get filed tomorrow, the financials will be stale and we'll have to start from scratch."

I looked at him over there, sleeves of his Brooks Brothers shirt rolled up to the biceps, gold Cross pencil in his hand, crisp, self-confident, the battle-polished colonel among his troops. Maroon corduroy jacket was gone, bow tie was gone, the kid from the Penn State Sigma Chi house was gone. This was somebody else. Once in a while younger lawyers came in ("Harry, I'm sorry to bother you"), murmured into his ear, put papers in front of him: other deals, more important than ours, trouble with Chrysler's proxy

statement, with the Eurobonds of the Mobil Oil Company
. . . Twice he was called out to the telephone.

The work went on. "Okay, let's go to the 'Management' section," said Harry Hatch. "Do I understand these stock options are still screwed up? Why don't they tie into the financials?"

Tommy Sharp was at my shoulder. "Could I see you a minute?"

I got up and walked to the other end of the room with him.

"Ordway, I can't get any response from Hydroflo."

"What do you mean? Who'd you talk to?"

"Well, their treasurer was supposed to review the proof, but now they say he's on a business trip and nobody seems to know anything, and I tried to reach Mr. Sneed but he isn't there either. . . . I don't know these guys personally — "

"All right, let me give it a try." I was glad to have something to do. As I placed the call with the Iselin Bros. operator, she said: "Oh, Mr. Smith from Conyers & Dean? We've got a call waiting for you."

It was Marion. "Am I to understand you're still in New York? Do you know what time it is?"

The time was six-thirty, and had I forgotten about the Mahoneys' dinner? For the Shepleys? Buck's been made president of his company —

Of course I had forgotten. "I'm terribly sorry, but there's nothing I can do about it now. Will you call Mary and explain? These guys are used to terribly long hours, it's the only way they can get the job done. I'll write a note tomorrow."

"They really need you there, do they?"

"I feel it's my job to be here, yes."

"Are you going to be home tonight?"

"Well, I'm not sure how long it's going to take."

"All right, Ordway. I'll handle the Mahoneys." She hung up.

The call to Schwenkstown went through. It was a little after five-thirty down there, and they couldn't seem to find anybody. Mr. Sneed was gone for the day. Mr. Billington was also gone. Mr. Sneed's secretary was not answering her phone, but it's five-thirty, you see. Ahm truly sorry, operator, would the gentleman call back t'morrah?

"I want to speak to the highest ranking officer that's still in the building."

"The highest ranking officer?"

The long distance operator interrupted to confuse matters. Who did I want to speak to? I told them I would speak to anybody, put the call through.

The Hydroflo operator came back. Who was calling, please?

I gave my name.

A moment later: What was I calling in reference to, please?

"Young lady, will you tell that gentleman if he doesn't take this call *this instant*, he is going to regret it for a long, long time. Will you tell him I said that, please?"

Then I was talking to a wary young man who identified himself as an assistant vice president in the engineering department.

"Mr. Hollingsworth, do you know who Charles C. Conroy is?"

Yessir, he did.

"Mr. Hollingsworth, I am Mr. Conroy's personal attorney, I am working on a registration statement for a hundred-million-dollar bond issue that has to be printed tonight and filed with the Securities and Exchange Commission before five-thirty tomorrow afternoon. If it is for any reason not filed by then, certain information in it becomes stale, the job has to be done over, and my client's company, of which Hydroflo is a part, will have wasted a couple of months of work and maybe a hundred thousand dollars in expenses. Are you with me so far?"

He was trying to follow me, yes sir.

"Now some officers of Hydroflo are supposed to review a proof of the Prospectus contained in this Registration Statement, the thing we have to print tonight and file tomorrow. For some reason we can't get through to them, so I want to locate Oren Sneed. Do you know where Oren Sneed is? The operators have tried his home and he isn't there either."

Mr. Hollingsworth did not know where Oren Sneed was.

"Mr. Hollingsworth, I want you to find Oren Sneed and I want you to find him within the next hour. Is that clear? I don't care whether he's at a dinner party or on a business trip or where he is, but I want you to find him and have him call me at this number. Is that entirely clear?"

Yes sir. It was clear all right.

Tommy Sharp touched my shoulder. "Better give him the printer's number." He wrote it down and I gave it to Hollingsworth. I hung up.

"That ought to do the trick," said Tommy Sharp.

"I hope so," I said, but I was worried.

They worked over the Prospectus for another hour, then gave it to the printer's messenger. No word from Schwenkstown. At the Hydroflo plant, a watchman answered the telephone.

"Let's go eat," said Harry Hatch.

The brass plate beside the door says Delmonico's, but everybody calls it Oscar's, a lonely oasis in the desert that is Wall Street at night. At the bar, a row of overdressed young men with sideburns, talking big deals. In the dining room, red plush *à la* Diamond Jim Brady, violins, working teams eating dinner.

"Ordway, are you really coming to the printer?" murmured Tommy Sharp.

"If Graham were here, wouldn't he be going to the printer?"

"Not necessarily, not if there aren't any problems."

"I think I'll stick around. Is there another bed in your hotel room?"

"Oh sure, Ordway, but I'll go call for another room if you're really going to stay."

Cocktails, Oysters Rockefeller, Prime Ribs. Harry Hatch dominated the table with stories about other deals. I wondered how I could reach Charlie Conroy if I needed instructions. Larry Lenz, the comptroller, was working with us, but he hadn't seen Charlie for a week. They had told him we would file tomorrow, so he considered it as good as done. When Charlie gave an order, the order was carried out; no excuses were ever given or accepted. But why wait to file on the last day? "Timetable slippage," was Tommy Sharp's explanation; the underwriters blamed the Company, the Company blamed one of the accounting firms, that firm blamed the other accounting firm responsible for auditing Baxter Instruments, those accountants blamed poor inventory control at Baxter. . . .

Two limousines from the printer were waiting at the door. They drove us to a loft building in Little Italy. Elevators, security guards, another plush boardroom, telephones, a well-stocked bar. The proofs were coming down already, but the pages were out of order and soon the table was covered with what looked to me like a shambles. The younger men sat down to "slug" the pages, reading the first word of each line to make sure that no line had been dropped when changes were made. In one corner, Larry Lenz and the accountants pored over the financial statements. Harry Hatch, Tommy Sharp and one of the underwriters checked the changes methodically, still tinkering, still finding things ("Hey what's this Note 2 under the cap table? Didn't we decide to break out all the bank loans separately? . . ."), still sending changes back upstairs for new proofs. I tried to read the proofs for sense, to see if the Prospectus made any sense to fresh eyes, but I wasn't accomplishing much until one of the printers came in to report a long-distance call for me.

— Hello Mr. Smith, this is Oren Sneed, Hydroflo Washing Machines.

— Well, it's good to hear from you, Mr. Sneed.

— Been trying to get ahold of you. . . .

— That's funny, I've been trying to get hold of you too. Have you any comments on the proof?

— What's that?

— The proof of the Prospectus that was sent down to your treasurer. We'd like to have your comments on the Hydroflo section, are there any changes or corrections, did they describe Hydroflo correctly?

— Oh, I don't know anything about that, Mr. Smith, I'm calling about this lawsuit here?

— What lawsuit?

— Well, they served me with a complaint this afternoon . . .

— Who did?

— Well, the U.S. Marshal out of Fort Smith, he called and said could he come over and serve me with this complaint, and then he came over.

— Mr. Sneed, where is this complaint?

— Got it right here.

— Will you read it to me please?

— The whole thing?

— How long is it?

— Oh, looks like . . . ten, twelve pages —

— Start reading, will you please?

In the United States District Court for the Western District of Arkansas . . . Civil Action number . . . Long list of names, with the name Schwenk reappearing frequently . . . Annie Cantrell Schwenk, Rhoda Schwenk Donahue, Farmers National Bank of Little Rock as Trustee u/d/t Herman W. Schwenk . . . Clara Schwenk Billington . . . as Stockholders of Hydroflo Washing Machine Co. on behalf of Hydroflo Washing Machine Co. and all other minority stockholders thereof, *Plaintiffs*, versus Conroy Concepts Corporation, Charles C. Conroy, Jr. . . . all Directors and Executive Officers of Conroy Concepts Corporation, *Defendants* . . .

I listened as the flat homely voice droned on, feeling deep deep in my bowels the first twinge of panic: You saw this coming, subconsciously you *knew* something like this was in the wind, you knew it and you couldn't (or wouldn't) focus on it, bring it out, look at it, do something to avert it or at least anticipate it, make a plan, and now here it is, the muzzle pointed right between your eyes.

The others watched me listening to Oren Sneed.

One of Charlie Conroy's concepts was coming home to roost. When we first bought Hydroflo from the Schwenks, we bought the whole thing — all the stock. A few years later we copied what was really Jimmy Ling's idea; we sold about a third of Hydroflo's stock to the public, through underwriters. Hydroflo was going great guns, the stock in the hands of the public went to twenty-five times Hydroflo's earnings. Although the accountants would not allow Charlie to "write up" the book value of the Hydroflo stock retained by CCC, the market value of these shares was enormously increased. This in turn meant that Charlie could borrow more money for new acquisitions — especially for Darby Turbine.

What's wrong with that? What's wrong with that appears to be that the Schwenks have been buying back into Hydroflo, quietly buying Hydroflo stock in the open market.

Why would they do that? First they sell it to us, then they buy it back? The reasons came over the telephone, in the Arkansas twang of Oren Sneed, reading it .slowly, reading it like a laundry list, reading the careful paragraphs constructed by excellent lawyers — and I did not have to wait for the signature on the complaint to guess which lawyers they were. We're just country boys, Mr. Smith. Just country boys trying to get along!

The Schwenks thought that Charlie was ruining Hydroflo.

The complaint stated what we call a derivative action, brought on behalf of Hydroflo itself and all minority stockholders against Charlie Conroy and CCC and CCC's top people; the charge was mismanagement. It was the same story that Morehouse poured out over the bottle of Virginia Gentleman, plus a good many other things. CCC was destroying Hydroflo's dealer network; CCC was destroying Hydroflo's principal asset, the reputation of its washing machines, by selling too many defective ones; CCC has forced out Morehouse as a scapegoat for its own mistakes, thus impeding Hydroflo's future growth; CCC had borrowed money from Hydroflo — at lower than bank rates — to buy other companies for CCC; Hydroflo was forced to pay an excessive percentage of CCC's own operating costs "including lease rentals and operating costs of one Gates Learjet corporate aircraft used exclusively to transport said defendant Charles C. Conroy, Jr., for personal and CCC business unrelated to the business of plaintiff Hydroflo Washing Machine Co. . . . ."

The plaintiffs prayed the court for relief: CCC was to repay the loans and pay bank interest for them; reduce Hydroflo's share of its corporate charges; elect three directors to represent the minority stockholders; restore Morehouse to the presidency; and repay to Hydroflo what plaintiffs claim Hydroflo *would have* earned if left alone during the preceding four years — a sum computed by the plaintiffs at eight million dollars.

"That's the end, Mr. Smith. Do you want me to mail it to you?"

"I don't think that's going to be fast enough, Mr. Sneed. Will you hang on for a few minutes, please?"

Everybody was looking at me. I put the receiver down and gave them a summary.

"Jesus Christ," said the older man from First Hudson quietly.

Harry Hatch looked at me, but said nothing.

I explained my theory that the Schwenks had come back in the open market . . .

"But why?" asked Tommy. "If they thought we were ruining the company, why buy stock in it? When they sold it, presumably because they didn't want it any more."

"Well, they live down there," I said. "Sit around that country club they built, listening to everybody bitching about those bastards in Philadelphia, those carpetbaggers ruining the biggest employer in town — "

Harry Hatch spoke up. "The jewel in Conroy's crown. I believe that's how Hydroflo was described to us." His people had postponed their trip to Schwenkstown a couple of times and then decided to leave it until after we'd filed; there would still be plenty of time, and Hydroflo was an old established business making plenty of money . . . Harry's face was covered with egg too.

"Does this mean we can't file?" the younger First Hudson guy asked him.

"I can't speak to that until I see the complaint."

"I just told you what it said, Harry."

"You gave me your résumé of what somebody in Arkansas I've never seen says he's reading from a complaint. We don't operate like that, Ordway."

Why you little son-of-a-bitch! *We* don't operate like that? Mo Patterson was right all along. . . . "He's on the other end of this line, Harry. Do you want him to read it to you?"

"I do not. Which side of this case is Mr. Sneed on, do you think?"

"Well, then, what do you want to do?"

"I'm not prepared to do anything until I see the complaint."

Everybody looked at me.

"Where's the Learjet?" I asked Larry Lenz.

"I guess it's in Frisco, Ordway. That's where Charlie is."

What the hell is he doing out there? I almost asked but didn't when I saw Larry's expression. Whatever that may be, forget it, we've got enough problems now. "If Sneed gets himself on a commercial plane at eight o'clock in the morning — "

" — maybe he can get as far as Chicago tonight."

" — No, it's after ten o'clock."

" — only nine o'clock there . . ."

"Could we send somebody down?"

"What about the Xerox telecopier?" asked one of Harry's young men. I was amused to see that Harry didn't know what that was either, but all of the boys did, and they eagerly explained: transmission of written materials over telephone lines . . . just hook the telephone into this machine . . . papers roll around a cylinder . . . six minutes per page . . . the printer here has one . . . just have to find one in Schwenkstown . . .

The printer even had a book listing all the telecopiers in the United States. None in Schwenkstown.

"Mr. Sneed, are you still there? I'm sorry to keep you waiting so long. Now I'm even sorrier to tell you that you'll have to send somebody to Hot Springs, and you've got to wake up the Xerox sales manager . . ."

He didn't like it, but he didn't give me much of an argument. The poor guy was scared to death.

Then Harry Hatch began to cross-examine. He started on Larry Lenz, the only Company officer in the room, but Larry only knew about the numbers so I was able to deflect the fire to myself. How long had we known about this situation? Why hadn't it been mentioned before? An unpleasant courtroom atmosphere developed: we were crooks concealing facts from the underwriters, from the investment community. . . . What's the matter with him? Is he mad because his people are going to blame him for having overlooked something? Is he just mad at himself? Or is it that they've gotten cold feet, they don't want to do this deal after all but they don't want to walk away from it, so here's a great excuse, they can wash their hands of us and it's all our fault . . . No, that's nonsense, that's paranoia, they're hungry as hell this year, think of the commissions for running a hundred-million-dollar deal . . . Harry is putting on a little show for the First Hudsons and the accountants and for his own guys too.

I told him what I knew about the background, about Charlie's dissatisfaction with Hydroflo's performance; Hydroflo was growing, but it wasn't growing fast enough to meet Charlie's targets, Charlie's game plan. Larry Lenz supplied the numbers for my argument. Charlie was demanding growth, pushing his people very hard to achieve certain growth objectives, and in this case he had to make some changes at Hydroflo. Morehouse was a protégé of the Schwenks. Naturally they resented what had happened, naturally they think they did a better job when they were running the show.

We sat there and looked at each other for a moment.

The other First Hudson guy said: "I think we'd better have a huddle."

Harry nodded, and they all left the room.

"We'd better get word to Charlie," I said. That took a while. He was staying at the Pacific Union Club, but it was still dinnertime in California and they had trouble finding him. When he came on the line, he began to talk without listening: "Good you called, Ordway, I think we may have a deal out here — "

"Charlie, for God's sake, will you please not make another deal until we get this one out of the way? We've run into some trouble down at Hydroflo." I told him what happened, gave him my *Reader's Digest* of the Schwenks' complaint.

A pause. Then: "That's a crock of shit."

I said nothing.

"What was the name of the kid down there?"

"What kid?"

"The wise-ass Harvard one, the one who drank sherry."

"That's Billington."

"Right, Billington. He's behind this."

"Could be."

"Young Billington is pulling my chain."

I told him we were having trouble with the underwriters. "Why?"

"Well, in the first place Hydroflo is supposed to be one of your best companies. In the second place, here's a claim for eight million dollars; even a fraction of that would put quite a dent into CCC right now. . . . And in the third place . . . well, I guess it raises some question about . . ." Well, Christ, am I a lawyer or an ass-kisser? " — about your ability as a manager."

"Oh it does, does it? Some corn cobblers down in Arkansas file a complaint and right away everybody pees in their pants. I'm not some fast-buck operator, I've got a track record and they damn well know it. You tell them if they want out they're out, as of right now this minute, and this deal is going straight to Goldman, Sachs, and I happen to know they'd be delighted, and that's the last business First Hudson ever does with CCC! Is that clear?"

"Yes, it's clear, Charlie. But it won't help us much tonight."

"Well, that's my position. You're running the show back there, don't take any crap from these people and let's get this thing through the SEC. The bank loans come due in October. So long, Ordway, gotta get back to work." He hung up.

Larry Lenz and the accountants returned to their financial statements. One of Harry's lawyers came back and we began to look at proofs again.

Should I be calling somebody for advice? Graham Anders? In the hospital? Ellsworth Boyle? It was two o'clock in the morning by now. What would they tell me? I know more about this situation than they do.

The older First Hudson guy came back. Would I come in the other room and talk to their boss on the telephone? I sat down beside Harry Hatch and took the receiver from him.

A Big Fish was on the line. When you are dealing with Wall Street investment banks, you mostly work with Little Fish. Big Fish appear at ceremonial occasions — post-closing lunches and the like — and when there is Trouble. This particular Big Fish sounded pretty smooth despite the fact that they had got him out of bed in the middle of the night. Called me Ordway.

"Ordway, I've one question to ask you. Is this, do you think, a strike suit?"

I tried to sidestep. "I don't really know what a strike suit is. That's a layman's expression — "

" I am a layman, Ordway. To me a strike suit is a suit that's brought without grounds, to block something or buy a settlement. Is that what you've got here?"

What do I tell him?

"No, that's not what we have here. These people think they have a claim."

"I see."

"That doesn't mean they're going to get anywhere with it. We haven't seen the complaint, of course, but it was read to me and I didn't hear anything about bad faith, about conscious wrongdoing on anybody's part. What they're really saying is they would have run Hydroflo differently. Better, presumably. Now, you're going to rely on your own counsel to advise you on this, of course, but is a federal judge, even down in their own bailiwick, going to interfere in the management of a company, if nothing improper is alleged? I don't think so. Okay, I'll give you back to Harry now."

I walked out of the room. Tommy Sharp shouted down the hall: the complaint was coming over the telecopier. They brought us a new page every six minutes and just after three o'clock we had the whole thing on the table. Harry and the First Hudson people returned, saying nothing. Harry read the complaint, took off his glasses, rubbed his eyes, sighed: "Okay, Ordway, we've decided to file. Now we've got to stick in some language describing this situation."

The rest was anticlimax.

It took us another hour to work out a short paragraph headed *Hydroflo Derivative Suit*, which outlined the complaint and ended with a statement that counsel for the Company had no opportunity to evaluate the merits of the claim. This had to be set in type, and the pages of the Prospectus adjusted to make room.

At quarter to five we gave the printer clearance to assemble the filing package, print order, distribution lists, signature sheets, check for the filing fees, covering letter . . .

"Where's the covering letter?" asked Harry Hatch.

"What covering letter?"

"Counsel for the issuer has to write a covering letter to the SEC explaining what's being filed, what the proposed timetable is — "

Tommy Sharp flushed. "I'm sorry, Ordway. Graham always does that himself. . . . I forgot about it." But then he moved fast, improvising with skill and imagination. We had no letter paper and no secretary. Tommy took a C & D letter from our files, had the letterhead Xeroxed onto a sheet of blank paper, wrote out the covering letter on a yellow pad, and sent both upstairs to the print shop. Twenty minutes later the letter was back, ready for my signature, immaculately printed on what looked exactly like Conyers & Dean stationery. "Most expensive letter you've ever signed," was Harry's comment.

I signed, and we all stood up. It was after six o'clock. My pants were sticking to my legs. A partner of the accounting firm was coming in at 8:30, on the way to his office, to "sign off" on their report, and the printer's messenger was taking the filing package to Washington on the 9:30 plane. The registration statement would be filed before lunch. For the moment, we were finished.

Down on the silent street a cool breeze blew into our faces. The sky was pink. The limousine drivers woke up, got out, opened the doors for us. Harry Hatch was going back to his office, to have a nap before his next meeting. The accountants were going to Grand Central. Larry Lenz and Tommy Sharp were going to Penn Station, getting the first train back to Philadelphia.

I didn't want to go back to Philadelphia.

"I think I'll stay here and get some sleep," I said. "I've got errands to do in New York." Tommy gave me a funny look. Long training with Graham Anders, I guess. The hell with you, buster! After Grand Central I was alone in the car. It took a couple of stops to find a telephone that worked.

"Want to cook me some breakfast?"

"Ordway! Where are you?"

"Park at 57th. I'd like to see you. Want company for breakfast?"

A pause.

"No?"

"No? Oh no, *yes*, Ordway. I'm just trying to think of what to tell the doorman."

12.

Northeast Harbor

"Somehow I never think of you as a lawyer," said my father-in-law.

"Why not, may I ask?"

Mr. Ellis was painting my portrait, a birthday present for Marion. He had me slouched back in a wicker chair, practically prone, white shirt open at the collar, white trousers, arms folded across my chest — the gentleman at ease. With a bottle on the table it could have been an advertisement for expensive gin.

"Well, one thinks of the proverbial steel-trap mind, lawyers tend to be aggressive . . . they know about *things,* one finds them . . . oh, awesomely *competent.* . . ." He put more paint on his brush and dabbed at the canvas.

"If you don't see me as a lawyer — "

A bleak smile. "You're more like me."

"An artist?"

"A courtier."

That hurt. I couldn't think of a polite reply and shifted my position, making the chair creak. The studio is a shingle cottage, a hundred yards through pine woods from the house, just one bare room under the rafters. Sunshine streamed through enormous windows. I could see across the rocky beach, the Cranberry Islands, the blue Atlantic to the horizon — and the sky. The place smelled of pines and sea air and oil paint and wood smoke from the Franklin stove.

In this room he's not a courtier. The pin-striped suit, the Legion of Honor ribbon, the balanced teacup are replaced by a paint-smudged work shirt, ancient knitted cardigan, blue jeans, dirty tennis shoes; the affable old gentleman who goes to so many parties is replaced by the cool professional, the expert absorbed in doing something he is very good at.

He worked in silence for a while, looking at me, looking at the canvas, apparently not conscious of having hurt my feelings. He didn't use a palette, but rather mixed his paints on scraps of cardboard that lay scattered over the top of a high counter.

A courtier? He's right, of course. Painters, musicians, waiters, all purveyors of personal service. Lawyers are supposed to be counselors, purveyors of advice, advocates. May it please the court, ladies and gentlemen of the jury, my client's future, his whole life is in your hands. What I really am — am getting to be — is a *broker*, just like Ellsworth Boyle. My job is to bring people with legal business together with lawyers who can do it for them.

Out on the glittering water a black sloop was standing south against the tide, moving on her engine, her sails furled. I was very tired, although I had slept reasonably well. The sea air was good for sleeping but Marion's feet kept touching me —

"Painters study faces," said Mr. Ellis.

"Yes, I would think so."

"Are you worried about the boy?"

"Which boy — you mean Teddy? No, I'm sure they'll be all right, a bicycle trip up the Rhine isn't that exotic, these days — "

"I'm thinking of this damned war."

"He's just turned eighteen."

"They're taking them at nineteen now, and I don't see any end to this mess, do you?"

"Well, it's *got* to end, we can't keep grinding along like this, every morning the box score of how many Chinamen we've supposedly killed — "

Mr. Ellis painted in silence again, then suddenly put the brush into a glass and walked across the room to an old cupboard. He unlocked the door and rummaged under disorderly piles of books and papers, then found what he wanted and brought it over to me. It was a battered spiral notebook, apparently some kind of sketchbook.

"Take a look at it," he said, as he wiped the turpentine from his brush and resumed his work.

I opened the book. On the first page was a vivid watercolor portrait of a young man's face, or rather half of his face, because one cheek had been shot away so that his jawbone and his remaining teeth were exposed in a heart-stopping grin.

I turned the pages: A naked man with bleeding stumps where his legs had been; a chalk-faced French soldier trying to push his own intestines back into himself; a face without a nose . . . and in between pictures of surgeons operating in bloody aprons, pictures of bandaged soldiers playing cards, pictures of bodies being loaded on a truck — primitive but brilliant pencil sketches, filled in watercolor, pictures crammed with detail.

"How old were you when you did these?" I asked.

"Eighteen. They kept me from losing my mind. Until it was over."

I knew he had gone to France with American Field Service ambulances, long before we entered that war, but I had never heard him say a word about it.

Mr. Ellis painted, apparently absorbed. I knew better than to ask why he had shown me this notebook. I waited.

"Teddy was up here in May, to help us open the house."

"Yes, sir. I knew that."

"Ordway . . ."

Why the hesitation?

"He doesn't want to go to Vietnam. In fact he's made up his mind to become a Conscientious Objector, but he isn't at all sure he can get that kind of a classification. I gather he hasn't talked to you?"

"Not a word! Hasn't he said anything to Marion either?"

"Sometimes it's easier to talk with a grandfather. I think he's worried about how you'd take it, with your own record — "

"*My* record?"

"You spent years overseas, you have decorations — "

"Mr. Ellis, you know how I got my decorations. You just called me a courtier. Are you under the impression I want to see Teddy sent into combat? Is that why you show me these pictures? I admit I was never shot at, but I have seen wounded men. You really think I want my own boy — "

"You misunderstand me, Ordway. We've never discussed this subject, I have no idea what your views might be, I only know that I've got an absolute horror about how men destroy each other's bodies, have had this horror since Verdun, where they ground up a whole generation of Frenchmen and a whole generation of Germans like so much hamburger meat, and for no purpose. Stupid arrogant old men who didn't know what else to do, so they kept feeding bodies to Mammon. I've never forgotten it . . . and this thing now . . . I know it's different, but in some respects — " He stopped to collect himself. I had never, ever seen him excited.

"Ordway, I think part of the problem is that he fears he

won't get a deferment, he doesn't even want to register, he's thinking of going to Canada — "

"No *sir!*" The wicker chair protested as I rose to my feet. "That's out! He'd be an exile, a refugee, a man without a country." For some crazy reason I thought about Alfred von Waldstein. Why? What possible connection? "Mr. Ellis, you're not encouraging him in that proposal, are you?"

He looked down at the tip of his paintbrush. We both saw that it was quivering. He dropped the brush back into the glass, and wiped his hands on the legs of his trousers. "Have you got a cigarette?"

"Yes, of course." I produced one, lighted it for him, watched him settle into the other wicker chair.

"I haven't looked at that notebook since . . . I don't know, many many years. I really didn't have the courage, because it brought back — well, a time of great spiritual crisis. Did you know I was institutionalized for a short time after I came home? Yes. Nineteen-nineteen. I don't think the girls know about it. After Teddy had that talk with me I forced myself to look at it again. It's much more real to me, even now, than the stuff you see on television. It brings it all back, Ordway. The *pain!* When you think of the complicated machine a human body is, every muscle, every nerve ending, every brain cell is a miracle . . . and then you see it blown apart and splattered over the landscape by other men who have exactly the same organs . . . and to *no purpose!*" He took a long drag at the cigarette.

"But that doesn't mean Teddy has to run away," I said. "There must be other solutions. When I think about our friends, our friends who have boys this age, boys in their twenties, I can't think of one that's gone to Vietnam. This war is being fought mostly by professionals and by the sons of the poor. That's hellishly unfair, but that's how it is, and I can't see encouraging a kid to run away if he doesn't have to. I'll talk to him about it, Mr. Ellis, and we'll work something out for him. I'll look into it as soon as I get back to the office . . . but I wish you'd tell the boy it's all right to come see me about it."

Mr. Ellis smiled.

"I feel a little better." He stood up. "You know, that's a really splendid boy you have there. Want to take a walk along the beach?"

I didn't feel better. I felt worse. I hadn't given Teddy a thought in months. A good steady boy, kind to everybody, good-looking, good athlete, unfortunately the inheritor of my brains instead of his mother's, unhappy in the knowledge that we're disappointed to have him at a tiny college nobody ever heard of . . . and I'm treating him just the way my father treated me, with benign neglect.

We had just stepped out of the cottage when we heard somebody running down the path from the house. My daughter Ailsa appeared, cheeks flushed, breasts moving, my God she's become a woman, she's beautiful! Freckles, high cheekbones, black hair, the face of an Indian maid, where did she get that black hair?

"Hey Dad, there was a call for you." She stopped in front of us, panting a little. She was dressed for tennis: tight white shorts and a white boy's polo shirt — neither entirely clean — long brown legs, white sneakers. "They want you to call back, it's Mr. Conroy, he's in San Francisco and he wants to catch a plane!"

In some cultures she'd be married by now, a couple of children.

"Mr. Ellis, I guess I'd better — "

"Oh sure, you go ahead, I'll just walk down to the point and back. I'm glad we had this talk, Ordway. In fact, I'm relieved."

Ailsa skipped beside me on the path.

— Hey Dad? Does this mean you're going to leave again? You just got here.

— I don't know, Puss. I hope not, but if they need me —

— 'Cause, like, there's something . . . I kinda want to ask you something —

— Well sure, go ahead.

— Dad? I don't want to go back to school in the fall. Can I come home and go to Shipley again?

— You don't want to go back — you mean to Farmington? Why not? I thought you were doing so well — You're not in some kind of trouble, are you?

— Uh uh.

— Well then —

— I don't like it, I want to come home, Dad!

— But why? Why don't you like it?

— I don't know, I mean I don't know how to say it. . . . They got all this chickenshit, all these rules, you're cooped up with all these dumb girls all the time, they just sit around and talk —

— What do you mean? What do they talk about?

— They talk about what they do with boys, you know, stuff like that —

— That bother you, when they talk about —

— No, I don't know, I can't explain it, but they're all cooped up, see, like in a henhouse —

— But you do a lot of riding —

— Yeah, but it's not the same, it's not like riding with you at home, they make you do all this horse-show crap, they have this team, you're supposed to get points, and they make you turn the lights out at eleven, they wake you up at the same time, and everything is the same every day, you do the same thing at the same time every day, all these girls doing the same thing together every day —

— Have you talked to your mother about this?

— Uh uh. I know what she'll say.

— What will she say?

— She'll say it's good for me, I need the discipline.

— Well, Puss, you did give her a pretty hard time last year —

— But I was young then, Dad, I was just a kid, it wouldn't be like that now, I *promise* —

— Well, if you really hate the place that much, I can't see the point of forcing you to go there —

— Oh Dad, I *knew* you'd see —

— No, wait a minute, I'm not promising anything, I've got to discuss this with your mother, and I don't see how we're going to get you back into Shipley this year, they've made up the class by now.

— If you talk to Mrs. Epes, she'll let me come back.

— What makes you say that? If they're full, they're full.

— Okay, so I'll go to public school, I'd like to try that.

— Better let me talk to your mother. Where is she, anyway?

— She's gone into Northeast to get some stuff.

— Okay, I'll discuss it with her. No promises. Now where's that telephone number? Hey listen . . . come on, Puss.

— I love you, Dad!

— Okay . . . Okay, I love you too, now where's the telephone number?

— Thanks for calling back, Ordway. Only got a minute, I'm taking a commercial flight back to New York but this thing out here is really beginning to cook, I don't think we can keep it on the back burner any longer or we'll lose it, they want to sign a letter of intent this week, you'll have to put a couple of your best guys on this right away. I want the tax aspects checked out, their lawyer claims they have to get a ruling but we can't wait for that, you'll have to talk them out of that one, but the reason I'm calling now, Ordway, I've got to send the Learjet up for you.

— Today?

— Tomorrow morning. The underwriters are going to start their dog and pony show, the first meeting's at the Bankers Club tomorrow afternoon, then Chicago, then Dallas, they want to have us talk about CCC with all these guys they're inviting into the syndicate, they think you ought to be there in case there are questions, especially about that Hydroflo situation, and maybe you ought to go down there for a couple of days too, find out what's really eating those people anyway —

— I've told you what's eating them, Charlie, and there's nothing I should say to the underwriters beyond what we say in the Prospectus, and I've only been with my family for a couple of days —

— Yeah, I'm sorry about that, it can't be helped, I'll square it for you with Marion and I'll send you back up as soon as we get some of these things straightened out. . . .

"I've never heard anything so ridiculous," said Marion. "A dog and pony show!" She was driving me to the airport in her mother's old station wagon.

"That's just what they call it. They trot a company's executives around to all these meetings so the underwriters can ask them questions."

"And you're the little puppy who comes wagging his tail when master sends the Learjet."

"Couldn't very well say 'No,' could I? 'I'm sorry, Charlie, I'm busy with my vacation, you'll have to get another lawyer.' "

"You can't seem to say 'No' to anybody."

"Let's not get started on *that* again."

We were running up against the tailgate of an old pickup truck. Marion glanced in her mirror, swung left, pressed the gas pedal to the floor. The station wagon inched past the pickup — two boys in T-shirts and sideburns — and up ahead a yellow Volkswagen appeared, coming the other way. The boy in the truck accelerated, grinning at me. Marion, her jaw set, kept her foot on the pedal and squeezed into the right lane in front of the truck just an instant before the Volkswagen, honking wildly, was upon us.

"The plane's got to wait for me, you know."

"You could have called a taxi. You know the real reason she wants to come home, don't you?"

"Haven't we been all over this?"

"Because at school they make her toe the line while at home she can do anything she likes. At home she's Daddy's Pussycat."

"We haven't had any trouble with her."

"*You* haven't had any trouble with her. You don't care what her room looks like, you don't care if she talks like a platoon sergeant, you don't care if she fails all her courses. You don't think for one minute Isotta's going to take her back, do you?"

"No harm asking, is there? I thought she did pretty good work, actually."

"You call failing French and math doing pretty good work? I'll grant you she won a lot of tennis tournaments."

"Well, I'll grant you she won't get into Bryn Mawr, but what difference does it make? She's a pretty girl, she's supposed to have a good time."

"And she's not supposed to learn anything — except how to manipulate a man into giving her what she wants?"

"Aw, come on!"

"That's what she's learning, Ordway. That's exactly what you're teaching her. And in a year or two she's going to apply the lesson — to other men."

"For God's sake, what's wrong with that? Don't all women do that? Hey, slow down, we've got to turn — "

"I know my way to the airport. . . . All right, look, there's no use arguing with you, but you're going to be sorry, Ordway. You're spoiling her, and spoiled people are unhappy people, later. You're really just indulging yourself now, and it isn't good for *her*, but I give up. . . . My God, is that Charlie's plane?"

"Looks nice, doesn't it? See the initials on the tail?"

"How could I miss them? . . . Okay, is this where you want me to stop? Are you going directly to New York now?"

"Yeah, that's the schedule. And then Chicago."

"You're not going to get home at all? You're going to run out of shirts."

"I'll get some in New York. Okay, thanks for bringing me over. . . . I'll give you a call in a couple of days, as soon as I know where I'm supposed to be, in Chicago or Arkansas or where. . . . Bye . . ."

"Bye, Ordway."

I felt her eyes upon me as I handed my bag up to the co-pilot, but by the time I had climbed the ladder and turned around in the door, the station wagon was driving back toward the highway.

13.

Dog and Pony Show

The Securities Act of 1933 imposes heavy penalties for misstatements or omissions in offering prospectuses, but it permits some defenses. For example, if an underwriter can prove that he made a reasonable investigation and had reasonable grounds to believe that the statements in the Prospectus were true and that there was no omission to state a material fact, then the underwriter can get off the hook.

Hence the "Due Diligence" meeting: company officers, lawyers, accountants, top men of the lead underwriter behind a long table, facing a room full of analysts and customer's men who are smoking, looking at their watches, and reading (with various degrees of boredom) their copies of the "red herring," the Preliminary Prospectus which was handed out by the pretty girls at the door, each copy bearing on the cover, printed vertically and in red letters, the magic incantation required by the SEC: "A registration statement relating to these securities has been filed with the Securities and Exchange Commission, but has not yet become effective. Information contained herein is subject to completion or amendment. These securities may not be sold nor may offers to buy be accepted prior to the time the registration statement becomes effective. This Prospectus shall not constitute an offer to sell or the solicitation of an offer to buy nor shall there be any sale of these securities in any State in which such offer, solicitation or sale would be unlawful prior to registration or qualification under the securities laws of any such State . . ."

I've been to lots of these ceremonies and they are usually a crashing bore. God only knows why they have them; by no stretch of the imagination would a court ever hold that attendance at such a meeting constitutes a reasonable investigation. "The standard of reasonableness shall be that required of a prudent man in the management of his own property," says the Securities Act, and that does not mean sitting slouched back in your chair, listening to a speech, leafing through a Prospectus, maybe asking a couple of questions about projected earnings which you know the lawyers won't let the company officers answer anyway.

So why do they still have these meetings? Partly because it has become a custom they are afraid to stop, and partly because the right kind of meeting can actually be used as a sales tool, not so much to let the underwriters exercise due diligence as to persuade them to join the syndicate in the first place. For a very big and perhaps a very difficult issue, the company is taken on the road, to give syndicate managers, analysts and salesmen all over the country a look at the product they will be trying to sell.

The format was pretty much the same in New York, Chicago, St. Louis, Dallas, Los Angeles. Little speech of welcome from the senior guy in the local First Hudson office . . . so glad all of you could come, a bad year for underwriting in general but always room for high quality deals . . . want to show you first hand why we're so excited about this one . . . you've read our preliminary prospectus but we want the management to give you their insights in depth . . . my pleasure to introduce these gentlemen at the table, starting at the other end, Mr. Renfrew, chief operating officer, Mr. Lenz, comptroller, Mr. Lundquist from Pennypacker Poole, the company's accountants, Mr. Smith, counsel for the issuer, and here beside me the man you've all come to see and hear . . .

Charlie was uniformly terrific. He had always been at his best in this element, glowing with self-confidence and enthusiasm, communicating this enthusiasm to the audience. Expensively dressed, carefully barbered, hands in his pockets, he seemed almost shy as he warmed them up: He always looked at the local paper when he came to town, he said. This morning he'd seen an interesting item in the Personals column of the Chicago *Tribune* (or the Los Angeles *Times,* or whatever). The item read "Widower, age 85, smokes and drinks, seeks acquaintance with attractive widow, age 85, who smokes and drinks. Objective: Smoking and drinking." When the roars of laughter died down he launched into an explanation of his Concepts, with special emphasis on decentralization. Two young men from First Hudson stood by the easel and turned huge pages as Charlie explained bar graphs and pie charts, dealing mostly with government studies predicting what might happen in various industries and sectors of the economy. Cynics have been heard to call these things Gee Whiz Graphs. (*We're* not making projections; these are government reports showing what is supposed to happen in the power generating industry, in cable TV, in home appliances, in electronics, in real estate . . . Of course we're in those industries, and if you want to conclude that we will grow with them . . .)

But then came the questions. A great many were always about accounting, technical questions which Charlie could easily have handled himself but which he usually referred to John Lundquist from Pennypacker Poole. I rarely understood either the questions or the answers, but the message seemed always to be the same: CCC used whatever "generally accepted" accounting principles would make the bottom line — the earnings per share — look better. What's wrong with that? If the Messrs. Pennypacker Poole & Co. give their blessings, what more do you want?

— Well, but is there not some dispute with the accountants at the SEC about how the fully diluted earnings should be computed?

— No sir, there was some discussion with the staff but the matter has been resolved.

— And the diluted earnings in this red herring have been computed in accordance with APB 15?

— That is correct.

All this was getting too technical for the customer's men, who shifted in their chairs and fidgeted until the analyst asked what the dilutive effect on earnings per share of future acquisitions might be. Then they woke up.

Acquisitions? Did somebody say acquisitions?

One way or another the question came up at every one of the meetings, and Charlie's answer was always the same: Why gentlemen, you know I'm in registration! What would Mr. Smith over there say, what would your own lawyers say, if I mentioned any pending acquisitions at this time? They'd throw a fit, wouldn't they? (Laughter) But I guess I'm free to say that we're looking at companies all the time, we're talking to people all the time, and the minute we make a deal we'll announce it.

— Does that mean an announcement is imminent? Before the Debentures come out?

— My lips are sealed.

Philosophical questions: Have not conglomerates peaked by now? Isn't the bloom off the rose? Look at LTV . . . look at Leasco . . .

— Gentlemen, you really flatter me: Jimmy Ling is a

friend of mine, he's one of my heroes, as you know I've copied some of his ideas . . . and Saul is a brilliant boy, a prodigy, fantastic mind . . . but I'm not in the same ball park with those guys, I'm just not that ambitious. . . . No, don't laugh, I mean it, that's on the level. . . . Imagine trying to take over the *Chemical Bank!* They're just scaring everybody to death, they're shaking the pillars of the temple, and so they're bringing the government down on their necks, the Congress and the Department of Justice . . . but that hasn't got anything to do with CCC, we're not fighting with anybody, we're just trying to run a lean, clean operation —

— What about Darby Turbine?

— Well okay, Darby Turbine was a big hunk to swallow, no doubt about that, and we're having some problems, they are spelled out in the Prospectus. But, as all of you know, Darby was having those problems before we took over and I think we're making damn good progress in solving those problems, we've worked out a game plan for Darby and we're right on target. Now let's come back to the energy crisis for a few minutes. Have you gentlemen got any idea . . .

In Los Angeles somebody asked: What about Hydroflo? What's happening about that lawsuit you mention in the Prospectus?

— Ordway, will you take that one please? Mr. Ordway Smith, Conyers & Dean, Philadelphia.

— Well, a complaint had been filed, the complaint is carefully described at page thirty-five of your Preliminary Prospectus, the Company and its counsel are now working on an Answer denying the allegations and expect to file Motions to Dismiss. Beyond that, we feel the matter is *sub judice* and further comment would be inappropriate . . .

Somebody at the back of the room: People at our Memphis

office hear reports that there may be something to the case, there's a lot of feeling that Hydroflo's being mismanaged —

Charlie on his feet: So far as I'm concerned there's absolutely nothing to the case, but of course we're making a full investigation and as a matter of fact Mr. Smith is going down to Arkansas tonight to look into all the details. . . .

I am?

Our host from First Hudson: All right, gentlemen, if there aren't any further questions, I want to thank you all for coming but don't rush away, the bar back there is open now, we hope you'll stick around and visit with us for a while. . . .

Charlie was shaving with an electric razor. We were alone in the back seat of the enormous black Cadillac, hurtling along the maze of freeways toward the airport. There was another meeting in San Francisco that evening. He had hung his jacket on the hook by the window, loosened his necktie, opened his dispatch case, plugged the razor's cord into the cigarette lighter and now he was shaving, leaning forward to examine his face in the little mirror inside the lid of the razor box.

He looked tired, drained, the actor in his dressing room between matinee and evening performances. So far he had said nothing more about my going to Schwenkstown. For all I knew that was just baloney for the brokers and I was still headed for San Francisco with him, but I knew better than to ask questions when he was in this mood.

Was Charlie changing? Hadn't he always been this way, burning with energy and enthusiasm one minute, slumped into slack despair the next? But weren't the troughs getting deeper now? A couple of incidents on this trip made me wonder.

One night we were in Chicago, at one of those monstrous new motels beside O'Hare. The air conditioning was broken and my room felt like a steam bath. I managed to open a window but that let in the shriek and thunder of jet engines so I closed it again. I took another shower, drank another bourbon-and-water, switched back and forth between Johnny Carson and Dick Cavett, finally dozed off naked on my bed watching Bob Hope and Bing Crosby chasing Dorothy Lamour down The Road to Somewhere.

Telephone.

"Mr. Smith? Brooke-Templeton here. Terribly sorry to wake you at this hour but it's of the *utmost* importance." A British accent, indeed a Sandhurst accent, Darby Turbine's European manager. I'd met him once, in London, and got along well with him. He looked like what he had been the first half of his life, a professional soldier: six foot six, Grenadier moustaches, a face burned by tropical sunshine and whiskey. He served in the Indian army until the British left; then he retired, married an American girl, moved to Philadelphia and applied to Darby Turbine as a trainee. A forty-year-old trainee, late lieutenant colonel in the 30th Punjabis, no business experience? They had the good sense to try him. He began at the bottom, rose quickly through all those ice water–and–slide rule types at Darby Turbine, and by the time CCC got control he had been running their European operations for years.

"It's good to hear from you, Colonel. Are you in London?"

"I'm right here in this furnace of an hotel. Just got in from London, got a couple of Dutch bankers with me and that's the problem. Might I come up for a moment? I'm in a bit of a fix and I'd like your advice."

Of course I had to let him come up. I put on my pants and my shirt and then he was there, filling the little room with his presence. We sat sweating through our shirts, drinking highballs, and he told me his story:

As we doubtless knew, Darby Turbine's European operations were not doing well. On top of the problems associated with nuclear power plants — local fears of radiation and explosion, insurance difficulties — Darby was trying to compete with European contractors on their home grounds, and the local governments — French and German especially — were doing everything possible to favor their own companies over the Americans. Brooke-Templeton's people had just wangled the chance to bid on a job in Belgium, and they had every hope of getting it. The hooker was that it would cost a great deal of money to prepare the bid, and they also had to demonstrate their financial ability to finish the job. In other words, Darby Turbine's European venture needed a large infusion of cash — something like $40 million — and they were having trouble finding it. After months of effort, a private bank in Amsterdam had worked out a Eurodollar loan agreement, under which a syndicate of banks in Holland, Belgium and England would put up the money required for the Belgian project.

Brooke-Templeton stopped talking for a moment, wiped his brow with his handkerchief, took another drink. He was thin and well preserved, and yet he must be well over sixty . . . flight over the Pole . . . time zones. . . . He looked tired.

"I'll come to the point, old boy. You know of course, that I've worked entirely with our Darby people all these years, I've no experience whatever with your CCC establishment, but our Philadelphia headquarters insist I must go directly to the top for this — around them, so to speak, because this whole arrangement's been negotiated in London, we know about it whereas the Philadelphia crowd do not . . . and that's why I've come directly to Chicago to see Conroy. He's got to okay the thing, of course, and CCC must guarantee the loan."

"I guess that makes sense," I said. "What's your problem?"

"Can't get in to see him."

"What do you mean by that?"

"Just what I said, old boy. We've flown from London to Chicago to confer with Conroy, but his ADC or whatever he is, the fellow with sunglasses, won't let me speak to him, nor may we see him tomorrow because your road show (as I believe he termed it) is leaving for Texas at eight o'clock in the morning, and Conroy won't see anyone before he leaves. Now, am I to ask these bank chaps, these Dutchmen who've spent months putting this thing together — am I to ask them to fly on to Texas in the hope that we might be granted an audience down there?"

I had a feeling of *déjà vu*. Another motel room, another bottle of bourbon, another report on how CCC is governed. I reached for the telephone and called Charlie's suite. The Frenchman answered.

"Is he there?"

"He's not seeing anybody, and that means *anybody* — "

"I'm on my way up, Frank. You'd better not keep me standing in the hall!"

I told Brooke-Templeton to get some sleep. After he left I walked up the fire stairs one flight, and knocked on Charlie's door.

The Frenchman opened it immediately. Sunglasses at night. "I told you, Ordway, he's not gonna see anybody — "

I'm six inches taller than he is. I brushed right by him. "What's going on in here?"

The living room was a shambles: glasses, overflowing ashtrays, paper cups, a room service table piled with dirty dishes.

"We've been working out the numbers on the Frisco deal all night," said the Frenchman. "Larry Lenz and the accountants just left a little while ago — "

"Well, is Charlie asleep? What are you doing here?" I moved toward the bedroom door.

"*Stay outa there, counselor!*"

I stopped. I knew he didn't like me, but he had never raised his voice to me before. We just stood there and looked at each other for a moment. Voices behind the door, the door opened, a girl came out and closed the door behind her. A pretty girl, maybe twenty-five, teased black hair, brown eyes, jangling bracelets, blue cotton pants suit, large leather handbag slung over her shoulder with a strap.

"What's all the hollering? Who's this?" she asked.

"This is our lawyer, Ordway Smith. You're not going, are you?"

She had taken a cigarette from the handbag and was applying the flame from a golden lighter. "Too hot," she said. "I'm sweating like a horse. I'm going home to my air conditioner."

"You're supposed to stay all night."

She looked at him and blew out a cloud of smoke.

"That was the deal, Mona!"

She said nothing and headed for the door to the hall.

The Frenchman put his hand on the doorknob. "What the hell is the matter with you?"

"There's nothing the matter with *me,* you asshole!" She narrowed her eyes. "If I stayed here all night you'd have to fly your boss to Dallas in a straitjacket tomorrow." She slapped his hand away from the door, opened it, and was gone.

"Oh Jesus," said the Frenchman, very softly, and for the first time I felt that maybe he was human. I tried to pretend that nothing had happened. "Frank, he must be awake, I've got to talk to him about Brooke-Templeton — "

"You really want to make him crack?" asked the Frenchman through his teeth. "Is that what you want? It's three o'clock in the morning now, he's been working for — let's see, twenty hours. You think maybe that's enough? Does he have to do *every* goddamn thing in this company? Can't those limeys — "

The bedroom door opened and Charlie came out, fully dressed except for his coat and tie. He looked terrible.

"What limeys?" he asked.

As quickly as I could, I told him about Brooke-Templeton.

He sat down in a chair and put his head in his hands.

"Fix me a drink."

The Frenchman began to busy himself with a glass, the ice bucket, a bottle of Scotch . . .

"What time's the flight?"

"Eight o'clock, Charlie. Commercial. You sent the Learjet home because — "

"Yeah, I know." Charlie's hand shook as he lifted the glass to his lips. "Can we take a later flight?"

"They got a big lunch set up for us down there."

"All right, we'll take Brooke-Templeton and his bankers with us, we'll talk to them on the plane."

"Charlie, they just came over from London, Brooke-Templeton thinks it would look funny — " I stopped talking because Charlie's hand was trembling as he put down the glass, Charlie was suddenly on his feet, moving across the room, grabbing a huge lamp off the table so hard that the cord snapped, hurling the lamp against the wall with a shattering crash . . .

Motionless, the Frenchman and I watched. Charlie stared

at the mess on the floor for a moment, then walked back, picked up his glass and took a long gulping drink.

"All right, we'll see them at breakfast. Six-thirty in the coffee shop. Now both of you get out of here."

The Messrs. Ten Holter and van der Steenbock were clearly not accustomed to negotiating deals in airport coffee shops, yet here they were, crowded amongst traveling salesmen and waitresses and stewardesses, identically dressed in blue suits and white shirts, cheerful, polite — and puzzled. They were puzzled because they had spent many weeks negotiating a complicated loan involving forty million dollars, and now they were hearing it explained — apparently for the first time — to the man who would have to guarantee the loan.

A couple of tables had been pushed together in one corner and we surrounded them: Brooke-Templeton earnestly addressing Charlie across the cups and plates and open dispatch cases; Charlie smoking cigarettes, listening, staring into the distance with hooded eyes; Larry Lenz listening, frowning, shaking his head; the Frenchman, listening, glancing at his wristwatch. . . .

When Brooke-Templeton finished his story, Charlie turned to Larry Lenz, who was still shaking his head. "That would put it right in our financials, wouldn't it? Notes to our cap table?"

Larry Lenz kept right on shaking his head. "No way, Charlie, *no way*. Forty million additional debt! Just what CCC needs!"

Brooke-Templeton broke in: "Gentlemen, these negotiations have been approved step by step by our management, it's been understood all along — "

"The hell it has," said the Frenchman.

"Lay it out for them, Larry," commanded Charlie, lighting another cigarette.

Larry laid it out: Darby Turbine's European operation was not included in CCC's financial statements because it was not technically a subsidiary. From the beginning, Darby had maintained a minority position, leaving the English and Dutch partners at least theoretically in control. This was supposed to make it easier for Darby to compete in the European markets, and avoided American taxes. CCC had never changed this setup. Consequently the financial statements of Darby's European operations did not appear in CCC's Prospectus.

"But now you want us to guarantee your forty-million-dollar loan? That would mean we'd have to footnote it on CCC's financials, we'd have to put it into our Prospectus. And the whole point of selling our Debentures is to *pay off* our bank loans! How can we suddenly stick in forty million of *new* bank loans? It would look crazy as hell. The underwriters wouldn't touch it. They couldn't explain it. *We* couldn't explain it."

Silence around the table. Brooke-Templeton looked sick, physically sick. "These negotiations have been cleared at every step by our management, a tremendous amount of time and effort has been expended — "

"Cleared by what management?" demanded the Frenchman from behind his sunglasses.

"By my employers, the Darby Turbine Corporation," snapped Brooke-Templeton.

"They know we don't include your numbers," said Larry Lenz. "They set it up that way themselves. We don't control you, we don't include your results, why the hell should we guarantee your bank loans?"

Another silence. The Dutch bankers studied their coffee cups. The Frenchman looked at his wristwatch.

"Time to go?" asked Charlie. The Frenchman nodded and got up to find the waitress.

"This leaves matters in a rather awkward posture," said Brooke-Templeton. "We've already begun work on the Belgian proposal, on the assumption that the funds would be available — "

"Somebody's dropped the ball, all right," said Charlie.

Brooke-Templeton closed his dispatch case and snapped the locks. He was fighting to control himself. "May I ask for instructions then? Will you gentlemen advise me how we are to obtain funds for the Belgian project?"

"You'd better ask your bankers, hadn't you?" said Charlie.

Mr. van der Steenbock spoke for the first time. "In the light of these developments, we will of course confer with the other members of our group."

Charlie stood up, so everybody else stood up too. He shook hands with the two bankers. "Delighted to have met you gentlemen, I'm afraid we didn't put our best foot forward on this deal, but when you get to know us better you'll find out we know what we're doing. Most of the time." He turned to Brooke-Templeton. "Back to the old drawing board, eh Colonel? We're going to have to kick some asses at Darby Turbine for you. Have a good trip home. Come on, Ordway, we're going to miss our flight."

Charlie finished shaving, unplugged the cord of the electric razor from the cigarette lighter, wrapped the cord and the razor back into their little box, and slid his tie back up into his collar.

"What are you looking so gloomy about?" he asked me.

"I was thinking about Brooke-Templeton."

"Forget about Brooke-Templeton. Just one more fuck-up at Darby Turbine. We could spend all our time playing nursemaid to those guys. Here's something more interesting to think about." He reached into his dispatch case and presented me with a small black object, a flat black box about the size of a transistor radio, with a little glass window and a panel of numbered buttons. It was a tiny calculator. I pressed the buttons and watched the little green numbers flash in the window: $2 \times 2 = 4$ $4 \times 4 = 16$ $16 \times 16 = 256$ $256 \times 256 = 65536$ $65536 \div 256 = 256$ . . .

"Nice toy."

"Toy? Ordway, that's going to be the hottest item in American retailing within a year. That baby can do anything a desk calculator can do, and it's going to open up markets that have never been thought of before. This is going to be a breakthrough like the portable typewriter, only more so, because you have to type a little to use a portable typewriter, but look at this thing, all you have to know is to punch a couple of buttons, my God, Ordway, just think! Construction engineers on a job, estimators, the housewife who can't balance her checkbook, the housewife at the supermarket, kids in school, anybody who can't do arithmetic in his head — we won't sell them like office machines, through dealers, we'll sell them like radios, through all the consumer outlets, department stores, discount stores. . . ."

"*We'll* sell them? Who's we?"

Charlie grinned. He had recovered. His enthusiasm for this gadget had stimulated him more than a double martini. "This is the San Francisco deal I've been spending my time on. Ordway, it's going to be great, just great, the sweetest little outfit you ever saw in your life — " A glance out the window, a glance at his watch — "Look, I'll tell you all about it when you get back but we've only got a few minutes to talk about Hydroflo, there's an American flight at six o'clock for Dallas, I've already told them to have the Learjet in Dallas to meet you, they'll take you right in to Schwenkstown."

"And what do I do when I get there?"

"You get rid of this crazy lawsuit."

"Oh, is that all?"

"Right. And then you come back out here, to San Francisco, and we'll sign up the deal with the Brombergs. Your tax guys did a good job on that, by the way, they're not going to hold out for a ruling — "

"Wait a minute, Charlie. One thing at a time! Will you please tell me how you expect me to get rid of the Hydroflo suit? Do you remember what they're asking for? They're asking for eight million dollars in damages, that's what they say they want you to put back!"

"Well they're not going to get that, and they know it."

"Okay, maybe they know it, but how much are you willing to give them? What am I supposed to offer them to make them drop the suit?"

Charlie was looking out of the window again, looking out at the smog and the Avis billboards and the stream of cars all around us.

"What do you think we should offer them? What is it they really want?"

"Well, first of all they really want Morehouse back."

"Should we give them that?"

"Yes."

"Why should we?"

"Because you say you want to get rid of the suit. When you fired Morehouse, blamed him for what really wasn't his fault, that's what brought on the suit. They had other grievances, but that triggered the suit."

"You believe that?"

"Yes."

He was still looking out of the window. "All right, give them Morehouse."

"They would insist on a contract."

"Yes. Okay. How much?"

"Well, I guess what he was getting before, until sixty-five, with regular pension benefits. I guess they'll take that, I'm sure he will. But that won't be all. The main thing is they want to run their own show down there. You promised them that in the first place. After all they did a damn good job on their own."

"Well, what does that mean, run their own show? Are they a sub of CCC or are they not? How can I promise anything like that? I've got a duty to the stockholders of CCC, we've bought this property, we can't just sign over — "

"Aw come on now, Charlie! Did I just listen to a beautiful speech about your Concepts, about decentralization? What does decentralization mean to you? Now the facts are right in front of you, I don't care what Renfrew or the Frenchman have told you, the Hydroflo crowd was doing fine until your people starting running their business for them, starting to increase the net so hard that the product suffered . . . look, I'm not blaming anybody, I'm not trying to rub it in. You made a mistake. It's time to admit it — if you want to get rid of this lawsuit!"

We were coming into the airport complex now, huge motels, signs for the various airlines. Apparently the driver knew that my flight was first because he headed directly for the American Airlines terminal. It was twenty to six when the car stopped. Charlie still hadn't said anything. The driver got out, walked around the car and opened the door on my side. I just sat there and looked at Charlie while he lighted a cigarette. The driver looked at me and I looked at Charlie, and behind us a taxi began to honk.

"Use your judgment," said Charlie.

"Come on, Charlie, what's that supposed to mean? What's the use of sending me down there without any instructions? Suppose they insist on a lot of money? They've got to pay their lawyers. . . ."

"They can pay their lawyers, but I'd better not hear another word from that bunch of — "

"They're simple country boys."

"Beyond the legal fees, work something out. Talk to them. They seem to like you. See what else they want. If it's within reason, we'll give it to them. If you can't reach me at the Pacific Union Club I'll be at Bromberg's."

"You'll be where?"

"Bromberg Instruments, in Oakland. Remember the name. Okay, you'd better catch your plane, Ordway. Now get rid of that goddamned lawsuit and come on back out, because I need you."

— Are you trying to tell me you won't be back this weekend? You won't be here for the Yacht Club dance?

— How can I be? I've told you I won't be finished down here until tomorrow evening, and Charlie insists he needs me back in San Francisco on Saturday.

— Ordway, that's *ridiculous!* You must be able to send somebody else out to do that sort of thing. Why don't you send Tommy Sharp?

— He's already out there. He's been working with these Bromberg people for a week, but Charlie insists that I be there to review the agreement. I just can't help it, Marion, I'm sorry to miss the dance.

— Well, all I can say is it sounds pretty fishy to me. You always had somebody like Graham or Tommy to do the paperwork, you've never shown much interest in working all night, you've tended to ceremonial occasions —

— I think this signing in San Francisco is sort of a ceremonial occasion. Charlie is red-hot to buy this Bromberg outfit. I don't know much about them yet —

— When *are* you planning to come back, if I may ask? Do you realize the summer's almost over? Do you remember that you promised Ailsa you'd get her back into Shipley? Am I supposed to start something about that?

— Marion, I'm sure I'll be back before next weekend, but you go ahead and call the schools about Ailsa. You can handle it much better than I can. I'm really sorry about the dance, but there's nothing I can do about it.

— Okay, Ordway. Give me a call when you get to San Francisco.

— Okay, kiddo. Good night.

Not one question about what I'm doing down here in Arkansas. Could have told her I did a pretty good job down here. Get along all right with these people, Billington, Billington's wife, Morehouse, even their lawyers, the barefoot country boys. Wasn't so hard after all, but could Tommy Sharp have done it? Could Graham Anders have done it? Did I give them too much? All I gave them was a chance to repair the damage CCC has done to them, really. They have to get court approval to stop the suit and they have to give notice to all the other Hydroflo stockholders, so maybe we're not out of the woods yet. But I think it looks pretty good.

Shall I call her?

Why not?

Want to boast about what a good lawyer I am.

She'll ask me all about Hydroflo, she'll know what I'm doing down here, she'll understand what this is all about.

And then I'll ask her to fly out to Chicago and meet me in that motel at O'Hare. Have they fixed the air conditioning yet?

You're getting to be like Graham Anders.

Would he do that? Goddamned right he'd do that.

Suppose Westphal answers the phone?

Still in London.

Maybe not. Suppose he answers.

Then you hang up. Come on now, pick up the phone.

She works. She doesn't have time to run off to Chicago —

An hour on the plane. She could leave after work, be back next morning.

Would she do it?

Ask her.

Come on, this is kid stuff.

Be fun though.

Book Three

FAMILY BUSINESS

14.

The Brombergs

Tommy Sharp was at the gate when I arrived in San Francisco. It was only eleven o'clock out there, and his instructions were to get me checked into the Fairmont and then to drive me to a restaurant in Sausalito, where we were to eat lunch with Charlie, Mr. Bromberg, and Mr. Bromberg's lawyer.

Blue sky. Sunshine. The San Bruno Mountains, yellow and dry, rose in front of us.

Tommy had rented a little yellow Mustang. As he drove me north along the glittering bay I leafed through the financial statements of Bromberg Instruments. People like Tommy and Graham Anders can tear these things apart, can read notes about depreciation policies and tax accruals the way Leonard Bernstein reads a music score, but even I could see that Bromberg was making a lot of money — and that the earnings stopped growing last year.

"A damn nice operation," Tommy was saying. "Of course some things are coming out of the woodwork, the usual things we find in smaller companies: inventory used to be understated to keep the taxes down, family trust owns the factory and leases it to the company — but that's all par for the course."

"Tell me the story," I said, putting the financials back into his briefcase. "There's always a story. Who are the Brombergs?"

Delighted, Tommy took a deep breath.

"Okay, the Brombergs. They're Jews, of course, but well established, been in San Francisco over a hundred years, they're even in the *Social Register*. Originally made their money in dry goods, sold ship supplies, sold pickaxes and guns to the miners, then real estate, all kinds of things, a bank, lost a pile in the Depression because the bank failed, made it back in the war, an interesting family. The one we're dealing with is Bernard Bromberg. I guess he's in his fifties, late fifties, a pretty smart, tough guy. Carrier pilot in the war, torpedo bombers off the *Saratoga,* he told me, came back in 'forty-five and started a little company to make airplane instruments. Borrowed money from his relatives, hired a bunch of smart engineers, they branched out into specialized instruments for rocket machinery and got in on the space boom. They're small but they're good. They've got a hell of an operation over in Oakland and as you can see they've made a lot of money."

"And now?"

"The usual story. Bromberg's one of these barrel-chested athletic types, a boxer in college, rides horses, plays tennis, flies his own plane, I've never seen him get mad but he gets red in the face, maybe he has high blood pressure, maybe he's had heart trouble, and his eggs are all in this one basket, he's got to get some cash or listed securities because if he keels over now the IRS would value his Bromberg stock at maybe twenty-thirty million and there wouldn't be enough cash to pay the estate tax and then they'd be forced to sell under pressure. So the choice is to sell more stock to the public or merge with somebody that has listed stock. Well, he can't go to the public now, not at any sexy price-earnings ratio, his earnings are flat and this year nobody wants this kind of issue anyway. I guess he's afraid to wait for a better market, and Charlie's offered him one hell of a price in CCC stock."

"Why are his earnings flat?"

"Because the private airplane business is in a slump, they're not making many private planes, so that part of his business has suffered, and then the government is beginning to slow up the space program."

"The space program? I thought we were in the Age of Aquarius."

Tommy shrugged. "Brombergs say they're cutting back. We're on the moon, now everybody is saying 'national priorities.' If we can get on the moon, why can't we run a profitable commuter line into the big cities? Out here they're building a mass transit system, they're going to run computerized electric trains all over the Bay Area — "

"Go on about Bromberg. Who are his lawyers?"

"Just one lawyer, Justin Silverstone, pretty decent older guy."

"Give you any trouble?"

"Not really. He's been tough when he's had to be, he hasn't taken any crap from Charlie or from our people, but he's done his job. He's got some Bromberg stock, too."

"No big law firm, eh?"

"Well, that brings up one problem we *do* have. Bromberg's got a son, Bob, a guy in his thirties, went to Harvard Business School, smokes a pipe, good-looking guy but a bit of a wise-ass. He's giving us trouble. Wants to bring in Sutter's firm, they're one of the biggest out here — "

"Sure, I know them. Why does he want them?"

"Because he's against the deal — our deal. He wants to run the show himself, be his own boss when his old man quits. He's the one who got them into this pocket calculator business. Did Charlie tell you about that?"

159

"Yes, that's the whole point as far as Charlie's concerned."

"Right, but that's the funny part. Bromberg Senior is lukewarm about these gadgets — he claims anybody can make them, if they catch on everybody *will* make them, the Japs and the big American electronics firms, and they'll glut the market, but Bob and some of his younger guys think the old man's afraid of trying something new, something he hasn't made before."

"And Charlie agrees with them?"

"Charlie's red-hot for the calculator, but Bob Bromberg doesn't want to work for Charlie, he wants to be his own boss."

"You can hardly blame him for that," I said, as the Fairmont's doorman approached.

"Well, Charlie's bringing up his heavy artillery, I guess the deal is getting serious," boomed Bernard Bromberg as Charlie introduced me. They were sitting around a table drinking Bloody Marys, and they rose as Tommy and I came across the terrace. A big umbrella protected the table from the blazing sunshine. A soft wind blew out of the west. Directly in front of us, blue water and whitecaps and sails. In the distance, docks and skyscrapers, the crowded hills of San Francisco.

Tommy's description had not prepared me for Bromberg's size. He was a bull of a man, several inches taller than me, at least 250 pounds, completely bald, deeply tanned, the profile of a Roman emperor. He wore an expensive blue suit, blue shirt, blue Gucci tie, enamel lapel pin of the Navy Cross. Justin Silverstone, his lawyer, looked like a sad but friendly spaniel, a lined face and the spaniel eyes behind horn-rimmed glasses.

"This is quite a view you have here," I said as we sat down.

"We've been cooped up in conference rooms for days so we thought we'd show you some fresh air and scenery," said Bromberg. "Have you been out here before, Ordway?"

We chatted politely, ordered a round of drinks, ordered lunch, but Charlie began to fidget, to tap the table with his fingers, to draw diagrams on a napkin. Charlie wasn't interested in the view or in my knowledge of San Francisco, and he soon got them back on the track. They were obviously close to making a deal, and now they returned to it, so I drank my drink and ate my poached salmon and listened.

The mechanics were clear enough: CCC would organize a new subsidiary and Bromberg's stockholders would vote to merge their company into it. As part of the merger plan, Bromberg stockholders would get CCC stock — a block right away, then more if Bromberg's earnings met certain goals over the next three years. Bernard Bromberg would continue to run the business.

The sticking point seemed to be how much power he would retain. Apparently he was insisting that during the three-year pay-out period, Bromberg's present directors would remain, Bromberg's present management would remain under employment contracts, and CCC's management would keep their hands off Bromberg's operations.

Of course Charlie was resisting these conditions. If he announced an acquisition to the world, he said, the world expected that he had acquired something. This way he was paying out a ton of money in CCC stock and the other CCC stockholders had a right to expect that he was buying something with it, obtaining control.

I knew that wasn't the only reason, though. If Charlie

gave in on this matter of management, then every other potential acquisition would demand the same terms Bromberg got. They would be filed with the SEC for the world to read, and thereafter nobody else would sell a company to CCC without retaining management control.

"I'm sorry, Charlie," said Bromberg. "It's not negotiable. The whole outfit looks to me, they're like members of my family, there's no way I can sell the right to keep them or get rid of them — "

"Speaking of your family, what about Bob?" asked Charlie.

"What about him?"

"Bob's been dead against me all along. If he can't talk you out of this, what's he going to do? Is he going to take all his minicalculator guys over to Texas Instruments?"

A pause. The wind blew down from the hills behind us. Bernard Bromberg unwrapped a cigar and lighted it. "Charlie, I've managed to handle Bob for over thirty years. Suppose you let me continue to handle him. Bob isn't going to Texas Instruments, Bob isn't going to compete with his father, Bob is going to stay right here."

"How do we know that?" asked Tommy Sharp. *Shut up!* said the look I gave him across the table.

"You know that because I'm telling you that," said Bernard Bromberg quietly.

"Let me make a suggestion," said Justin Silverstone. "What you've got here is a basic business decision, how much authority will the present Bromberg management retain. You don't need lawyers to kick this around some more, to work out a compromise. I'm confident you've got a deal here, it's 99 percent agreed to, and what the lawyers should do is get the papers ready, or 99 percent ready, with maybe this one hole left. So why don't I take Ordway and Tom back to my office, there's plenty of paperwork for us to do while you stay here and drink some more coffee and see if you can't arrive at a compromise."

That seemed like a good idea. We rose.

"Don't forget you're all coming over to Berkeley for dinner tonight," said Bernard Bromberg.

I crouched in the back seat of the Mustang, Tommy drove, and Justin Silverstone sat beside him, turning to address me.

"Now let me tell you about Bobby Bromberg, because I've known him all his life. He's really a good kid, a very nice boy, but all his life he's felt . . . I don't know how to explain it for you. . . . He's felt that he's got to prove something to his Dad, to Bernard. Prove everything. He was only eleven when Bernard came back from the navy. I guess Bernard felt he had to make up for all those years when the kid didn't have a father, so the way he did it was to spend time, to direct, to push . . . little Bobby had to do everything: horseback riding, polo, tennis, special lessons, had to be the *best* at everything, the best tennis player in the school, push, push, push . . . flying lessons when he was seventeen, boxing lessons . . . then they sent him to military school, to Culver, so he could ride all the time, then they sent him to Amherst — Berkeley or Stanford weren't good enough — then they sent him to Harvard for business school so he could take over the company someday, then of course he had to start right in at the company, and he made some mistakes and Bernard gave him *hell* for it!

"You know, if I had a son — we've got one girl, she's adopted, my wife had some problems — if *I* had a son, I wouldn't take him in to work for me. I wouldn't take the risk, wouldn't subject the boy to the strain. Well, maybe if it was a big firm, a big law firm like Sutter's office, then you don't have the contact, or if Bromberg had been a big outfit, like CCC, with operations all over the country, but the whole show's right over there in Oakland, they see each other every day, and he won't let the boy learn by making mistakes. You see, he's so afraid people will say he's easy on his son, he favors the son over others, so he leans over backwards and he's *harder* on the son! If the kid does something good — like this calculator thing, I think that's going to be a great thing, don't you? Conroy thinks so, he never stops talking about it. Well, that was Bobby who picked it up from the engineers, who talked Bernard and the others into putting up money for prototypes, for production machinery. Okay, so there isn't much patent protection but Bromberg got the head start, Bromberg's on the inside track, and Bobby ought to get some credit for that."

We had crossed the Golden Gate and were moving up one of the steep hills of downtown San Francisco.

"Turn right at the second light, Tom. You'd better get in the right lane now. . . . Okay. . . . What was I saying? Yes, Bobby getting credit. What does Bernard do? Bernard decides to sell the company. He brings the boy up to think he's going to run the company someday, and just as he gets ready, he's learned the business, he's ready to expand into an exciting new line — Bernard decides to sell the company! No offense, gentlemen. Nothing wrong with your deal, with CCC. I'd say the same thing if we were merging into General Motors."

I was amazed at all these personal revelations. "You mean you're opposed to our merger?"

"No, I'm in favor of it, if we can come to terms, because the family needs liquidity. Bernard isn't getting any younger, he's spent twenty years building this business and now he's got to cash in some of that work, he's perfectly right to make the deal, but I'm trying to show you how it looks from Bobby's point of view. It looks like his father doesn't trust him to run the business by himself."

"And he doesn't?"

"No," said Justin Silverstone sadly, "he doesn't. Pull right into that garage, Tom. We can take the elevator up to my office."

Silverstone had a small comfortable suite, a few younger lawyers, a few secretaries, law books lining the walls, papers spread all over the desks, several telephone messages. Conyers & Dean, Philadelphia: Mr. Harry Hatch in New York very anxious to get in touch with Mr. Smith. I looked at my watch. It was after six o'clock on the East Coast, but I was confident that Harry would still be at his desk. He was.

"Say, Ordway, what's going on out there? First Hudson tells me that Conroy's about to sign up another acquisition. Is that true?"

"Well, we're getting close to a deal, I would say. Your people know all about it."

"Yeah, but from what they tell me it sounds like we'll have to recirculate. What are the numbers?"

I held my hand over the phone's mouthpiece. "What does he mean 'recirculate'?" I asked Tommy Sharp.

"The preliminary prospectus for the debentures. We'll have to include Bromberg's numbers on a *pro forma* basis, and send an amended Prospectus to everybody who got the first one." With no invitation from me, he picked up the other telephone and cut himself right in. "Hello Harry, this is Tom Sharp. Have they shown you Bromberg's financials yet?" I listened to them discuss the problem. The point seemed to be that we would have to republish CCC's earnings, showing how they *would have looked* if Bromberg had belonged to CCC over the last five years.

In New York, Harry Hatch sighed a little. "This isn't going to make things any easier. The people at the SEC are just about to issue their comment letter, and now we'll have to go back to them with all these changes. . . ."

"But Bromberg's earnings make CCC's look one hell of a sight better," protested Tommy.

"That's true," said Harry Hatch. "And that's why my underwriters are so hot to include them. But it almost means starting over again. When do you plan to close with — what's their name? Bromberg?"

"Same time we close with you — with the underwriters," said Tommy.

"*What?*" I couldn't believe my ears.

"Sure," said Tommy. "We had to agree to that. Brombergs don't want CCC stock unless CCC gets the proceeds of the bond issue, gets the bank loans paid off, gets enough working capital in the till . . ."

Silence from New York.

"Still there, Harry?"

"Boy-oh-boy-oh-boy!" He didn't sound happy. "Oh, we can do it all right, but you understand what it means, don't you? It means the two deals will be contingent on each other. If we pool in Bromberg's earnings — even on a *pro forma* basis — then the underwriters are going to sell the debentures on the theory that you're going to *have* those earnings, that you've got Bromberg on stream with CCC. And if something goes wrong at the last minute, if you *don't* close with Bromberg after all, then you won't be able to close with the underwriters either!"

"Oh sure, we realize that," said Tommy airily.

I certainly had not, and I wondered whether Charlie had.

"And a simultaneous closing," said Harry Hatch. "Oh, we've done plenty of them, you understand, but it'll be a Chinese fire drill, the Normandy landings and the Marx Brothers at the Opera — all at the same time. It always is."

I was getting irritated now. "I guess we'll manage somehow, Harry. We always have."

"Sure thing, Ordway. Will you let me know the minute you've made your deal out there? We should clear the announcement with the SEC, and I want to send my boys out for the due-diligence investigation. So long, fellows, and happy hunting."

We rolled up our sleeves to attack the draft of the CCC–Bromberg plan of merger.

The Brombergs lived in a big rambling old house set amidst Monterey pines and eucalyptus trees in the steep hills above Berkeley. The house was made of weathered red-brown shingles. From the driveway one approached on graveled paths winding through ancient overgrown shrubbery and hedges. Beside the front door, Mayan statuary. Inside, polished teak floors, Persian carpets, redwood paneling, enormous modern paintings, a gigantic room filled with people, doors open to the terrace, and from the terrace a breathtaking view.

"Of course that's the University right here below us," said Bernard Bromberg. "The Bay, the City . . . Nob Hill's only nine miles as the crow flies . . . over there's Sausalito, where we had lunch . . . up above there is Marin County . . . the sun's going to set behind Mount Tamalpais . . . okay, if you've seen enough scenery I want you to meet some of these people. . . ."

He piloted me and Tommy through the crowd of guests, introducing Charlie Conroy's Philadelphia lawyers. Bromberg executives, Bromberg engineers, university professors, a bank president, all with wives. Everybody cordial: Is this your first visit to San Francisco? A black butler in a white jacket carried drinks on a silver tray. Charlie Conroy stood by the mantel, surrounded by earnest-looking men. He waved to me. Tommy wandered off.

Mrs. Bromberg, gracious but very, very cool, was tall, suntanned, dressed in a white silk suit and silver bracelets. I asked about her paintings. I had obviously been billed as a broken-down steeplechaser, so she was surprised to hear that I was a trustee of our museum. We walked around the house and she showed me her Miró, her Kandinsky, her two Pascins. She knew much more than I about the Arensberg Collection and how Fiske Kimball's persistent persuasion had got it for Philadelphia, from under the noses of the University of California and every other museum in the country. By the time we finished the tour, she was less cool. The butler stood in front of us with his tray. We each took another glass.

I told her I would like to meet her son.

"Well, he's late," she said, looking at her watch. "I can't imagine what's keeping them, we'll be eating in a few minutes — Oh here he is now. . . . Bobby, I want you to meet Mr. Ordway Smith from Philadelphia. . . ."

He was ascending the stairs — tall, thin, dark, loafers, flannels, blue blazer with silver buttons, pipe taken out of his mouth, kiss for mother, handshake for me, perfunctory smile but dark angry eyes.

"Where's Karin?" asked Mrs. Bromberg.

"I'm sorry, Ma, she asked to be excused. She called from the ranch, they were late getting back from the ride and she had to pick up Margy on the way back, but she'll try to come over after dinner. . . ."

A flicker of displeasure showed in Mrs. Bromberg's features, but only for an instant, and she left us to start the movement for dinner.

"Well," said Bob Bromberg, puffing on his pipe. "We've certainly been hearing a lot about Mr. Smith of Conyers & Dean."

"Nothing flattering, I trust."

"Oh, very flattering. So flattering, in fact . . ." Pause. Puff, puff. "Well, you've met old Justin Silverstone. Been representing us since Christ was a corporal — "

"Seems like a fine lawyer, I just met him today, but we've been working all afternoon. He's been representing your interests very tenaciously."

"Hmm." Puff, puff. "There's going to be another meeting tomorrow morning, right?"

"So I understand. They're typing up what we hope will be the last draft of the plan of merger, and we're all going to go over it with your father and Charlie — and with you, of course. . . ."

"Yeah, well, I've told Dad this and now I might as well tell you, I've decided to get special counsel in on this, to look at this thing for me and for my mother, too. Justin is a wonderful old guy, Dad doesn't want to hurt his feelings, but Justin is a general practitioner, knows a little bit about everything. I'm not saying anything against him, but frankly he's not in the same league as Conyers & Dean. . . ." Pause. Puff, puff. "I assume you've heard of Sutter & Monroe?"

"Oh, yes indeed."

"Well, I've got a classmate there, fraternity brother, Sandy Simon, Alexander Simon, do you know him? He's younger, of course, but he's a partner there, went to Harvard Law School, he's handled a number of other things for me, a brilliant legal mind, and so I've given him all these agreements and things to look over, all the things you people have submitted to us, and I think he has a few questions, so I've asked him to attend tomorrow. That's all right with you, isn't it?"

"Why sure," I said. "The more the merrier."

The butler was standing beside us. It was time to go in to dinner.

The guests sat around small tables on the terrace. Again the overwhelming view, this time stars, the Bay at night, the glittering lights of San Francisco and its bridges. Candles shielded from the breeze by glass chimneys. Clear turtle soup, fried abalone, artichokes, California Pinot Chardonnay.

Mrs. Bromberg sat between me and Charlie Conroy. Apparently Bob's wife was supposed to have been on my other side, but the table had been rearranged and I was with the matronly Mrs. Justin Silverstone, blue hair, passionate praise of California — she was originally from Hartford — and worried reports about a granddaughter who brought her boyfriend home from Columbia and expected to sleep with him right in her own bedroom, right next door to her parents. . . .

Charlie and Mrs. Bromberg were not enjoying themselves. He had no small talk, no interest in paintings or food or the geography of the Bay Area; he looked tired and bored and was clearly drinking too much. She, on the other hand, was as cool with him as she had been at first with me, and by now something in her manner — I can't explain exactly what — gave me the feeling that she was on her son's side. She didn't like Charlie and she didn't want to sell out, but she was a good hostess, making the required effort.

To give a little help I leaned into her conversation and asked Charlie to describe what Captain MacDiarmid was doing to the Hyde Place. That seemed to wake him up, he launched into an enthusiastic description of the project, and Mrs. Bromberg gave me what seemed a grateful smile.

On my other side Mrs. Silverstone was on another tack: "I must say that Karin might have made an effort to be here. She knows how important they consider this evening. She rides horseback all the time, they wanted her to talk to you about their horses. . . ." I learned that the Brombergs owned a ranch in the foothills above Sonoma, and that Karin was spending more and more time with her horses out there instead of attending to what Mrs. Silverstone considered her wifely duties at home in Berkeley.

As the butler passed a silver bowl of strawberries and a dish of sour cream, the table turned again. Mrs. Bromberg told me about the student riots in Berkeley, then we talked about the younger generation generally, the protest marches, the war in Vietnam, the same things everybody talked about at every dinner party that summer. Where will it all end? Charlie smoked a cigarette, glumly answering questions from the bank president's wife on his other side.

A spoon clinked against a glass somewhere. At another table Bernard Bromberg rose: Don't worry, everybody, no after-dinner speeches, just a word of welcome to our friends from Philadelphia, enjoyed meeting you, enjoyed working with you, look forward to a long successful marriage. Thought we might have an announcement this evening, but now Charlie has brought in his Philadelphia lawyers and you know what *that* means!

Laughter.

No, in all seriousness, Charlie — and Ordway too — we

think we're very close to making a deal, we've got a few more kinks to iron out, a few more points to nail down, I'm confident that we'll settle all the terms tomorrow, and I just want to tell you again how pleased we are to have you here.

Applause.

Charlie rose — a little unsteadily, I thought. Mrs. Bromberg, Bernard, ladies and gentlemen, just a couple of words to respond to those gracious remarks.

Hands in his pockets, looking down at his empty plate. A long pause. Silence on the terrace. He *can't* be drunk! He's never drunk.

His head came up and he spoke again: Traveled a lot around the country, talked to a lot of people. All over the country. Bought a lot of companies, too. Some of them very good, some of them not so good but we made them good.

Another pause. Mrs. Bromberg and Mrs. Silverstone looked up at him, expressions fixed, waiting.

Met a lot of people, all different kinds of people, all over the country, but never met a group like this, never been so impressed with a company or with the people who run the company.

Made it plain from the beginning that we're eager, CCC is eager to make a deal. Paying what we think — what we know everybody thinks — is a high price, but we're glad to pay it, because we know we're getting *quality* — quality management, quality products — and we expect to make a lot of money — for you, for us, for everybody.

Now sitting here, on this beautiful terrace, thinking about the future, I just had an idea: I'm going to give a party too, and I want you all to come! You see, I've just bought myself a house, a pretty big house out in the country near Philadelphia, and I've been fixing it up and in a few weeks it'll be ready for a housewarming — it's hot back there now but after Labor Day it'll be cooler and we'll have a party to open the house and to celebrate the marriage of CCC and Bromberg, and I want you all to come. All of you! I'll charter a plane — I've got a plane already but it isn't big enough — I'll charter a regular commercial jet and it'll bring all of you east for the party and bring you home again too. How does that sound?

A moment of stunned silence, then Bernard Bromberg shouted: "It sounds great, Charlie!" and began to applaud, and then everybody applauded while Charlie sat down, looking flushed and pleased with himself.

We rose. The ladies followed Mrs. Bromberg into the living room, the men regrouped in a loose circle around Charlie and Bernard Bromberg, the butler passed cognac and cigars. The conversation was stock market (terrible), student riots (terrible) and Vietnam (terrible). Bernard Bromberg was a Hawk, his son was a Dove, the professor of history weighed the alternatives for us, Charlie withdrew into himself and smoked a cigar.

In the living room the voices suddenly rose, then the door opened, a young woman and two tiny girls appeared on the terrace. All three were so blonde that their hair seemed almost white; all three were identically dressed in navy blue dirndls, white blouses, white aprons. All conversation stopped: the effect was overwhelming.

The little girls dashed to Bernard Bromberg and tried to climb into his lap. Beaming, his face transformed, he hugged them, kissed them, and rose to kiss their mother.

"Oh Dad, I am so terribly sorry, I explained to Mother it just couldn't be helped — "

She had some kind of an accent. She shook hands with all the men except her husband, to whose lips she presented her cheek for a perfunctory kiss.

Bernard Bromberg couldn't take his eyes from her. "Karin, where did these dresses come from, these matching costumes?"

"You like them, Dad? My mother sent them, they come from Lanz in Salzburg."

"They're beautiful!" said Bernard Bromberg, carrying a little granddaughter on each arm. "They knock me out. Come on, let's join the other ladies."

As we moved into the living room Tommy Sharp whispered into my ear: "What a piece! Wouldn't that be something for Graham Anders!"

"What the *hell* do you mean by that?"

"Sorry, Ordway, just popped into my mind."

"Just popped out of your mouth, you mean. You'd better stick to tonic water from now on."

Bernard approached, moving Karin toward me. "Ordway, they tell me you're a good rider, I always thought *I* was a good rider, Boy, you ought to see this girl! She's really *something!*"

She really was something. I spent the rest of the evening talking with her. When Charlie gave the signal I didn't want to leave.

Tommy drove us back to San Francisco in the Mustang. I sat in the back seat.

"Charlie, would you turn off that radio for a minute? I want to talk to you."

He turned it off and lit another cigarette.

"Charlie, I want to be sure you understand what we're

174

getting into here. The underwriters want to amend your Prospectus to include Bromberg's earnings *pro forma*, to show what we'd look like if we'd had Bromberg's earnings over the last five years — "

"Of course they do, that's the whole point!"

"Okay, but what if something happens at the last minute? Bromberg says he won't close with us unless we sell the Debentures and pay off the bank debt. Now suppose for some reason Bromberg backs out just before we close with the underwriters? Then we don't have Bromberg's earnings after all, we've told people we *would* have them — or at least we will have implied it — so we've got a misleading Prospectus and we can't close with the underwriters either! Then what do we do? How are you going to pay off the banks?"

Charlie turned in his seat and squinted at me. "What are you trying to do, scare me?"

"No I'm not, I just want to be sure you understand — "

"Look, Ordway, if I backed off from everything because there was a risk . . . maybe even a big risk . . . you know where I'd be now? I'd be in the accounting department of International Bond and Share, that's where I'd be! Making thirty-six hundred a year, or whatever the guys in that room get now."

"It's my job to explain these things — "

"It's your job to get things *done!* Do I pay Conyers & Dean — what was it last year? Three hundred thousand? Just to tell me not to do things? Now goddamnit, I want Bromberg on stream, I *need* Bromberg on stream, did you know that? The market is lousy, First Hudson says they may not be able to sell the Debentures *at all* if we don't show that we're still picking up good companies, so I don't want any more talk about deals falling through, or misleading prospectuses. That's mechanics, that's your job, and if you can't do it I'll find somebody who can!"

We were under the bright lights of the Oakland Bay Bridge. Tommy drove the car, looking straight ahead.

In my room at the Fairmont I lay awake, first staring at the ceiling, then walking around the room, looking out at the lights across the Bay, then back on my bed.

I was worried about Charlie. He had never lashed out like that before, at least not at me. There is too much for him to think about, too many companies, too many problems. He *can't* keep all these things in his head and he hasn't developed the organization to do it for him. Where is Renfrew, for example? Don't even know where he is, but he isn't here. What's going on at Darby Turbine? What's going on in Florida? Does Charlie know? How many problems like Hydroflo are there, scattered all over the country — all over the world, for all I know — simmering away, ready to explode any minute *and we don't even know about them!*

And here we are walking into this Bromberg mess, a complicated family thing, son against father. It's a trap, I can feel we are walking into a trap, but nobody will listen to me. What's going to happen if we can't pay off the banks in the fall?

Why can't I make him listen?

Forget about it, there's nothing you can do tonight. Think about something else.

Think about Karin Bromberg.

At first she told me about her ranch in the foothills of the Sonoma Mountains. I listened well enough to ask questions, how many horses? what kind? but I was watching her talk and wondering. Where had she met Bob Bromberg?

I asked her.

"I'm supposed to be telling you about our horses."

"Why?"

"That's what they thought you'd be interested in."

"I'm interested in people, too."

She laughed and told me a little about herself. She was born in Hamburg, during the Second World War. Her mother was Dutch. Her father was a German engineer, a specialist in rocket instruments. After the war the Americans brought the whole family to Alabama, where her father worked with Wernher von Braun, developing the rockets for ballistic missiles and for the space program. When Karin was a child her parents were divorced, she and her mother returned to Holland. Her father took a job with Bromberg. Karin was occasionally sent out to California to visit him. In her twentieth year she met Bob Bromberg at a company picnic.

But why had she married him? I asked myself, looking at the lights reflected on the ceiling of my hotel room. It's not a question you ask a lady at a dinner party, especially if you intend to make a deal with her husband and her father-in-law. Why shouldn't she have married him? Was her father a Nazi? Did the Brombergs accept her? Well, they hired the father. That's a little different, not the same thing as having your son marry . . . But I was thinking why did *she*? Loved him. No. What do you mean, No? You don't know a damn thing about it. She doesn't love him, though. What are you, psychic? Just because you didn't like him. . . . Good-looking, rich, well-connected in San Francisco, going to inherit his father's business, the boss's son, after all. Maybe the old man liked her. Yes, he still likes her. Crazy about her. Not the mother, though . . . The mother doesn't like her; didn't like her coming late, didn't like the matching costumes, the way all eyes followed her, the way Bernard kept his arm around her waist. . . .

15.

An Irish Lullaby

Sandy Simon, Esquire, reminded me of a teddy bear, a chubby curly-headed teddy bear in black-rimmed glasses and a navy blue Brooks Brothers suit with vest and Phi Beta Kappa key. And a pipe, just like his client, who brought him around and introduced him to the rest of us.

We settled down around the table in Justin Silverstone's conference room: Charlie, both Brombergs, all the lawyers. In addition Charlie had summoned Jack Renfrew and Larry Lenz. This was because the exact degree of Bromberg's operating independence after the merger was to be worked out — the missing link in the merger agreement. They had apparently been called west after the meeting in Sausalito, had been on planes all night, and looked it.

The latest draft of the merger agreement had been typed and Xeroxed. A copy lay in front of each place. Sandy Simon went right to work, turning the pages, running his gold pencil down the lines as he read. Bob Bromberg, pipe clenched in his teeth, moved his eyes from his father, who sat at one end of the table and listened, to Charlie, who sat at the other end and talked.

Well, Charlie hoped this would be the last session, because he was confident that he and Bernard had come to a meeting of minds on this management question, the thing was academic anyhow because the whole reason for the acquisition from our point of view is Bromberg's management, but Bernard feels that his people need it down in black and white, so Jack and Larry have come out to see if we can live with this from an operating standpoint, and then the attorneys can get it down on paper and we can sign it and then we can all go back to work and make some money.

Charlie outlined the agreement he and Bromberg had made, ticking off the points on his fingers, and as he spoke I felt a curious mixture of dread and relief. Dread because the Bromberg acquisition was apparently going ahead as planned, right in the middle of the Debenture deal; relief because the doubts I was beginning to have about Charlie's mental health seemed to be unjustified. The old blarney was still working. He had romanced Bromberg out of the more extreme "independence" points which were supposed to be non-negotiable. Instead of the commitment to keep Bromberg's business untouched after the merger, Bernard himself would go on the CCC Board, and Bromberg's Board would be half their people and half ours. Their top executives, including both Brombergs, were to get ironclad employment agreements — but only for the three-year period during which the total purchase price would be computed. In exchange for these concessions, this particular "Conroy package" was being sweetened: on top of CCC common, the Bromberg stockholders were to get ten million dollars of convertible preferred.

I looked at Bernard Bromberg, who sat with his elbows on the table, chin in his hands. Why had he given in? For the Preferred, for the supplemental income it would provide? Or was he more eager for this deal than we suspected? Was there really something wrong with his health?

"One more thing," said Charlie. "In addition to joining our Board, Bernard is going to accept a new position that we're going to create for him at CCC. He's going to become Executive Vice President and Chief Operating Officer–West, reporting directly to me, in charge of everything out here on the Coast. Jack, my theory is this will take some of the pressure off you, you'll be able to spend more time on our other divisions, especially Darby Turbine. We've got a number of problems out here on the Coast, and we're looking at a couple of other acquisitions out here, and I think Bernard with his track record and his contacts in the business community will be invaluable to us. As for the day-to-day operations of Bromberg Instruments — well, do you think you could handle that, Bob? As President, I mean. Your Dad would move up to Chairman, be available whenever you need him, be based out here of course, but you'd actually run the company. What do you say?"

Too-rah-lu-rah-lu-rah, I thought. It's an Irish Lullaby.

Are they going to buy it?

Bernard Bromberg, chin still in his hands, looked at his son. His son, sucking the pipe, looked down at the table, then directly at Charlie:

"Is that the kind of a deal you offered Billington?"

"Who?" asked Charlie, genuinely puzzled.

"You don't remember Bill Billington?"

"Not offhand — "

"Sure you do, Charlie," I interrupted quickly. "That's the Schwenk son-in-law down at Hydroflo, the one who's been giving us such a hard time. . . ."

"Oh *that* guy. Well sure, what about him?"

Sandy Simon had reached down into his briefcase, and now he produced a copy of our Preliminary Prospectus for CCC's $100 Million Debenture issue. "Could I ask you a few questions about this Hydroflo situation, Mr. Conroy?" He was very polite.

"Certainly," said Charlie, his voice like iron, all traces of blarney vanished. "But you'd better ask Ordway here, he's the resident expert on that situation."

Sandy had done his homework. He had read the Prospectus, picked up our reference to the Hydroflo lawsuit, sent for a copy of the complaint and apparently talked to the country boys in Little Rock.

And that wasn't all. When he reported his findings to Bob Bromberg, the name Billington came up. "Bill Billington?"

Sitting there, trying to field their questions, I could imagine that conversation. Billington and Bromberg had been classmates at the Harvard Business School, it turned out. There must have been telephone calls, apparently a meeting, too. They had the full story — the Schwenk version of what we had done to Hydroflo — and now Justin Silverstone's conference room was turning into a courtroom, with Charlie and his men on trial, Sandy Simon prosecuting, I trying my best to defend, and Bernard Bromberg, silent, scowling, drumming on the table with his fingers, both judge and jury.

In one corner of my mind I wondered what he thought of Bob's tactics. You might expect a son to go straight to his father with such a discovery. No, here we unveil it at the most dramatic moment, right in front of the enemy, throwing the enemy into confusion and making the father (and the father's old lawyer) look stupid. See, Dad, I'm just as sharp as you are — maybe sharper. *Not* a lovable guy.

"Well, Mr. Conroy, were you unaware of the fact that during this period Hydroflo was losing dealership franchises?" Sandy Simon was working through a list of prepared questions now.

"I can't involve myself in all the operational problems of every subsidiary! We're a decentralized operation, the Hydroflo people were supposed to run their own show — "

"That's just the point," said Bob Bromberg. "They tell us you *didn't* let them run their own show, you had somebody riding them the whole time — "

"All right, now wait a minute." It was time for me to interrupt again. "I don't think we came out here to submit to a cross-examination about complaints from our companies. What happened is a matter of public record, you've got the pleadings right in front of you, I assume you also know that the whole thing's been settled, it's all cleaned up, as a matter of fact I was just down there before I came out here, Billington and his wife took me to dinner at their country club, we had a pleasant evening, and I'm surprised to hear they still have hard feelings."

Sandy Simon took off his glasses and began to polish them. "I wouldn't say they have hard feelings down there. They say you threw in the sponge."

"We gave them what they asked for, which was to have their old president hired back and a promise of more independence. Now the fact of the matter is, some mistakes were made — can I say that, Charlie? The lines of communication were not as clear as maybe they could have been, there was an intermediate level of management — "

"Which has been removed," said Jack Renfrew, taking the cue.

"Fired, he means," said Charlie. "We were trying to put the divisions under group v.p.'s at that time, sort of a pyramid setup, we put one guy in charge of all consumer divisions, so Hydroflo reported to him. . . . It seemed like a good idea at the time but he wasn't the right guy for the job."

I fed him another one. "Do we claim we never make mistakes?"

"Hell *no*, we don't claim that! Everybody makes mistakes. I do claim that we don't make the same mistake twice, though, and I wonder if we can get on and talk about Bromberg instead of Hydroflo. I thought that's what this meeting was going to be about."

Silence. Everybody looked at Bernard.

"Gentlemen, I think you'd better let me have a talk with my son," he said.

— Poor Ordway, she must have been *furious*.

— Can't really blame her, I've spent exactly three days with them all summer.

— And how long do you have to stay out there now?

— Christ, who knows? The deal nearly blew up this morning, but Charlie's determined to get this company no matter what concessions he's got to make. I mean he seems to be obsessed, he's just got to have this company! And Bromberg, the old man, I don't know . . . This morning I thought he was going to throw us out, but he didn't, he's still willing to listen, which makes me think he's more eager to sell than they're letting on, so at any rate we've all got to hang around here and wait while Charlie lays out a few more goodies on his tablecloth. . . . So I was wondering —

— What are you wondering, Ordway?

— You know.

— Oh no. . . . No, no, no, Ordway!

— Why not?

— Oh don't be ridiculous! All the way across the country —

— I'll pay for it, if that's the —

— No, dear, it's out of the question.

— Why is it? This is a great town, have you ever been here?

— But you are supposed to be working, you're with all those other people, Charlie Conroy and the Brombergs —

— They wouldn't have to see you, you could stay in a different place and tomorrow we're not going to meet, it's just Charlie and Bromberg, they're going to talk by themselves again, there's nothing for us to do but hang around and wait, as long as they know where to get me on the telephone there's no reason we can't be together for a while. . . .

— No, Ordway, it would be nonsense, and I can't come anyway, I have too much work. I have to decide before Monday if I should recommend that we pay the advance this crazy woman is asking for her novel, you just can't imagine what dirty books women are writing these days. . . . Ordway, you know that I'd like to come out, don't you? The other night was . . . It was very nice. Such a strange feeling, a rendezvous with airplanes. I've never done that before.

— Well, it *was* very nice, that's why I'd like to do it again.

— We'll do it again, but not on a business trip so far away. We can see each other right here in New York.

— Marie?

— Yes, dear?

— What are we going to do about all this?

— All what?

— You and me, this whole thing?

— I don't know.

— Are you sorry?

— About what? That I didn't marry you?

. . .

— Is that what you mean? Ordway, I . . . I don't think I want to talk about it now.

— You've always been my girl, you know that, don't you?

. . .

— Don't you know that?

— Yes.

— You do?

— Yes.

— Remember the time you hit me, said I wanted seignorial rights? Remember that, in the stable?

— Yes.

— Remember that first time at the Plaza, when you made the reservations?

— Yes.

— We took two rooms, to be careful? You already knew to do that.

— Ordway, why are you —

— I want to know what's going to happen.

— What do you mean? Nothing's going to happen.

— Is Bill staying in England?

— What difference does that make?

— Well, I should think it might make some difference.

— Why should it?

— Well, if he comes back, where would I call you? Where would I see you?

— You would call me at my office and you would see me where you've seen me for the last twenty years — in restaurants and in hotels, or motels, more recently.

— Is that what you want?

— Is what what I want?

— To see me in motels?

— Are you offering me something different?

— Do you want me to?

— What?

— Do you want me to offer you something different? I did once, you know.

— Oh Ordway, I think this is getting too complicated for the telephone, don't you? I don't understand what you're saying now, and I would have to look at you, so let's not say anything now that we'll be sorry for, let's wait until you're back. There isn't any hurry, you know. We have known each other such a long time. And you say you want to know what's going to happen. Why? Who knows what's going to happen? We have known each other since we were children, and our lives keep touching, and we are just growing older every day, so let's just live from one day to the next and not worry so much about what's going to happen. It *is* happening. All right?

— Marie . . .

— No, I think that's enough for tonight. Let me know when you're coming east, or when you can get to New York. You know I'll always be here for you. I'm going to hang up now, Ordway, I don't feel like talking anymore. Good night, dear.

16.

Karin

"Oh man, this is the life!" Tommy Sharp yawned and stretched and reached for his whiskey sour. Dressed only in bathing trunks we had bought that morning, he and I were reclining in deck chairs at the edge of the aquamarine swimming pool. A few feet away, Jack Renfrew and Larry Lenz bent over a checkerboard. A breeze stirred the branches of the massive oaks surrounding the pool, the patio, and sprawling whitewashed ranch buildings. A couple of acres around the houses were green; the grass and the bushes were constantly sprayed with water pulsing from buried pipes. Beyond this oasis, brown grass, fields and eucalyptus groves sloped down into the valley and the town of Sonoma. More brown hills rose on the other side.

"My-oh my-oh my-oh," murmured Tommy, and I turned my head to see Karin Bromberg coming out of the living room, her sandals clacking on the flagstones as she walked toward us. She had put on a white bikini. Even Renfrew and Lenz looked up for a moment, then quickly back to their checkerboard.

"Have you had a swim?" she asked. "How is the water?"

"Just right," I said. "We're basking here wondering what we've done to deserve this."

She smiled, unwound the black silk scarf that bound her hair, dropped the scarf on the table beside my drink, and dived into the pool without a splash, like a seal. A moment later she surfaced, hair darker now and plastered back, brown arms methodically chopping the water, brown back glistening.

I still didn't understand why we were here. Last night Charlie had announced that he was going to meet with both Brombergs at their plant in Oakland. "Just the three of us, no lawyers, nobody else, we're going to settle this once and for all."

"Charlie, do you really want us all to hang around here . . ."

He scowled at me. "Yes, goddamnit, I've told Jack and Larry I want them to stand by, and I want you here too, both you and Sharp, because the minute I shake hands with Bromberg I want the agreement drawn up and signed. We've had enough delays on this thing and I want you to start your due-diligence investigation so you can amend the Prospectus in a matter of days, is that clear?"

"Well, days? I don't know about — "

"I said *days*, Ordway! When I sign with Bromberg I want to hit the deck running, is that clear?"

Right after that Karin Bromberg telephoned. Did I want to see the ranch? She had heard that I'd have some time on my hands. . . .

"I'd love to see your ranch, but I've got Tommy Sharp with me, and two of Charlie's executives."

"Oh bring them along, we will have a swim and some lunch." Then she gave me careful directions for the forty-mile drive across the Golden Gate and up through Marin County. "Stop and buy yourselves some bathing suits. We will see you about eleven."

Renfrew and Lenz had been diffident at first, they didn't have the right clothes and they were getting telephone calls with problems from all over the country and maybe they'd go down to North Beach and check out the topless bars if they had any free time — but the fact was they just didn't know how to stop working for a few hours. Next morning Tommy got the Mustang out of the garage and I went up to their suite (undershirts, open briefcases, mimeographed financial statements, overflowing ashtrays, a room service table piled with dirty dishes) and made them hang up their telephones and come with us. I drove the Mustang this time. The sky was blue and the sun glittered on the water at the Golden Gate. We roared away from the tollbooth, up Route 101, past Sausalito, past Mill Valley, past San Rafael, then down toward San Pablo Bay.

"Hey Ordway, you must really want to see that ranch!" remarked Tommy from the back seat.

"I don't think Charlie's going to like this," muttered Larry Lenz. "I promised I'd show him the Darby Turbine results just as soon as they've got them worked out — "

"Well, they don't have them worked out, do they?" said Jack Renfrew. "I think it's time we kick a few asses over there."

"Chop a few heads, you mean! I don't understand what's *wrong* with these guys. I *told* them, I said to Robinson only last week — "

"Hey fellas?" I tried to put it tactfully. "I'm sure you realize this, but any talk about kicking asses or chopping heads isn't going to help us with the Brombergs right now."

"Jesus, Ordway! You don't think we would . . ."

I only got lost once, in the brown dusty hills near a place called El Verano, but we were close then and got directions at a gas station. From the highway the place looked modest enough: A clump of oaks, an ordinary RFD mailbox marked "Double B Ranch — Bromberg," a narrow gravel road disappearing over a hill. Half a mile down the road Renfrew had to open a gate. Then we drove through another grove of trees and emerged among a group of whitewashed stable buildings, barns and silos. A couple of Dalmatians came bounding toward the car, barking and running in circles.

I parked the Mustang beside a pickup truck and we climbed out.

"Good morning," called Karin Bromberg, walking out of the stable toward us. She wore tight faded jeans and cowboy boots and a denim work shirt with sleeves rolled high on her strong brown arms. A Mexican boy of fifteen or so walked shyly behind her, holding a straw cowboy hat. She shook hands very formally with all of us and introduced Miguel, who also shook hands. Then they gave us a guided tour of the ranch — the stables; the tack room full of western saddles and a couple of silver-studded Mexican saddles, but no English saddles; the riding ring; the corral; the house where Miguel's family lived; the bunkhouse for the other hands; the empty guest house; and the main house, with its enormous cool living room, with french doors leading to the patio, the swimming pool, the oaks, and the whole valley spread out beyond.

"These people know how to live," said Jack Renfrew as we were putting on our bathing suits in one of the guest rooms.

The stables and the tack room had done something to me, and the sight of splendid horses standing in the shade of some oaks at the end of the field. We used to have four horses when I was a kid.

Watching Karin swim the length of the pool and back again, I thought about a lot of things: my Old Man, who knew how to live as well as anybody, and the Brombergs who also do, and Charlie Conroy, who does not. Bob Bromberg senses what would happen if he has to work for Charlie, so why is he having his wife entertain enemy troops this way?

A trick? Baloney. Maybe he doesn't even know she's doing it. I hadn't seen many traces of Bob around the place anyway.

"Are you ready for some lunch?" she asked, holding on to the gutter and looking up at me.

"Sure. . . . Does Bob drive all the way over to Oakland from here every day?"

"Oh no, of course not, he stays in Berkeley during the week."

"So you only get to use this place on weekends?"

She looked amused, let go of the gutter and kicked herself into the middle of the pool. I got to my feet, finished the rest of my Bloody Mary, and dived in. We swam back and forth a few minutes, passing each other. When I stopped beside the ladder she stopped, too.

"Would your friends like to go for a ride later?"

"No, but I would."

"Yes, I thought you would. I usually go first thing in the morning or just before sunset, because it is cooler." She climbed out of the water. "Shall we have lunch in our bathing suits?"

We sat around a glass table, underneath a blue-and-white striped awning. The Mexican lady served gazpacho, deviled eggs, shrimp, asparagus vinaigrette, melon with prosciutto. Renfrew and Lenz didn't like the food, didn't like eating in their bathing suits, and had very little to say for themselves in a situation where nobody talked business. In self-defense they helped consume two huge pitchers of sangría, and by the time we finished they were having trouble keeping their eyelids up.

"Ordway, we'd better be getting back," said Larry Lenz, looking at his watch. "By this time Charlie may need us, and if we're not there when he calls — "

"Oh, don't worry, he knows where you are," said Karin, and it flashed through my mind: they want her to fill us full of booze so we won't be able to —

Baloney. They're just being hospitable. I'm supposed to be an expert on horses, they have beautiful horses and they're proud of them.

"I usually take a siesta at this time," said Karin. "We have plenty of rooms, or you can sleep right out here under the trees if you'd like."

"That's the nicest suggestion I've heard in a long time," said Tommy Sharp.

They were coming down the trail in single file. They're crazy, I thought. Don't they know better? Don't they teach them anything? The faces under the camouflaged helmet covers were the faces of little boys, though several wore moustaches. Maybe the jungle is so thick that they have to stay on the trail, but they shouldn't be so close together, and why have they got him in front? Shouldn't the lieutenant or somebody be in front? He carried one of those stubby guns they use now, more of a submachine gun than a rifle, and he wore a cloth-covered armored vest — the kind of thing we used to call a flack jacket. They all wore them, and they all were sweating as they picked their way along the trail, stumbling over roots, cursing and sweating, and then I saw him coming up to the wire, it looked just like another vine but I knew it wasn't a vine and I yelled but of course I wasn't there and he didn't hear me and I could feel the heat and the blast and I could see him thrown up into the trees

. . . and she looked down at me, frowning. "I think you are having a bad dream."

"Oh boy!" I rubbed my eyes. She had adjusted the venetian blinds so that the afternoon sun slanted into the room, a bare whitewashed little guest room. I had a headache and a terrible taste in my mouth, and I still wore my bathing trunks.

"If you want to go riding," she said, "I think we better go now, because your friends will be getting restless." She had put on her jeans again, and her cowboy boots. She carried another pair of jeans and a checked shirt. "Do you want to see if you can fit into these? They are Bob's."

I took the clothes. "Are the others still asleep?"

"I think Tommy is. The other two are watching a baseball game on television. I don't think I have a pair of boots to fit you, but you can ride in your shoes, can't you?"

"Yes, sure."

"All right, I will help Miguel get the horses ready. We'll be in the paddock."

Western saddles are designed for roping cattle and sitting ahorse all day, and since you can't very well jump fences or post I never understand why they insist on using them for ordinary riding, but they do. The big black mare had a comfortable gait, a gentle almost quarter-horse trot, and I didn't have much trouble sitting down to it, the same way we used to trot bareback when I was a kid.

Karin rode a light brown gelding, a beautiful horse that must have been partly Arab. She led the way along the first road, a dusty ranch road curving gently up into the hills, cool in the shadow of the oaks and laurels. We passed over the same creekbed a couple of times, the hooves drumming on the wooden planks. A shallow draw led us out to an open hillside: blazing sunshine, wind, the smell of hot dry grass.

She stopped her horse and turned to me. "What was your dream about?"

I shook my head. "Crazy dream. About my son, getting hurt in Vietnam. He's not in Vietnam, he isn't even in the army, he's still in college."

"But you must be worried about it."

"Well, I guess I am, but actually he doesn't want to go, he's going to ask for a deferment when he's old enough to get drafted, at least that's what he's told his grandfather. . . ." My God, what am I babbling to this girl for? "Where are your children, by the way?"

"With their grandmother, in Berkeley."

"You know, I can't help wondering . . . I know I shouldn't ask you this, but was it Bob's idea to have us out here today?"

"What makes you think it wasn't my idea?"

"I don't know, I'm just wondering."

"Why?"

"I have the impression that your husband isn't too crazy about the deal I'm out here to accomplish. . . ."

"If you were Bob, how would you feel?"

Touché! "Okay, then why did you . . . Didn't he . . . ?"

"If you want to know, I didn't even ask Bob, I asked his father if it would be all right, and he said 'Sure!' Does that answer your question? You see that big rock, sticking out up there . . . all the way out on the point? I will race you up there." She touched the gelding's flanks and he shot ahead, but my mare was right behind him, bounding out of the draw, hurling rocks and pebbles with her hoofs, stretching her neck way out, stretching herself into a long rolling gallop. I let her have her head because she obviously knew where she was going.

The wind blew into my eyes, the sky was clear, the mare's

shoulders surged in front of my knees, the headache was gone, the dream about Teddy was gone, and for the first time in weeks I forgot about Charlie Conroy.

Of course the gelding was stronger and Karin was lighter so they pulled about a length in front of us, but we stayed right with them all the way up the long gentle slope. As we neared the big elephant shape of the rock I saw Karin really kick him, but she couldn't get away from me, and as we raced around the outside of the rock she called, "Okay," and reined in.

She was red-faced and sweating now, grinning, her eyes shining with excitement. "Well, you *can* ride, can't you! Now we will walk them for a few minutes, through the woods down there, and then we do a little jumping." She touched the gelding again and we moved toward the trees.

Another hillside, this one sloping down.

"You want to see if you can follow me?" she called.

I nodded. Why not?

"Stay back a little. This time it's not a race." She moved off at a slow gallop, going sideways down the slope. I stayed well behind, then suddenly she disappeared. When I reached the lip of the hill I saw that she was already far below, cantering hell-for-breakfast down what looked like a forty-five-degree slope. I sat all the way back, letting the mare catch herself and slow to a walk, because this is a good way to break a horse's leg — and the rider's neck — but Karin was still cantering, almost down on the flatland. There seemed to be some water down there, a slow-moving creek or irrigation canal.

By the time I got down she was galloping directly at the canal. I thought, cow horses aren't taught to jump! The gelding flew over. Karin grinned at me over her shoulder and headed downstream. I put the mare into a gallop and hoped she wouldn't balk at the water, which was only about six feet wide here. She didn't. We made the grass on the other side with a foot to spare, and set off after Karin.

I saw what she was doing now. The canal was getting wider all the time. She jumped it again, made it. I followed, made it too. The third time the canal seemed like fifteen feet. Karin turned away from the water, raced around in a huge semicircle, came back as fast as the gelding could run — and barely made the other side, the gelding's hind legs sinking into the mud as they landed. I tried the same maneuver but this time the mare balked just as we reached the water and I had to grab the saddle horn to keep from flying over her head — looking like a fool, of course.

I could hear Karin laughing as I kicked around and retreated for another try. "Okay, my girl," I said to the mare. "We're just going to do this over and over until it works," and I guess she understood that I meant it, because this time she galloped harder and I could feel she wasn't going to balk and she didn't, she pushed off bravely but it was just too far for her and we came crashing down in a great spray of water and mud.

She's a little crazy, I thought, still soaking wet and sticky with mud, riding behind her through the tall irrigated grass. We were cantering again, even though the grass was up to the horses' bellies and they couldn't see where they were putting their feet. This isn't how *we* treat horses.

She turned and pointed to the range of hills in front of us. "Do you want to ride to the top? We have a beautiful view from there."

Far below us in the valley, some lights were coming on. "How much longer will it be daylight?"

"Less than an hour. Do you want to start back? Your friends will be so anxious about Mr. Conroy."

"The hell with them. You know something? This is the nicest day I've had in a long time."

She had tethered the horses in the clearing behind us. We sat on the grass just at the edge of the cliff, our backs propped against a smooth rock.

"Well, I'm glad," she said. "But you're still a bit suspicious, aren't you?"

"Oh no!"

"Oh yes! You have very good manners and you try not to show it but you don't understand what you're doing here. You think there must be some deep purpose, something to do with Bromberg Instruments and Conroy — "

"Oh no — "

"Oh yes, I think you look for diabolical motives, Machiavellian schemes, Oriental business methods. It never occurs to you that I liked the way you looked and wanted to go riding with you."

She turned to look at me. Easy does it! Tommy was right, this is a role for Graham Anders, not for me. I still wasn't sure if she was absolutely fearless or just crazy. The chances she took with herself (and with the Arab gelding) had made my flesh creep, although she did it with style, in full control of herself and the horse. Looking into those sapphire eyes — three inches from my eyes — I wondered what Graham Anders would do right now. Hell, I knew what he would do. I could smell her. Although I'd ridden behind her most of the time, I had seen her face when she made the gelding jump that last arroyo — ten feet across but fifty feet down if you didn't make it. That second in the air her face was contorted, a grimace, a mask, not of fear but of unbearable pleasure. She wanted danger because danger gave her pleasure — pure sexual pleasure — and Anders would have her pants off by now and a finger up her — at least a finger . . . She's closed her eyes already, waiting for it. . . .

"Tell me about Bob," I said, because I'm not Anders.

She opened her eyes and moved back a few inches, regarding me carefully. "What would you like to know?"

"Does he like horses, too?"

She shrugged. "He was sent to military school, you know. He hated it. I think the horses remind him."

"Why did he buy a ranch?"

"Oh, he didn't buy the ranch, it belongs to his father. His father is the one who loves to ride. He's owned it . . . I don't know, for many years."

"And he rides out here a lot?"

"Whenever he can get away. You saw that stallion . . . I would have put you up on him but he's quite difficult, he likes only Dad — "

"That's all right, I understand, the mare is fine. . . . Tell me, where does Bob spend his time?"

"At the plant, with his engineers, they are developing this little calculator, you can hold it in your hand, it can multiply and divide — "

"Oh yeah, we've seen them, they're the reason we want your company. But I get the feeling that Bob's against the merger."

She said nothing for a moment. Both of us knew this conversation had gone too far.

"Can you blame him?" she asked. "He expects to inherit the company, to succeed his father, and his father decides to sell it instead."

"How do you feel about it?"

"I know nothing about business."

"You know about men, though."

"What do you mean by that?"

"Which one is right?"

"They're *both* right! Dad thinks that Bob won't be able to run the company alone, and he's probably right, so it's just another thing that has gone wrong for Bob, he never had a chance to show he could run it alone — "

"What else has gone wrong for him? He looks like a pretty lucky guy to me."

She gave me a long look, a trace of a bitter smile. "Oh, he looks like a lucky guy to you, does he?"

"Sure he does. Beautiful wife, beautiful children, tons of money, interesting important work — "

Abruptly she stood up, brushing dirt from her jeans. "I think we better go back. It is really getting darker and your friends will begin to — "

"Karin, I'm sorry if I've been — "

She touched my arm. "Don't be sorry, I invited it. But if you see Bob Bromberg as a lucky guy, you are *much* less perceptive than I had thought." She turned away and walked toward the horses.

17.

An Arm and a Leg

Sandy Simon's law firm has automatic typewriters; Justin Silverstone does not. Ostensibly for this reason, the meetings continued in one of the oak-paneled conference rooms of the Messrs. Sutter & Monroe. Except for the view of San Francisco Bay, the atmosphere reminded me of Conyers & Dean: long dim hallways, rather used-looking furniture, old expensive Persian carpets, oil paintings of distinguished old men — but also the most modern equipment, such as typewriters that can store a fifty-page merger agreement on magnetic tape and copy it automatically, so that the girls need only retype the changed sections. This meant we could see a clean draft right after each session instead of waiting hours to have the whole thing done over with human hands.

I had talked with Charlie a few minutes the night we returned from the ranch, but I didn't learn much. He sat in his suite at the Fairmont, subdued, sipping Scotch, staring at the eleven o'clock news. "Had to up the ante a little," was all that he would say about the negotiations. "They'll show us a new draft of the agreement in the morning." The Frenchman had arrived, with a briefcase full of problems from Philadelphia. Jack Renfrew and Larry Lenz went into a huddle with him, but they couldn't seem to get Charlie away from the television. I went to my room, so I didn't know anything about Charlie's concessions until Sandy

Simon explained them next morning, sitting between the two Brombergs, looking more than ever like a teddy bear.

Item: Both Brombergs will go on the CCC Board.

Item: Both Brombergs will receive ten-year employment agreements, in form attached. Minimum salary $85,000 per year for Bob, $110,000 for Bernard to age 65; maximum for both keyed into Bromberg Instrument earnings as determined by independent accountants to be selected by the Brombergs. Bob agrees not to work for any manufacturer of computers or calculators for five years after leaving employ of Bromberg or CCC, if he should leave.

Item: After the merger, Bromberg Instruments Board will remain intact. All replacements appointed by CCC must be approved by at least one of the Brombergs. No change in corporate structure for ten years after merger without approval from both Brombergs or their survivor.

Item: Options to buy CCC stock at current market price granted to the Brombergs' treasurer, their vice president for sales and six of their top engineers. CCC will guarantee bank loans required by these men to exercise their options.

Item: In addition to CCC common, Bromberg stockholders will receive $10,000,000 in CCC preferred stock, convertible into common.

Item: Bromberg stockholders will receive a block of CCC stock right away, then much more if Bromberg Instrument earnings meet certain projections.

The last condition had been in the deal all along, but the formula was now changed. As Sandy Simon talked, both Larry Lenz and Tommy Sharp produced their slide rules, played with them a few seconds, then glanced at each other. Tommy scribbled a note and passed it to me: "If they make projected earnings, Bernard will become the biggest stockholder in CCC!"

Sandy Simon stopped talking. Larry Lenz's face was white. Jack Renfrew's face was purple.

Charlie had gotten up and walked to the window where he stood now, his back to the table, looking out across the Bay.

"Those are the changes that have been agreed to," said Sandy Simon, "as I understand them. Now I want to emphasize that Justin Silverstone hasn't had a chance to review this either — "

"That's correct," said Justin Silverstone, leafing through the agreement, looking sadder than ever.

" — but Bob just gave me the changes by telephone last night and I put this together by myself, so I'd like you all to — "

"That's what we're here for, isn't it?" asked Bernard Bromberg. It was the first time he spoke. "Charlie, I think that Ordway and the rest of your boys might like an opportunity to read this new draft carefully, so why don't you come upstairs to the Bankers Club and drink some coffee with Bob and Justin and me. You too, of course, Sandy."

"Good idea," said Charlie, who had also been very quiet during Sandy's explanation.

"Just one minute, gentlemen." Everybody turned to me. "Look, these are obviously very major changes. Before Charlie signs this thing for CCC, I think our directors should — "

"They'll ratify it later," snapped Charlie.

"I think we ought to at least discuss it with them, Charlie. It really could cause some trouble if we don't. And what about the underwriters? If they can't live with this thing — "

"They're all for it, they've been pushing this deal all along. . . ."

"But have they seen these terms? With all due respect,

Bernard, this is beginning to look as if you're buying CCC, instead of the other way around — "

"Goddamned right," muttered Jack Renfrew under his breath.

"Just *one* minute, Ordway!"

Charlie's voice sounded too loud somehow, but I went on anyway. "My point is how long will it take to get this agreement into final shape? Maybe a couple of days — and in the meantime some other things have got to be done. In the first place, we've got to make some kind of an announcement. If we're this close to an agreement, we've got to tell people that negotiations are continuing, and that it looks like the deal is going through. In the second place, the underwriters and their lawyers are coming in from New York this afternoon, and we've all got to start work on revising our Prospectus to reflect the Bromberg acquisition. And your people — I mean Justin and your financial officers and your accountants — have to start right in on your proxy statement — "

"I think we should do one thing at a time," said Bob Bromberg. "When we've got a *signed* agreement of merger — "

I interrupted: "Bob, I'm sorry, you're wrong about that! We've got a very tight timetable. Charlie's instructions to me are to hit the deck running, because your stockholders have got to vote on this merger before we can sell the Debentures to the underwriters, and before they can have a meeting you've got to send them your proxy statement, including all of our stuff, and before you can send it you've got to clear it through the SEC — "

"Not to mention our California Corporations Commissioner," said Justin Silverstone. "He can be more trouble than the SEC."

"What's your point, Ordway?" asked Bernard Bromberg.

"My point is you've got to let the underwriters and their lawyers and our people start to work with your people in Oakland today. *Tonight*. Even though the agreement isn't signed. We've got to assume it's going to be signed and get started on the amended Prospectus and the proxy statement right now, or they won't get done in time."

Nobody said anything for a moment. Bernard Bromberg lighted a cigar and turned to Justin Silverstone. "Is he right?"

"He's right."

Bernard Bromberg blew out a cloud of smoke. "Okay, Ordway. Tell the underwriters we'll have our treasurer and our production guys available in Oakland at six o'clock. They can start with them."

Bob was on his feet: "Wait a minute, Dad — " but his father was already following Charlie out of the room.

"My God!" said Larry Lenz when the door was shut. He had taken off his glasses and was massaging his eyes with his fingers.

"Playing checkers!" Jack Renfrew glared across the table at me. "You had us swimming and playing checkers and watching TV, you were out horseback riding with that — "

"He needs them," said Tommy Sharp, trying to defend me. "He knows he's got to have them. The underwriters can't sell the Debentures without these extra earnings pooled in, and the Brombergs know it, too."

"Horseback riding with who?" asked the Frenchman from behind his sunglasses.

"You guys believe he's serious about this agreement?" I asked them.

No response. They looked down at the papers on the table.

"Well, in that case I think we'd better settle down to Sandy Simon's draft."

Larry Lenz sighed, put on his glasses, and turned the first of fifty pages.

18.

Hitting the Deck Running

Oakland. Chain link fence. Security guards. Long dark halls. Conference room. Young men from New York, with briefcases. Balance sheets. Earnings statements. Cash flow statements. Employment agreements. Collective bargaining agreements. Bank loan agreements. License agreements. Stock option plans. Pension plans. Tax returns. 8-K reports, 9-K reports, 10-K reports. Title reports. Plant leases. Articles of incorporation. Minute books. Questions. Answers. Cigarette smoke. Coffee in paper cups.

To bed at four in the morning, up again at eight, breakfast in coffee shop, back across the Bay Bridge to Oakland, lower level of the Bridge, dark, steel girders flashing by, the tunnel, the grimy port, long lines of army trucks being loaded on the freighters. Why *not* send him to Canada? What if everybody went to Canada? Security guards again, this time a tour of the plant: offices, laboratories, machine shops, brightly lighted halls, rows and rows of women in slacks and hair curlers, smoking cigarettes, talking, bending over their work tables, knitting snarls of wire and transistors, assembling gauges, fitting printed circuits together like jigsaw puzzles, electric trucks moving parts and materials from the locked storage areas, more rooms full of conveyor belts and women packing instruments into cardboard boxes — and everywhere the Muzak speakers: ". . . drifting along with the tumbling tumbleweeds . . ."

Bob Bromberg and two young engineers draw diagrams on a blackboard: the minicalculator made possible by two technological breakthroughs: (1) readout devices that light up or reflect light to show numbers in the little window (2) tiny silicon squares, large-scale integration chips, no bigger than your fingernail, contain thousands of transistors, diodes, capacitors. Everybody nods, indicating familiarity with diodes and capacitors.

The young engineers interrupt each other in their enthusiasm: All logic functions combined into single chip, four hours' work reduced to one, we can buy the chips from Texas Instruments, the displays from Burroughs. Direct labor three dollars, overhead four dollars. Even if the Japanese could get labor down to zero, they'd have shipping costs from Japan plus 5 percent import duty. Price themselves out of the market unless they build plants in the U.S. And we've already got a plant!

Bernard Bromberg behind a mahogany desk, glad to answer any questions you gentlemen might have. Photographs: Mrs. Bromberg by Bachrach, a teenaged Bob buttoned into cadet uniform, blonde grandchildren, Karin in wedding dress, Karin in white bikini, Karin at full gallop on Arab gelding, grinning officers of Torpedo Squadron 9 lined up three deep on flight deck of USS *Saratoga,* President of the United States shaking hands with Bernard Bromberg . . . How about some lunch in our cafeteria?

In the hallway after lunch: "Ordway, our lawyers are finally satisfied with the merger agreement. We're prepared to sign whenever Charlie's ready."

"Where's Charlie?"

"Search me, counselor," said the Frenchman, who was hanging one of Charlie's suits in the closet.

"We've got to find him. The Brombergs are ready to sign. We can get the deal signed up this afternoon."

"All I know is he's off someplace with the fruitcake of yours. The decorator with the beard."

"MacDiarmid? What's he doing out here?"

"What's he ever doing, counselor? Trying to peddle something to the Boss."

"Will you tell him to get in touch with me the minute he comes in?"

"Absolutely, counselor."

We broke the group into smaller working teams. Two of the accountants from Pennypacker Poole and one of the young men from First Hudson settled into the office of Bromberg's treasurer to review the tax returns and the financial statements. In the conference room at Sutter & Monroe, Tommy Sharp, Larry Lenz, another accountant from P-P and one of Harry Hatch's young lawyers worked out the changes in the Prospectus for the CCC Debentures to show how CCC would look if it acquired Bromberg. Justin Silverstone sat in his own office and drafted the proxy statement explaining the proposed merger to Bromberg's stockholders.

I went back to my hotel room and waited for Charlie Conroy.

— Conyers & Dean, good afternoon.

— Hello, Harriet, this is Ordway Smith.

— Hi, Mr. Smith, are you having fun out there?

— Oh yes, great fun, Harriet. I hear there are some messages?

— Yes sir, Barbara's gone home but I have them down here. She said the only urgent ones were Mr. Canby at Ordway Chemical, and Commander Ordway, she said your uncle, sir? He'd like you to call him, he's at his summer place, I think it's Jamestown, Rhode Island, I've got the number . . .

— I guess the Chemical Company would be closed, wouldn't it?

— Yes, sir, it's after six here, I was about to close the board, do you want me to find Mr. Canby's home number?

— No, he won't be home yet, let's try my uncle. Listen, Harriet, if you want to shut down, just give me the number and I'll call him from here. . . .

— Oh no, Mr. Smith, that's all right, I'm not quite ready anyhow. . . . Just a minute, please. . . .

— Hey Ordway, how are ya?

— Just fine, Uncle Jack. How's the weather?

— Great. Just great. Had a shower last night, cooled things off, now we got a steady breeze, four-five knots outa north-north-east and it never got over seventy-five all day. . . . Hey listen, I'm glad you called, there's something I want to talk to you about.

— Go ahead.

— You know this Greek, this Pappas fella wants to buy the Chemical Company, he's not such a bad fella, it turns out.

— Oh it does?

— Yeah. Remember that big Alden ketch *Orion* that Freddie Pratt had built before the war? Thirty-foot beam and all that holly inlay in the main cabin?

— No, Uncle Jack, I don't think —

— Oh yeah, he was a big fan of your mother's, she'd remember the *Orion* . . . well anyway, old Freddie died and they couldn't get a crew during the war and the boys were in the navy so Anna sold her, I guess she changed hands a couple of times, only time I saw her — oh, must have been ten years ago, Shelter Island — she'd been let go all to hell, I mean it was a goddamned shame, Ordway, everything was peeling, they had a *tin* patch on the afterdeck, can you imagine?

— Uncle Jack, I'm not sure I'm following —

— Well just listen, Ordway, this guy has bought her, and he's completely restored her, must have spent a fortune, she looks just about the way Freddie had her except he's got a regular bar rigged up in the main cabin. Of course you got to make some allowances —

— Pericles Pappas owns the *Orion?*

— That's what I'm telling you, and he took us for a cruise in the Sound the other day, picked us up right at the foot of Wall Street, right where the helicopter lands —

— Who was on this cruise, Uncle Jack?

— Well, Ted Canby was, and that Englishman that represents your sister's people, and the fella from the Trust Company, I always forget his name, and Pappas himself, and his lawyer. . . . Hey, you know who his lawyer is? Old Billy Underwood's boy, he's in the firm now too, he must be about your age. . . .

— Sounds like a nice party, Uncle Jack. I'm kind of hurt that I wasn't asked.

— Oh you *were*, Ordway! Canby said he tried to get the message to you but you were out in Texas or someplace with your boy Conroy and your office didn't expect you back for a week, at least. They all said they were sorry you couldn't join us.

— I see. Well, tell me what happened.

— Well, that's the reason I wanted to talk to you, Ordway. . . . You know this Greek isn't such a bad apple. He told us all about how he started out in the junk business, didn't have a pot to piss in, then the war came and metal got scarce, then Allied Bolt owed him a lot of money, then they went into receivership — well, I couldn't follow it all but I kinda got to like the guy and I sure do like what he did to the old *Orion*. I mean he's got her looking just the way Freddie had her —

— Uncle Jack, was anything decided? About the Chemical Company?

— Well, of course we didn't sign anything, I said I wanted to talk to you, and of course we've got to have a board meeting and make it official but . . . Yeah, I guess you might say we made what they call an agreement in principle. . . . He's going to give us two shares of his common stock for each share of ours, and on top of that he's going to give us debentures at seven percent, convertible into more stock. . . . The whole package makes our Chemical stock worth about forty bucks a share, Ordway. Now how can we turn that down?

— Uncle Jack, I keep telling you it isn't forty bucks; it's *paper* that happens to be valued at forty today, might be worth zilch tomorrow!

— Well sure, anything might happen, but the others all think it's a good deal.

— And they've convinced you.

— Ordway, you know I'm not a lawyer, I'm not a financial guy. I've spent all my life playing with boats, I've got to listen to the experts when it comes to all this big-time stock market stuff, but I think I know something about people, and this Greek looks all right to me. I mean I wouldn't want to spend six months in the same wardroom with him, but I don't think he's trying to screw us. He's going to keep Canby, he's going to let Canby run the show, and all of our employees will be kept. So the answer is yeah, they've convinced me, and I thought I'd better tell you right away.

— I see. . . . Well, that's very nice of you, Uncle Jack.

— Canby said he'd tell you as soon as he could get hold of you.

— Uh huh.

— And your Aunt Emily sends her love. When are you all going to stop over for a sail with us? We haven't seen your kids since I can't remember when.

— We'll try to do that very soon, Uncle Jack. Not this summer, I'm afraid, but as soon as we can. Thanks very much for calling, and give my love to Aunt Emily.

As soon as I hung up the telephone rang again. It was the Frenchman with orders from Charlie Conroy.

The place looked undistinguished although all the other shops along the street seemed both elegant and expensive. *Rosenthal and Co. Objets d'Art* was all it said on the plate-glass window, through which I saw a blue tapestry and a table with an ormolu clock and a few jade figures. When I walked in, a plump woman with glasses approached.

"Is Captain MacDiarmid here?" I asked her, and immediately he appeared from the back somewhere, bearded, immaculately dressed for town.

"Good afternoon, old boy, so glad you could come down promptly. Miss Rosenthal, may I present — "

"Is Charlie here?"

"Certainly, come along, I want you to meet Miss Rosenthal's father, he's one of the greatest experts on European tapestries . . ."

He guided me along a corridor, then into the back of the building. "Such a coincidence, couldn't let it pass you know, having Conroy right here when this *magnificent* treasure went on the market, belonged to Mrs. Carter Winslow, *she* got it from Hearst. . . ." We entered a huge empty room — almost a loft — dominated by an enormous tapestry on a white wall, illuminated by strong lights on the opposite wall. The thing must have been twenty feet high and thirty across. A border of what looked like grape leaves. Marble columns, steps, a stone railing, some figures by the columns holding back curtains to reveal a field or a meadow, a lot of men on horses, a lot of dogs, a running stag, and in the distance a castle . . . ? a château . . . ? the Hyde Place? Conroy's House? Could it be?

Charlie Conroy slumped in a deep leather chair, glumly contemplating the tapestry. Beside him stood a tiny bald man in a pince-nez and a double-breasted blue suit. MacDiarmid introduced us: Professor Doctor Rosenthal, late of the Kunsthistorisches Museum, Vienna. His hand was cold.

"Mr. Smith is a trustee of the Philadelphia Museum of Art," said MacDiarmid. "You've heard of the Walter Slocum Smith Collection, of course. That was Mr. Smith's father." Professor Rosenthal received this information without comment. Nobody said anything for a moment. We looked up at the tapestry.

"What do you think?" Charlie's question was apparently addressed to me.

"Is that supposed to be — "

"Tell him."

Professor Rosenthal cleared his throat and delivered a lec-

214

ture. He had a heavy accent and I couldn't follow the whole thing: Paris, Gobelin factory, high-warp looms, low-warp looms, Charles Le Brun, Colbert, Minister of Louis XIV, series of tapestries showing the royal palaces, also known as the Months, Château de Montmort (Île-de-France) *not* a royal palace, however series copied many times in hundred years following 1668, this one unquestionably genuine, note marking woven into border, apparently done in reign of Louis XV, detail of hunting scene more typical work of Jean Baptiste Oudry (1686–1755), probably commissioned by . . .

Finally he stopped, clearing his throat again.

"Guess what they want?" said Charlie.

"Oh, I haven't the slightest — "

"Tell him!"

"Mr. Conroy, you understand this does not belong to me," said Professor Rosenthal carefully. "This belongs to Mrs. Winslow's estate, I am acting for the executors — "

"Absolutely *fantastic* find," bubbled MacDiarmid. "Couldn't believe my eyes. Nothing like it outside the museums any more, be just the perfect thing for the front hall — "

"A hundred and forty grand," said Charlie.

"The estate isn't going to auction . . . ?"

"The executors possess the power to sell privately," said Professor Rosenthal.

"Professor Rosenthal will of course authenticate — "

"Not so hard in this case," said Professor Rosenthal. "There are only eight previous owners since the work was completed — I would say between seventeen hundred and twenty and . . ."

"William Randolph Hearst," said MacDiarmid.

"Gentlemen, I'd like to consult my lawyer for a few minutes," said Charlie.

"Why certainly, old boy," said MacDiarmid. "That's why we asked him to come over." They withdrew and closed the door.

"What do you think?" asked Charlie again.

"Charlie, I don't know a goddamned thing about tapestries, that's what you're paying MacDiarmid for. I've got to talk to you about the Brombergs. They have the agreement ready, they want to know when you want to sign."

Charlie looked at his watch, then shook his head. "No time now, got to catch a plane at three."

"Catch a plane? Where are you going?"

"Home. Got another deal cooking, guy just called me, there's a chance that Manayunk Steel might be for sale, right in our own backyard, what do you think of that? We've been trying to get our hands on them for years — "

"Charlie, for God's sake, what about the Brombergs?"

"What about them?"

"Well, you haven't even signed the deal with them, you've been working for weeks and weeks and now that they're ready to sign — "

"All right, so let 'em sign. Haven't I given the bastards everything they asked for? Let 'em sign the agreement, we'll sign it later, what difference does it make when it's signed? Now tell me what I should do about this tapestry."

"Come on, Charlie! They've taken us into their houses, they're selling their business to us, we've been working on this for weeks, you've invited them all to fly east to a party — "

"We're still going to have the party, I just told MacDiarmid to make arrangements — "

"But you can't run off without signing the deal! Don't you see, it's an insult to them. Why should they sign before you do? As a matter of fact they might *not* sign if you run off like this. Have you said anything to Bernard?"

"No, why should I?"

"Aw Charlie! Suppose they get mad and don't sign?"

"They'll sign."

"I'm not so sure."

"Want to bet?"

"Charlie, it doesn't make any *sense!* You can't make another deal now anyway. Are we supposed to amend the Prospectus *again*? You've got to sit still long enough to get the Debentures sold. Now, you *know* I'm right about that, don't you?"

"What am I going to do about this tapestry? Should I give this guy a hundred and forty thousand clams?"

"Oh Jesus, Charlie!" I sat down in the other chair and covered my face, feeling the panic rise.

"I have trouble making up my mind these days," said Charlie. "Come on now, you know about these things. Should I give them what they ask?"

"Honestly, I don't know, but I guess we could ask somebody at the Art Museum. I could call somebody. . . . But it sounds like an awful lot of money. Have you got it? In cash?"

He shook his head. "Have to sell something. . . ."

"Your CCC shares are in hock — "

"Sell some tax-exempts. . . ."

"How much income would that cost you?"

"Well, I'm furnishing the house anyway."

"Buy a lot of furniture for a hundred and forty thousand dollars."

"Hmm . . . Sure looks like the Hyde Place, doesn't it?"

"Charlie, the Hyde Place itself is a copy. . . . Why don't

you tell them you'll think about it, you want to get another opinion. . . ."

"They say some museum down in Texas is after it."

"Well, the executors will have to get the best price, so if the museum offers more — "

"They wouldn't even be showing it to me."

"That's right."

"MacDiarmid wants to have it for the party."

"You mean the party for the Brombergs? If you don't sign that agreement there might not be any party, Charlie. Can't I persuade you — "

"No, you handle Bromberg now, I've got to see those guys at Manayunk Steel before somebody else gets to them." He was suddenly on his feet, heading for the door, opening the door. . . . "Professor Rosenthal, have somebody call me a taxi right away, I've got to catch a plane — "

MacDiarmid and Rosenthal came in, both looking at me, but Charlie was still talking. "Now Ordway, you just tell Bromberg that I had to rush off on this other deal, sorry I couldn't stay to sign with him but that's just a technicality, we'll expect him and all his gang to celebrate as soon as the merger goes through, I'll be talking to him as soon as I get a chance. Professor Rosenthal, nice to have met you, very interesting to hear about the tapestry, wish I had more time, Ordway here will talk to you, I've got to run now, think I'll just grab a taxi in the street. . . . MacDiarmid, you'll call me about the plans for the party, we've got to have everything installed by then, no, don't come out with me, I'll find the way, so long. . . ." and he was gone.

"Remarkable fella," said MacDiarmid.

Professor Rosenthal just looked at me.

Walking up Powell Street in brilliant sunshine, the cable cars grinding past, what a beautiful day, what a beautiful town. *What am I going to do?*

The conference room table at Sutter & Monroe was covered with open briefcases, yellow legal pads, printers' proofs, typewritten inserts, handwritten financial statements, scissors, staplers, Scotch tape dispensers, overflowing ashtrays, the remains of a sandwich lunch. . . . Around the table, a tired working group. They had been at it since nine o'clock that morning. It was now seven in the evening.

Tommy Sharp reported. "Ordway, we've called New York and the printer is putting his messenger on a plane. We thought we'd go out and get something to eat, come back and finish up, we ought to be done about midnight, by that time the messenger will be here and we'll turn him right around. He can catch the red-eye express, be back in New York in the morning, they should be distributing proofs by tomorrow night."

"Sounds all right to me," I said. They wonder why financial printers are so expensive! "What about the Bromberg proxy statement? They going to print that out here?"

"Easier to print the whole thing together," said Tommy. "Justin Silverstone says he'll bring his copy over as soon as he's finished so we can send everything together. He should be here pretty soon."

"All right, I'll wait for him, I want to talk to him anyway."

The young lawyer from Iselin Bros. & Devereaux spoke up: "Mr. Smith, has the merger agreement been signed? Harry Hatch called, he thinks we should make an announcement right away and he wants to tell the SEC that we're coming in with this S-14 — "

"Sure, I agree, but it's ten o'clock in New York, he's not

going to put out a statement tonight anyway. I'll work it out with Justin Silverstone."

They all got up and put on their jackets.

"Are you having dinner with Charlie?" asked Larry Lenz.

I just shook my head.

"Bernard is not going to like this," said Justin Silverstone, regarding me mournfully across the littered table.

"I know it."

"It gives Bobby another chance to sink the merger."

I nodded.

"But *why*, Ordway? Why did he do it?"

"I told you, he's been offered another acquisition, he's afraid he might lose it if he doesn't — "

"But in the meantime he might lose this one. Does that make sense to you? Hmm?"

"Justin, you've been frank, so I'll be frank. I don't think he should have gone without signing the agreement. I think it was discourteous to Bernard, and I told him. But he went anyway. That's just the way he is. He's an extraordinary guy, he's subject to moods, but he's also a brilliant man who's built an empire from practically nothing, and I guess we've got to take our clients as we find them and do the best we can to help them do what they want to do. Am I right?"

Justin Silverstone sighed. "Yes, of course you're right. But how are we going to handle this?"

"I thought I'd let you handle it."

He considered that for a moment. "What's our timetable now?"

"They hope to distribute proofs tomorrow night. If they fly out yours you can review them the next day and give us your corrections by phone. Most of our people will go back tomorrow, next day at the latest, and from then on we'll be working at the printers' in New York. If there aren't too many changes we should be able to file before the end of the week."

"And we can't mail the proxy statement to our stockholders before the SEC clears it, which will be another week or two?"

"Justin, we can't even file with the SEC unless the merger agreement is signed. Not only that, we've just *got* to make an announcement now — if we have a deal. Or if it's fallen through, for that matter."

"So what you're telling me is that Bernard has to sign the agreement right now, even though Conroy hasn't signed it, otherwise we won't make the timetable, and we've got to issue an announcement before Conroy's signed?"

"Oh, he'll sign, Justin, it's just mechanics to him. If Bernard will only sign . . . I think we can get the thing done. Can you talk him into it?"

Justin's spaniel eyes regarded me. "Why *should* I talk him into it?"

"I guess I didn't mean that the way it sounded. . . . I've been under the impression that you were in favor of this merger."

"I was."

"But now?"

"But now I'm having second thoughts, Ordway. Charlie Conroy is beginning to look a little different . . . erratic . . . hard to deal with — "

"He gave your people everything they asked for."

"He gave them everything Bobby and Sandy Simon could dream up, that's what he gave them. How do you think that makes Bernard feel? And me?"

He was right, and there wasn't anything for me to say. We sat in silence for a while. Justin got up and walked to the window. It was dark outside. The others would be back in a few minutes.

"Justin, you've got to admit it's a very very good deal for your stockholders. The numbers — "

"Oh sure, the numbers." He turned around. "But life isn't just numbers, as you know perfectly well. Life is people, companies are run by people, we sell out for a pile of CCC securities, what are they really worth? What are they going to be worth five years from now? Ten years from now? Do we really want to entrust our futures to Charlie Conroy?"

"I thought you'd resolved that question."

"So did I. But now I'm not so sure." He returned to the table, opened his briefcase, put a manila envelope on the table. "Here's the draft of our proxy statement. Your people will want to go over it too. I'm going to drive over to Berkeley and have a talk with Bernard — Oh my God!" He stopped, took off his glasses and rubbed his hand across his eyes. "I forgot, he's out at the ranch tonight, I'll have to drive all the way out — " Again he stopped abruptly, but this time looking at me somewhat fearfully, looking as if he had said something he shouldn't, then recovering quickly and replacing his glasses. "Okay, I'd better get started then. I'll call you at the Fairmont."

— Marion, it looks like I'll be coming back, either tomorrow or the next day, I'll try to get a flight to Boston and —

— Ordway, there's no sense your coming up here now, we're going home this week, I told you that —

— Well, I thought I could drive you down, say hello to your father —

— No, that's not necessary, you just go on home, we'll be

there on Wednesday anyway, I've got an appointment with Isotta, I must say I think this business with Ailsa is something you might have handled yourself. . . . What's going on with Charlie Conroy, by the way? Did you know what he sent me?

— What he sent you?

— A mink coat, from Nan Duskin's, with a card, "Apologies for stealing Ordway's vacation." What am I supposed to do, Ordway? Can I accept a mink coat from Charlie Conroy? Can I send it back? And what's all this about MacDiarmid and a party?

— MacDiarmid is setting up a party at the Hyde Place, sort of an opening night, I guess, and an entertainment for the Brombergs, the people out here — but how did you hear about it?

— MacDiarmid called me, wants you and me to help organize the party. In other words, he wants us to see to it that our friends come. This is *exactly* what I predicted, Ordway, he wants me to tie his party into some function, something for the Museum or for one of the schools or the hospital, so he can get pictures into the papers. Of course it's a *preposterous* idea, things like that are scheduled a year ahead of time. He knows that, he's just trying to *use* us to get publicity for Charlie . . . and for himself, of course, and I will be everlastingly *goddamned* if I'm going to become Charlie Conroy's social sponsor even if you feel you have to be at his beck and call. . . . What am I to do with this coat?

— You can't very well send it back. Does it fit?

— It's a little short.

— Give it to Ailsa.

— Ordway, have you lost your *mind*? A mink coat for a fourteen-year-old girl?

— Well, then put it in mothballs, I don't know, but you'd

better write him a note, I guess it's the only thing to do. And I guess we should help out with his party. I'll talk to Mac-Diarmid, you won't have to do anything you don't want. Is there any word from Teddy?

— Yes, a postcard from Basel. They seem to be having fun. He's staying another week so he'll have to go up to college right after they get home. . . . We haven't seen much of him this summer. . . .

— No, we haven't. . . .

— Well . . . you think you'll be home when we get there, do you?

— Yeah . . . I hope so. I mean one way or another this thing out here has got to resolve itself, it's too complicated to explain but I'll see you in a couple of days. . . . Oh. There's one more thing: It looks like the Chemical Company will be sold.

— Ordway! My God!

— Don't talk about it, they haven't announced it yet, but they got to Uncle Jack while I was away, and he's tipped the scales. This time it'll go through.

— Well! . . . That's quite a piece of news.

— Thought you'd like to hear that.

— That means we'll get some money, doesn't it?

— Yeah. Some. Stock in another company. Debentures. Forty bucks' worth of paper, supposedly, for each of our shares.

— But you're mad about it?

— Sure I'm mad about it, but what can I do?

— Will it hurt you at the office?

— It won't help. My great-grandfather was one of Dean's first clients. Eighteen seventy-eight!

— Times change, Ordway.

— That's what everybody tells me.

— And God knows we can use the money.

— What happens when we've spent it? Or lost it in the market?

— Oh come *on*, Ordway! I think you're just dead tired. Why don't you get some sleep?

O. Smith sleeps.

O. Smith dreams. Steeplechase. Everybody in full gallop, too close together. Dust. Solid timbers ahead. Everybody over, but now two horses without riders, a big stallion and the Arab gelding. Gelding way ahead now, stallion right behind. Not on the course now, riding in the brown grass, high brown grass, ahead is the deep arroyo, the horses fly across but O. Smith is on foot now, can't get across, and on the other side the stallion is trying to mount the gelding and O. Smith is shouting, "No! No! You can't do that! That's not a mare!" But the stallion is doing it, doing it hard and O. Smith covers his eyes because he doesn't want to see, and someone pushes from behind and he falls down in the blackness, every muscle in his body clenched to bursting.

O. Smith is awake. O. Smith goes into the bathroom, urinates, flushes the toilet, goes to the window, looks out at the lights of San Francisco, lies down again.

O. Smith sleeps.

O. Smith dreams. Everybody is at a party on the ketch *Orion*, sitting in the main cabin: the partners of Conyers & Dean, the directors of the Chemical Company, his sister the Lady Stanhope, and the portrait of his mother hangs on the bulkhead, and his Uncle Jack, in blue blazer, explains that he put a bar in here, but you have to make allowances, and Charlie Conroy is behind the bar, he is the bartender in a white mess jacket, and O. Smith explains that Bromberg wouldn't sign and Charlie Conroy scowls: That was just mechanics. What are we paying all these legal fees for? And O. Smith tries to explain why Bromberg wouldn't sign, but nobody will listen, everybody turns away because O. Smith has made a mess of the Bromberg acquisition, everybody knows it's his fault, they are embarrassed for him, considering that Charlie Conroy has made it all on his own. Right now Charlie is working his way through school as a bartender, sweating in his white mess jacket, sweating as he mixes drinks for everybody, and nobody pays any attention to O. Smith, so O. Smith turns around and climbs the companionway to the deck but now they are sinking, the ketch is sinking and the black water is rising around him as he climbs and Charlie Conroy is behind him, grabbing him around the waist, holding on, pulling him off the companionway, pulling him back into the water, the water is warm and dark. Charlie Conroy will not let go, they sink into the darkness. O. Smith can't breathe, he knows that he is drowning.

O. Smith is awake. O. Smith
goes bathroom, eats two aspirin tablets, drinks a glass
of water with two shots of
bourbon in it, turns on the
television, turns off the television, goes to the window,
sees the sky growing lighter
above Oakland on the other
side of the Bay, closes the
curtains, lies down. O. Smith
sleeps.

The telephone woke me up. Justin Silverstone was calling.

I took a taxi in the morning rush hour, lower level of the
Bay Bridge again, steel girders and exhaust fumes, the
grimy Oakland waterfront, more freighters loading more
supplies for Vietnam — a parking lot full of howitzers, this
time — the security guards at Bromberg's gate, Bernard
Bromberg behind his desk, alone.

He didn't ask me to sit down. "Did Justin tell you what
we've decided?"

"No, he told me to be here at nine o'clock, that you'd tell
me."

He nodded, pushing a manila folder across the desk. "I
won't keep you in suspense. We've signed. Here you are, ten
executed copies."

"That's great, Bernard," said I, smiling with relief, reaching for the folder.

"But I want you to carry a message to your client."

"Certainly."

"Look at that picture there behind you."

I'd noticed it before: The faces of Torpedo 9, squinting into the sunshine of Ulithi Lagoon one morning in 1944.

"See anything unusual?" he asked.

I shook my head, perplexed, looking at the young faces.

"Well, you can't see it, but I can feel it. I'm the only Jew in that picture," said Bernard Bromberg.

I winced. "Now wait a minute, Bernard. I hope you don't think — "

"Ordway, I never know what to think, so I usually lean too far over backwards, I don't *want* to have a chip on my shoulder, I don't *want* to see slights where none were intended, maybe sometimes I don't recognize slights when they *are* intended."

"Oh no, now wait a minute, Bernard, there's *nothing* like that, Charlie hasn't got the slightest — "

He held up his hand to interrupt me. "I just want you to give him a message, all right?"

"He's setting up a big party for you, Bernard, it will be the housewarming for his new place — "

"All right, I know, I heard all the nice things he said at my house, the nice speech he made us, never been so impressed with the people who run a company — isn't that what he said? Going to charter a plane for us, isn't he?"

"That's right, that's how he feels."

"Is it? You tell him this, Ordway: You tell him I've signed this merger agreement on the representation that we're going into partnership together. I'm not taking him over and he's not taking me over, this deal was sold to me, in the end, as something of a partnership between equals. As you pointed out, if our earnings work out the way we hope, I'm going to be the biggest stockholder in CCC. And that's the way I expect to be treated, the way he would treat an equal partner in his business. If he wants to buy another company next week, he might have the courtesy to tell me about it before I read it in the *Journal*. And if we're going into business together, he might consider that important enough to hang around for another day while we sign the papers. Might even have a drink with me after we've signed!"

"I think he considers the closing the big moment — "

"No, he doesn't. He thinks Bromberg's in the bag now, just like Hydroflo and Darby and Baxter and all the others, so he can go on to the next. What I want you to tell him is this, Ordway: Bromberg is *not* in the bag. Right here in this agreement, there are a dozen ways for us to get off the hook, and if Charlie doesn't demonstrate his intention to treat me as an equal partner, I'm just not going to close with him, whether my stockholders approve the merger or not. And he can sue me till the cows come home. Is that clear?"

"Yes, it is, Bernard, I'll tell him."

"And after the closing, it'll be the same thing: I'll be a director of his company, but if he thinks he's going to treat me the way he treats his directors now, he's got another thought coming. If you think you've had trouble with the Schwenks — Ordway, you tell him he doesn't know the *meaning* of trouble until he gets into a fight with me! I may look like a nice guy, maybe I *am* a nice guy — I try to be — but this place wasn't built up from nothing by somebody who's just a nice guy! Honest to God!" He was out of breath, his face flushed. "Will you tell him that, Ordway?"

19.

Where's Charlie?

Since I had to change planes in Chicago, I called CCC headquarters from there.

"Good afternoon, Nancy. Is the great man available?"

"I'm sorry, Mr. Smith, I haven't seen him all day, he was out at Manayunk Steel this morning and now he's gone to New York. I'm sure he'll be calling me, though."

"Tell him I have good news. The Brombergs signed the merger agreement, I've got in my briefcase, would he please let me know when I can bring it over."

"Sure thing, Mr. Smith. Will you be in your office tomorrow morning?"

"Yes, I will, and I'd like to come over first thing, if I may. It's really important, Nancy. You might tell Mr. Renfrew too."

"Will do, Mr. Smith."

"Say, Nancy, I don't suppose the helicopter is available, is it? I'll be getting into Philadelphia just at rush hour, I've got to go all the way out to the country — "

"Oh gee, Mr. Smith, didn't Mr. Conroy contact you about that ordinance yet?"

"What ordinance?"

"Oh, Mr. Conroy is very angry about it. They passed a law out there in your township, Captain MacDiarmid called about it — "

"Captain MacDiarmid?"

"Oh yes, he brought some people over from New York, some people from a magazine to take pictures? And he brought them in the helicopter to save time because they're so busy and the police came — "

"This is out at the Hyde Place . . . I mean at Mr. Conroy's place?"

"That's right, and the police came and told the pilot he was not allowed to land there because they have this new law they just passed, the township supervisors, and Mr. Conroy was . . . I mean Mr. Conroy was going to speak to you about it when you got back. . . ."

So I rented a car.

You drive away from our airport over the Penrose Ferry Bridge and the first thing you see is an oil refinery belching flames and terrible stenches. The second thing you see is a gigantic contraption that hammers rusty old cars into little cubes. Graham Anders always claims the thing has aesthetic value, a piece of modern sculpture welcoming the traveler. At any rate the scenery is different from San Francisco.

The house was empty and cool. An old lawyer in West Chester is paid to keep me up-to-date about what goes on in this county, and the first thing I did was to call him at home, but of course he was still at the Shore. What are you going to do? He always handled my Old Man's real estate and zoning matters and I just kept him on retainer and now he's old and sick and asleep at the switch so Colonel Pickering and my other neighbors have made an end run. You have to advertise an ordinance before it goes into effect. I wonder if Marion heard about it and chose not to tell me?

I changed my clothes, went out and saddled up the mare Minnie. The sun had disappeared behind the trees on the ridge, but it was still hot. We moved along the creek, everything overgrown this time of year, trees and vines and weeds, a dank lush overripe semitropical jungle, patches of knee-high mint at the edge of the water. I reached down and grabbed a handful of mint and shoved it into my boot.

We passed the Old Mill. Window still broken. Crazy waste to let it stand empty. How much could I rent it for? Maybe one of the kids, someday? Old Peter Arno cartoon: Your mother and I think it's time for you to knock about on your own, my boy — Only on the estate, of course.

Up out of the valley, through the trees into the open hillside, I touched her flank and we moved into a trot, then right away into an easy gallop but only for a moment because it was still too hot. I thought about the hills above Sonoma but that ride seemed long ago, and so did Karin. I rode for twenty minutes. The leaves were not turning yet, not even on the highest branches, so there must have been rain. This is my home. This is where I come from. Everybody has to come from someplace. I'm staying here no matter what happens.

Back at the stable I rubbed down Minnie and talked to the farmer about the weather. Then I walked back to the house through the cicada-pulsing gloom. I went in through the kitchen door, crushed some ice into a glass and put it into the deep freeze, crushed some sugar and water and mint leaves in another glass and poured bourbon over it, went upstairs, took a shower, put on my pajamas, came downstairs, took the now frosted glass out of the deep freeze, poured the bourbon mix over the ice, added another sprig of mint, and carried the glass into the study.

There was a stack of mail on the table but I didn't look at it. I picked up the telephone and called Marie.

Our "big" library at Conyers & Dean occupies most of the thirtieth and thirty-first floors of the Franklin Tower. Real estate experts tell us it represents an unbelievable waste of space; you can't build rooms like that any more. But I love it, and I guess the others do too. The north wall is pierced by three tall Georgian windows looking across to City Hall. The other walls are filled from the floor two stories to the ceiling with books. A balcony circles the room twelve feet above the floor, and from the balcony railing hang gilt-framed portraits of deceased partners, including Judge Conyers (painted in 1935 by Marion's father) and Frederick Hamilton Dean. The crystal chandelier came from the dining room of the Hyde Place; Clarence Pickford Hyde supposedly got it from the real Château de Montmort. They keep telling me that we're running out of space in the Franklin Tower, but I wouldn't vote to move even if we have to stack young lawyers into double-decker cubicles!

First partners' meeting of the season: Ellsworth Boyle and his management committee behind the long refectory table, the rest of us scattered about at random, soft September sunshine streaming through the cigarette smoke, everybody now reading the financial report for the year past and the schedule showing each partner's percentage of the profits for the year to come.

In our middle-class world the new year begins after Labor Day: families come back from vacation, children return to school, clients return to their desks, business picks up, and the firm enters a new fiscal year. Of course nobody ever says anything about the percentage schedule, but everybody turns to that page first. You can't run a law firm as a democracy; I guess our self-perpetuating committee makes us technically an oligarchy. They govern by common consent. If you don't like the percentage they assign I guess you can object, but so far as I know that has never happened. And of course you're always free to quit. That's never happened either. The committee does a pretty good job, and in this particular year it was easy enough: Two new partners casually welcomed to the club, two old men retired to "of counsel" status — events announced weeks ago, to be celebrated at a fancy dinner later in the fall. Everybody turned back to the results of the year just ended.

"Well, nothing earth-shaking here," said Ellsworth Boyle, taking off his reading glasses. "Gross income up a little, which is nice considering there was hardly any underwriting work — but I guess people are still dying on schedule, are they, Taylor?"

An old joke, but Taylor Chew, sitting beside Boyle, talked earnestly about a couple of huge estates his probate lawyers had settled during the year, and the fees we received.

"That's splendid, Taylor," said Ellsworth Boyle. "The mortuary department as ever our solace and our strength. But fellows, I have to draw your attention again to the net, which as you see is barely holding its own, and that's what we take home. Net income has barely increased — Well, I know the year before was unusual, couple of windfalls, but the point is the *expenses* are growing faster than our fees are coming in, and the reason for that, as you all know, is the unbelievable salaries we've got to pay boys coming out of law school. I guess you've heard that in Wall Street they're starting them at eighteen thousand this fall. Eighteen thousand dollars! For kids just out of school!"

235

I knew what was next: billable hours. We have come to the point where every lawyer is supposed to write down how he spends every minute of his working day; these time records are fed into a computer which multiplies each lawyer's minimum hourly rate times the hours spent and then disgorges — every quarter or so — the dollars the clients are to be billed. And in order to justify the salaries the young lawyers receive, they are going to have to put in more billable hours. . . .

I had heard it all before and turned back to the percentage schedule. What would I be getting if it were not for the Chemical Company and Charlie Conroy? And now, as announced in the *Wall Street Journal*, the Chemical Company will disappear into the empire of Pericles Pappas — the next project for Graham Anders and Tommy Sharp, or maybe Lansing Merritt and Ben Butler. No one mentions it in my presence. No one has to. One more year of big fees for Conyers & Dean, but next September or the one after that O. Smith's percentage will be adjusted. Is that fair? What about the Museum? What about the GPM? What about the Bar Association? The Committee of Seventy? Don't bring in money. Not directly, but I fly the flag. Isn't that my job? How many billable hours? Who do we bill for flying our flag?

Ellsworth Boyle was talking to me now. ". . . running up one hell of a lot of time, Ordway. Does Conroy realize what this thing is going to cost him?"

"Oh, I imagine he's expecting a substantial bill, yes."

"When do we get paid?" asked Patterson Fox, the father. "After you close the deal?"

"That would be the normal procedure, yes."

"Better send a bill now," said Ames Mahoney.

"Why should I?"

"From what I hear, investors aren't exactly storming the brokerage offices to order these Debentures of yours."

"Well, it's a lousy market, we all know that, but I can't just send him a bill right in the middle of the deal like this — "

"No, I think we'd better leave this to Ordway's discretion," said Ellsworth Boyle. "Do you want to tell us anything about this San Francisco acquisition? The story in the *Journal* indicates they held out for a king's ransom. . . ."

I told them about Bromberg Instruments and why Charlie was paying such a price. While I talked I looked at them:

I've never had a brother. Are these my brothers?

Ames Mahoney wears a pinstripe suit, a carnation in his buttonhole. His face is the color of rare roast beef. He graduated from law school at eighteen. They had to get a special order from the Supreme Court to admit him to practice. He was a famous lawyer before he was thirty. He drinks too much. Taylor Chew's Phi Beta Kappa key glints on his bulging vest. Every law office in the state has his book on *Orphans' Court Practice*. Patterson Fox Senior, a tiny wrinkled gnome in English tweeds and high-laced army shoes, knows all there is to know about corporate mortgages; his giant son, most famous ball carrier ever to score for Penn in days when Penn dominated the Ivy League, now plays golf, raises money for the Republican Party, and wants to be president — not of the United States but of the Union League; Ben Butler used to watch Forrester; now he watches me. Harry Rex, putting a match to his pipe for the fourth time in ten minutes, has been litigating the Hammon Soap antitrust case for seven years; what will he do when they finally settle it? Lansing Merritt would rather be teaching corporation law but can't afford to because he divorced his wife, married his daughter's college roommate, and consequently must support two families; Graham Anders sits in an aluminum wheelchair. His eyes are hollow and his face is puffed up like a pumpkin from the cortisone they have been feeding him. . . .

So many faces, so many stories. Are you my brothers?

"Don't keep us in suspense," said Ellsworth Boyle. "Did Conroy sign the merger agreement?"

"Not yet, I can't catch up with him — "

"What?" Several people shouted at once. "For God's sakes, Ordway!"

"Well, what am I to do about it? I've been calling him — three times today — I've spoken to Renfrew — "

"What about his Board of Directors?" asked Graham Anders.

"They've approved it, they signed a record of unanimous consent we ran around to them."

"Has Conroy signed it?" asked Lansing Merritt.

"I don't know."

"Well, then it's not unanimous, is it?" somebody said.

"You all aren't being much help," I said. "I see the problems, all right. What I want is answers. Tommy is printing the registration statement tonight, we've really got to file with the SEC in the morning if we're going to get the Brombergs' proxy statement to their stockholders in time for the meeting — "

"My God," said Lansing Merritt, "you're not going to file an unsigned merger agreement!"

"If the Board's approved it, the signing is just a ministerial act," said Graham Anders.

"You'd better take another look at Section Fourteen-Oh-Two," said Lansing Merritt. " 'Consent in writing setting forth the action so taken shall be signed by *all* of the directors' is what I think you'll find it says — "

Ellsworth Boyle interrupted them. "Fellows, I think we're going to have to let Ordway handle this whatever way he thinks best, but Ordway, you'd better be pretty damn sure you're doing what the client really wants. If there's any doubt in your mind — "

"Who *is* our client?" demanded Harry Rex. "Are we working for the Company or for Charlie Conroy?"

"Charlie Conroy is the Company," said Pat Fox Junior.

"The hell he is," said Lansing Merritt. "The Company is the stockholders as represented by the Board. Take a look at — "

"*Fellows!* Come on now!" Ellsworth Boyle tapped his pencil sharply on the tabletop. "I think we've got some other things to talk about this afternoon — "

"No, Ellsworth, I beg your pardon, I think we got a problem here!" Lansing had the bit in his teeth. "I take it this firm will be expected to give an opinion — several opinions — as regards a hundred-million-dollar bond issue and a *very* large merger, in other words, we're going on the hook for those amounts if something goes wrong, and now it seems we've got Charlie Conroy's usual high-wire act — "

"Now wait a minute!" Graham Anders moved the wheels of his chair, but Lansing kept right on: "All due respect, Ordway, this isn't *exactly* your specialty, you've always had Pat Forrester or Graham actually running the more complicated deals — "

"Or Lansing Merritt," murmured somebody, way in back.

I said: "Indeed it's not my specialty, Lansing, but Tommy Sharp has a good deal of experience by now, and he's been doing most of the technical work."

Graham Anders said: "Ellsworth, these comments are entirely uncalled-for! I've been out of commission but I've kept in touch with what's going on, and Ordway's been running this deal exactly right, from everything that I can tell." His face was even redder and puffier now.

"Yeah, I think we've belabored this enough," said Ellsworth Boyle. "I've got a couple of other things on this agenda. . . . Harry, who's going up to Harvard to interview, this fall?"

Are you my brothers?

Some years ago they tore down Broad Street Station and the Chinese Wall that carried the railroad tracks in from Thirtieth Street, but when it came to developing the Penn Center complex they had trouble raising enough money in Philadelphia, so the first buildings were thrown up by some operators from New York, cheap glass-and-limestone boxes now streaked with dirt, looking forty years old instead of fourteen.

Somebody convinced Charlie that the change from Philadelphia Sheet & Tube to Conroy Concepts should be dramatized by physical change, a move from the old Arch Street offices, from their green paint, their dented olive filing cabinets, their Norman Rockwell calendars. Since this was before Charlie heard of MacDiarmid, the atmosphere at Penn Center is Executive Modern: glove leather, chromium, white rugs, cubist paintings, potted trees and water splashing somewhere.

It was seven o'clock when I stepped off the elevator. The receptionist was gone, but I rapped a coin against the glass and a young man in shirt-sleeves came to open the door. No sir, Mr. Conroy wasn't here, but Mr. Renfrew was still in his office —

Jack Renfrew, also in shirt-sleeves, sat behind a sea of

papers and talked on the telephone. As he looked up at me I remembered him in his bathing suit at Karin's pool, ill at ease, trying to relax. Now he looked tired, as tired as I've ever seen anyone. He was talking to somebody at Darby Turbine.

"Look, Hew, I keep telling you I told him, he knew about it, he said he'd be there, you want me to hit him over the head and *carry* him over? I guess something more important . . . I know it . . . I know it . . . I agree with you. . . . Right . . . Right . . . You guys will have to work it out on your own, I'm giving you the bottom line, Hew. . . . Who, me? Come on, you know better than that. No way, fella, no *way!* Just get your people together again tomorrow morning, I'll try to get him over there but I'm not promising anything, and if he doesn't show, you guys make the decision and give me a report. Okay? I know . . . I know, but that's the way it's gotta be. Go home and have a drink, Hew. . . . Have a second on me. . . . Okay, a third. So long, I'll talk to you to-morrow."

He hung up, leaned his elbows on the desk and rubbed his hands over his face. "Shut the door, will you, Ordway?"

I did. When I sat down again I saw that he had made up his mind to unburden himself. "That was Robinson, at Darby Turbine. They had a meeting this afternoon, executive committee, they've got to decide whether to go ahead with this Belgian project — "

"You mean Brooke-Templeton's deal? Is that on again? I thought that was shot down in Chicago — "

"Well, he's got it back on the track in some other form. They're doing a joint venture with a Dutch company, no guarantees from us, but of course they're gun-shy now, they don't want to lay it on unless Charlie's approved it, and so

241

they set up this meeting, the guys came over from London and from Amsterdam, Charlie promised me he'd go to the meeting, you know where he went instead? Went to the Parke-Bernet in New York to attend a furniture auction. With your buddy MacDiarmid. I hear they bought a cock-fighting chair for five thousand dollars. You know what a cockfighting chair is?"

"MacDiarmid's no buddy of mine."

"Thought you introduced him."

"I certainly did not. But you seem to be having the same problem I'm having, what I came over for." I opened my dispatch case and took out the folder of merger agreements. "Jack, we've got to get these Bromberg agreements signed. The registration statement has to be filed with the SEC to-morrow, otherwise it won't clear in time to mail the proxy statement to Bromberg's stockholders. . . ." I went through the whole song and dance again, while Renfrew lighted a cigarette.

"What do you want me to do?"

"Get him to sign them. Tonight."

"How?"

"My God, Jack, the two of us must be able to find him somehow. He hasn't disappeared, has he? Is he still in New York?"

"That's what Nancy thinks, but he didn't call her all after-noon, he's not at the Carlyle, he's not at his apartment, and he's not with MacDiarmid. Any other ideas?"

"Where's the Frenchman?"

"Good question."

"You think they're off on a toot or something?"

Renfrew shrugged.

"What's the matter with him, Jack?"

Renfrew blew out a huge cloud of cigarette smoke before he answered. "Damned if I know."

"You think he's having emotional problems, some kind of . . . maybe some mild form of nervous breakdown?"

"You said it, I didn't."

"You get the feeling that he can't make up his mind, can't decide things that have to be decided?"

Renfrew nodded, taking another drag.

"What are we going to do about it, Jack?"

"Any suggestions?"

"Can we get him to see a doctor?"

"You mean a shrink? He's already seen one. After the divorce he went out to Forty-ninth Street, to the Institute, twice a week, sat there and talked to the guy, only thing he ever said to me was he should develop other interests. So he went and bought that white elephant of yours — "

"It wasn't mine, Jack."

"You got him to buy it, now he's got other interests. Cock-fighting chairs!"

"Oh bullshit, Jack." I had enough now. "Don't try to tell me you think I'm the cause of Charlie's troubles. If he's sick I didn't make him sick and what's the use of us sitting here arguing about it. We ought to be working together doing something. People get sick sometimes. What happens if the captain of a ship gets sick? The first mate takes over, right? You're the first mate — "

"And you want me to take over the company?" He stared at me, incredulous. "Jeez, Ordway, maybe you're the one that needs a shrink."

"I'm not saying take over the company, Jack, I'm saying you've got to take some responsibility, you've got to see that decisions are made, you've got to keep the machine running.

We've just got to face one job at a time, and my job is to get the goddamned Bromberg merger agreement signed. I mean he still *wants* Bromberg, doesn't he?"

"Far as I know, yeah. The underwriters say we have to show their earnings to sell the Debentures — "

"Well then, one last time, Jack: How are we going to get this agreement signed tonight?"

He emitted a long sigh. "He might be coming back to the apartment. We could leave word with the doorman. . . ."

I took a taxi to the Parkway House and persuaded them to let me into Charlie's apartment — a dreadful place, furnished by his ex-wife at great expense to look like a hospitality suite in Miami Beach: indirect lights, tassels hanging from everything, fake heraldic emblems on the ashtrays, enormous television sets in every room. There is a nice view of the Art Museum and the Park across the river. I went to the leather-padded bar, poured some bourbon, and looked at the cars moving around the Museum circle.

What should I do about Charlie? What *can* I do about Charlie? Nothing. Sit right here and wait for him and do my best to get these deals closed.

I called the printer in New York and spoke with Tommy Sharp.

"Everything's under control," he reported. "We've got a whole team working here, I would guess we'll have everything cleared before midnight so that they can print and bind, the accountants are coming in before breakfast to sign off, if we get the messenger on the nine o'clock shuttle he'll be at the SEC before eleven — "

"But he's not to file until we tell him to."

"Jesus, Ordway, you don't mean — "

"You'll have to work out some arrangement where the messenger calls you every half-hour or so — "

"Ordway?" Tommy lowered his voice. "You know Sandy Simon's working here with us, don't you? Bob Bromberg's lawyer? He's in the next room, but I won't be able to keep this from him. He's not going to let us file if — "

"I don't *want* to file if the agreement isn't signed, that's the reason I'm telling you what to tell the messenger — "

"Yeah, but Ordway, what am I supposed to tell Sandy?"

"Tell him I'm right here in Charlie's apartment waiting to get the agreement signed when he gets home, no problem at all, you guys just get your registration statement down to Washington and I'll take care of Charlie." I hung up and made myself another drink.

When I finished that I realized I was hungry. The refrigerator contained a bottle of sour milk, a jar of mayonnaise, an open can of vegetable juice, an open bottle of liquid Maalox, a box of eggs and an envelope of bacon. I also found some bread and butter, so I made myself a fried egg–and–bacon sandwich. I ate it as I wandered around the place looking for some personal *thing*, some evidence of Charlie Conroy as a man, some sign that a human being lived here. Not a book anywhere — *Fortune, Forbes, U.S. News and World Report*, a stack of annual reports . . . This wasn't a place to live, it was a place to sleep and eat breakfast, a hotel room. They're right, I'm right, he needs the Hyde Place and maybe he needs MacDiarmid.

I called my house to see if Marion had returned from Maine. She had.

"Am I to understand you're just going to sit there in Charlie Conroy's apartment until he comes home?"

"I guess so. I don't know what else I can do."

245

"There's nobody at Conyers & Dean to whom you can entrust this vital mission?"

"Not really. Charlie's acting strange these days. I guess I'd better do this myself. . . . I'll be home for dinner tomorrow, though."

"Would you like to speak to your son? He won't be home tomorrow."

"Is Teddy there? I thought — "

"Hello Dad, how's it going?"

"Hey! Where did you come from?"

"We flew into Boston Sunday night. I caught a ride up to Northeast with Packy Fuller, so I drove down with Ma today but I've got to be back in school tomorrow, we're beginning practice — "

"Oh look, you've been gone all summer, I'd like to talk to you. When do you have to go?"

"I'm supposed to take a plane at two-thirty."

"Well come to the office, we'll have an early lunch. Bring in my car and I'll drive you to the airport."

"Sure, okay Dad, that would be swell, I'll see you at the office. Do you want to talk to Ma again?"

— I have a call for Mr. Ordway Smith?

— Speaking.

— Go ahead, please. . . .

— Ordway, this is Bernard Bromberg.

— Yes sir, how are you?

— I'm a little worried, Ordway. Am I to understand that Conroy still hasn't signed our merger agreement?

— He's going to sign it tonight, Bernard. I'm right here in his apartment waiting for him —

— What's the explanation for all this? Didn't you give him that message from me?

— Bernard, he's busy as a one-armed paper hanger, we just can't seem to catch up with him —

— Don't give me that kind of baloney, Ordway! What do you take me for? Is something the matter with him? Because I've really had enough of this, nobody's that busy, it's not normal behavior for a man who's supposed to be in charge of an organization this size —

— Bernard, just bear with me, will you? He's going to sign the thing, I promise you. He knows he's got to sign. The trouble is he thinks he *has* — I mean he feels as if — the deal's accomplished and he wants to go on —

— Well you better give him the message that it's *not* accomplished, Ordway, not by a damn sight, is that clear? Because if that agreement isn't signed tomorrow, if that proxy statement doesn't get filed tomorrow, this merger is *off*, we are withdrawing the agreement and we're not going to our stockholders with this deal. *Is that clear?*

— Bernard, I don't think you want —

— Is that clear, Ordway? My lawyers have appropriate instructions.

— Yes, it's quite clear, Bernard.

— The SEC closes at five-thirty, is that right?

— I guess so, Bernard.

— That's two-thirty out here. If I don't get a call from Sandy Simon or one of your people telling me you've filed, the deal is off, Ordway. I'm sorry it's come to this, but it has. Good night.

— Good night, Bernard. We'll file, don't worry.

I felt my heart beating when I hung up. I called Marie but a man answered. I drank another glass of bourbon, lay down on the couch, and watched Johnny Carson talking with a woman who teaches monkeys to play the violin.

What the hell am I doing here?
How did I get myself into this?
Is this my job?
Is this what a lawyer is supposed to be doing?
Am I a good lawyer?
How would a good lawyer handle this mess?

The hours passed. Errol Flynn with hairline moustache, Ann Sheridan with lovely legs, a hundred people rioting in a Dodge City honky-tonk, swinging from the chandeliers, hitting each other with chairs, whole balconies collapsing, commercials for deodorants and laundry soap . . .

When I awoke it took me a moment to find myself. Another ancient western was on the screen, people riding and shooting. I stood up, feeling cold and rumpled and lousy. Over Fairmount Park the sky was getting light but the streetlights were still on. It was raining and I had to walk almost to Logan Circle before I found a taxi. At the Racquet Club I shaved and showered and sent a man up the street to buy me a shirt and underwear. Then I sat up at a counter for breakfast, and went to the office.

Tommy Sharp didn't call until eleven-thirty. At six o'clock in the morning the accountants had caught a mistake in the notes to Bromberg's financial statements. The whole filing package had to be torn apart so that the corrected pages could be inserted, then the thing had to be re-bound, so they had only now sent off the messenger to Washington. Had the merger agreement been signed?

I called Jack Renfrew. Still no sign of Charlie, or of the Frenchman. I reported my conversation with Bernard Bromberg.

"What are we going to do, Jack? The messenger's on his way to Washington."

"You're the lawyer."

"This is a management decision, Jack. Are you going to sign the merger agreement or aren't you? Bromberg will withdraw, don't you see?"

"Don't push me, Ordway. You know I don't have any orders. I'll call you as soon as I hear something." He hung up.

The receptionist announced Teddy and a moment later he stood in my room: yellow Viking beard, hunting shirt, blue jeans, moccasins, sport jacket, duffel bag, rather long hair over his ears. . . .

"You look kinda worried, Dad."

"Yeah, well, we've got some problems here. . . . Look, old fella, I'm just as sorry as I can be, but I won't be able to take you to lunch, I've got to stay right here by the telephone and cope with something. Could we just talk for a few minutes?"

"Sure, Dad." He sat down, looking disappointed. The face behind the beard is his mother's, but he didn't inherit her brains. A wonderful kid, never a bit of trouble to anybody, a good athlete, varsity halfback, captain of the lacrosse team, a strong gentle boy. What am I going to say to him?

"Tell me something about your trip. Did you have a good time?"

Rather haltingly, stroking the new beard, he reported . . . heavy traffic and rain in Cologne, fog in Bonn, then sunshine, sleeping bags in the vineyards, at Coblenz somebody was bitten by a dog — The telephone rang.

— Ordway, the messenger is having trouble. There's been an accident at La Guardia, they're not clearing planes, he's got to go all the way over to Newark —

I hung up.

Teddy watched me, uncertain as to whether he should go on with his account, so I took the bull by the horns. "I hear you've talked to your grandfather — about Vietnam."

He swallowed. "Yes I did, Dad. I guess I should have talked to you first, but see, I didn't know . . ."

"Sometimes it's easier to talk to a grandfather than a father. I found it quite hard to talk to my own father. . . . Look . . ." Christ, what does one say? "I just want you to know . . . Well, generally speaking I think that if your country needs you, you ought to go, you know, I mean you belong to a country, you call yourself an American, and that carries some obligation with it . . . I mean that's my general reaction. But what I want you to know . . ."

What do I want him to know? I hadn't even thought it out myself.

"What I want you to know . . . this business in Vietnam . . . I think now it's different, I think they've made a mistake and they don't know how to pull themselves out of it, and it's just getting worse, all this business of sending more and more troops — drafted ground troops — it isn't going to work, they're just ruining that country and killing people for no damn reason, and if you don't want to go I don't blame you and I'll support you whatever way I can!"

He smiled with relief, but before he could say anything the telephone rang.

— Mr. Smith? I have Mr. Hatch, Iselin Brothers and Devereaux. . . .

— Hello, Ordway? I guess you've been getting the battle reports, have you? Talk about Murphy's Law, this must be Conroy's Law! Everything that could possibly go wrong, has. . . . Say, your clients have signed that agreement with Bromberg, I assume?

— I understand they're signing it now, Harry. In any event I have no reason to believe that it won't be signed —

— But you understand that Bromberg has given instructions that we're not to *file* unless CCC has signed?

— He told me himself.

— Well okay then, just wanted to make sure. . . . Ordway, I talked to the branch chief at the SEC, he promises they'll look at our amendment right away. . . . You know, our people are feeling a little more confident this week, they think they feel a little strength in the market . . . Maybe this deal will get off the ground after all. . . .

"I'm sorry for all these interruptions," I said as I hung up. "The point is, I don't want you to think you've got to run away, go to Canada or Sweden or someplace. It's not necessary. I haven't had time to look into it, but I know there must be ways — "

"I know some guys that got jobs teaching kids in Brooklyn, that got 'em a deferment."

"Exactly. That's the kind of thing I have in mind. Why don't you explore that? I'll find out what I can and when you come down for Thanksgiving we can decide the best course. But don't go running off in a panic, okay?"

He smiled his nice bearded smile again. "Okay, Dad. . . . Look, you're jammed to the eyeballs so I'll shove off, but I want you to know . . . I want you to know I feel . . . a lot better."

Jesus, I thought, thinking of the repulsive sons of some of my friends. Jesus, what a wonderful kid!

We both stood up and shook hands very formally and then he was gone. I looked out at the statue of William Penn for a minute, feeling an awful sadness, a sadness that didn't seem to have a cause or a focus that I could find . . . and then for the next couple of hours I tried to deal with the mail and the other things that had accumulated on my desk: Messrs. Pope & Underwood, 14 Wall Street, look forward to working with us in connection with merger of Ordway Chemical Company into their client ABC Industries Inc. and when would it be convenient to schedule first planning meeting? Taylor Chew forecasts heavy weather in the Orphans' Court if Museum auctions off a dozen nineteenth-century salon paintings it doesn't want any more. Twenty-five (by actual count) requests for money. The Lady Stanhope, Stanhope's Court, Mendip Bridge, Weston-super-Mare, Somerset, knows only too well what an awful blow this is to me, but she simply has no other choice, she can show me the figures in black and white if I want to see them and she has to listen to her financial advisors. . . .

I couldn't concentrate on those things, knowing as I watched the clock on City Hall tower that the question was coming, not knowing how I would — or could — answer it.

What happens if we don't file today? Why can't we file tomorrow? Because the deal will unravel, that's why. A deal is just a relationship between men. This relationship is hanging by a thread. If we don't file today the thread is broken, nothing will bring these men together again — and Charlie can't get that through his head.

Maybe I should ask somebody. Graham Anders? Ellsworth Boyle? What's the use of asking when I know what their answer will be? There is only one answer — but what happens if I give it? What happens to the Bromberg merger, the Debenture issue, the bank loans, Conroy Concepts Corporation and Conroy himself?

— Ordway, the messenger just called, he's at the SEC. Is it okay for him to file?

— No, have him stand by and call back.

— Ordway, it's after five o'clock!

— I know what time it is, I'm looking right at City Hall.

— Ordway, the others . . . they're going to ask . . .

— Tell them it's being taken care of, tell the messenger to call in fifteen minutes.

— Okay, but we may have trouble with Sandy Simon.

I called Jack Renfrew again, but they said he was out and they couldn't reach him. I called Charlie's apartment: no answer. I called the Frenchman's apartment: no answer. I called MacDiarmid's office: Captain MacDiarmid was on his way to Montego Bay to attend the opening of a golf-and-tennis club.

I looked at the clock on City Hall tower.

— Ordway, the messenger is on the other line, they're going to lock up the store —

— Tell him to file!

— You got it signed? Oh that's *great* —

— Tell him to file.

. . . . .

— Ordway . . . they won't . . . they won't let him file just on my say-so, it seems. . . .

— Who won't?

— Well, Sandy Simon, mostly. . . . Ordway, I'm really on the spot here —

— For Christ's sake, whose messenger is he?

— He's the printer's messenger.

— And he's filing our registration statement, is that right? We're the registrant, we're paying the printer, what the hell is going on over there?

— Ordway, he's only got a couple of minutes to get to the filing desk, it's too late to argue with him or get him con-

253

fused, if he decides to call his own boss he'll be told not to file —

— Have him call me direct.

— There's no time, Ordway, honest to God, won't you talk to Sandy Simon?

— Ordway?

— Put him on.

. . . .

— Hi, Ordway, how are you doing? This is Sandy —

— I'm just fine, Sandy, how are you?

— I'm fine too. Do I understand that the merger agreement has been signed?

— Yes.

— You're telling me that the merger agreement between Bromberg Instruments and Conroy Concepts Corporation has been validly executed on behalf of Conroy Concepts Corporation?

— You heard me.

— That's great, Ordway. We're delighted to hear it, we'll tell the messenger to sprint to the filing desk. . . . Tommy is telling him on the other line. . . . Do you want to talk to Tommy again?

— No, just tell him to come on home, Sandy.

— Will do, Ordway, and thanks very much. I guess we'll see you at the closing.

— Yes, I guess you will, Sandy. So long.

When I put down the receiver I noticed that it was slippery with sweat. My heart was beating in my throat. I didn't know what to do. I sat there for a while and stared out the window, feeling terrible, feeling about to explode. I got up and walked out through my secretary's room. She had gone. I walked along the hall looking into the offices, some dark, some still lighted as men bent over their desks. A burst of laughter: Graham Anders in his wheelchair amid his grandfather's furniture, surrounded by young lawyers recounting the excitements of the day. I always envied the way they drift in there, slouched on his ancient leather sofa, leaning in the doorway . . . usually one of them is in there to ask for advice, another stops by to listen, a third arrives with a report of what some judge just did to Ames Mahoney. . . .

They all looked up. "Come in, Ordway," called Graham. "What's the matter, did you lose your best friend?"

"Could I talk to you a minute, please?"

Ben Butler was up instantly, the others too, a hasty shuffle and the door closed behind them.

"Graham . . . I wonder do you possibly have something to drink in here?"

He looked at me quietly for a moment. Then: "Sure, certainly." He wheeled himself across the carpet to his grandfather's old rolltop desk, produced a key, unlocked the bottom drawer, and wheeled back carrying a square bottle of Ballantine's and a glass.

"Left over from the Christmas party," he said, pouring a huge shot. "Want me to call for some water?"

"No thanks." I sipped the Scotch, feeling it burn, feeling it touching my nerves, feeling just a little better, or at least calmer.

"Want to talk about it?" asked Graham.

"I don't know. . . . I don't think I should. . . . Jesus, Graham, I've done a terrible thing, and I don't even know *why* . . . I mean I wonder if I've gone crazy or something, I just did a crazy thing!"

Neither of us said anything for a few minutes. I drank the Scotch, Graham smoked a cigarette. We sat there.

"I think it would make you feel better to talk about it," said Graham, but then there was a knock at the door.

"What is it?" called Graham, irritated, and Ben Butler put his head in.

"Sorry, Ordway, but your client's out in the reception room, he says it's very important — "

"What client?" But I was on my feet.

"You implying your brother-in-law has only one client?" asked Graham behind me.

"Oh, I mean Mr. Conroy, of course — " and I was already past him, striding — almost running — down the long hall.

"Oh there he is," shouted Charlie, coming down toward my room dressed in a brand new navy blue suit, eyes shining, cheeks pink from a recent shave; "I didn't think you'd gone home yet, here's somebody I want you to meet," and he guided a chunky older man into the room. "Ordway Smith, meet Frank Ferguson, Manayunk Steel."

I shook hands, trying to smile. "Mr. Ferguson, it's nice to meet you, I wonder if you'd sit out here for just a moment, there's one matter I've got to take up with Charlie, but it'll only take a minute."

"Why certainly," said Ferguson, already moving out the door, but Charlie began to argue. "Wait a minute, Ordway, I want you to talk to him — "

"Come in here, please, Charlie." I knew my voice was shaking. I knew I had never been so angry in my life. I reached across my desk. "Do you know what this is?"

He took it, turned the pages. "This is the agreement with Bromberg, isn't it?"

"That's right. Will you sit down right there, please?" I turned to the execution page and handed him my pen. "Will you sign right here, on this line, please?"

He took the pen and signed. I gave him two more copies and he signed them too. "Okay? You feeling all right, Ordway? You look kind of funny. What's all this fuss about, I thought we signed this out in California. Now here's the reason I brought in Ferguson: I want you to explain that I can't make a deal with him right now because we'd have to put it in the registration statement, even if it's only a handshake, isn't that right? Hey, Frank, come on in here, we're all through, these lawyers and their goddamned paperwork, I swear we ought to pay them by the pound!"

Book Four

BOTTOM LINE

October 8, 1969

$100,000,000

CONROY CONCEPTS CORPORATION

8½% CONVERTIBLE SUBORDINATED DEBENTURES due 1984

The Debentures are convertible at any time prior to maturity, unless previously redeemed, into Common Stock of the Company at $12.00 per share, subject to adjustment in certain events.

———

Price 100% Plus Accrued Interest

———

THE WALL STREET JOURNAL
Wednesday, October 8, 1969

* * *

CONROY CONCEPTS ISSUE SELLS OUT

NEW YORK — Conroy Concepts Corp's $100 million offering of 8½% convertible debentures, due 1984 sold out on reaching the market at a price of 100, through underwriters managed by First Hudson Corporation.

The debentures are convertible into common stock at $12.00 a share.

Philadelphia - based conglomerate said about $65 million of the proceeds will be applied to paying short-term debt, and the remainder will be used for working capital.

Conroy Concept's latest acquisition is Bromberg Instruments, Oakland, California manufacturer of pocket-sized automatic calculators, whose stockholders have approved a merger to take effect next week.

Copies of the Prospectus may be obtained from such of the several underwriters, including the undersigned, as are registered dealers in securities in this State.

First Hudson Corporation

McTavish Bros. & Strauss

Lonsdale Jno. R. Breckenridge & Co.
Incorporated

William C. Luftschreiber & Co.
Incorporated

Nassau Securities Corporation

John J. O'Riley & Co.

Pell and Pell
Incorporated

A. B. Corcoran & Co.

Stolzfuss Strumpf & Co.

D. W. Benjamin's Sons & Rosenheim, Inc.

Mittersill, Taft, Von Gablenz & Peabody

The Penn Center Company

First Louisiana Company

W. W. Farr & Co.

Rienzi & Co.
Incorporated

Breasted Bros. & Co. Inc.

Threadneedle Securities Corporation

Port & Partners   Rothschild & Baring

Jones, Hopkinson, Bull & Co.

Yamashita International Corporation

Hansemann & Co. Incorporated

Dallas-Fort Worth Investors, Inc.

Knatchbull Spencer Cross & Co.
Limited

William Street Associates, Inc.

Puget Sound Securities Corp.

Untermeyer, Schmidlapp & C. H. Clapp
Incorporated

Schneider Schroeder & Schramm

Frankfurter Überseebank
Aktiengesellschaft   Crewson & Co.

The St. Lawrence Company

Mitchell & Selzer, Limited

Loup & Leclerc (Toronto) Ltd.

Jack Tuckerman & Sons, Inc.

Mr. Charles Clancy Conroy, Junior
requests the pleasure of
Mr. & Mrs. Smith's company

to meet

Mr. and Mrs. Bernard Bromberg
Mr. and Mrs. Robert Bromberg

Saturday Evening, October the eleventh,
at eight o'clock

R.S.V.P.
Conroy House
Chester Springs, Pennsylvania

20.

Conroy's Tower

Suddenly everything changed. A cool wind blew, the sugar maples turned to the color of fire, our farmer hauled a load of apples to the cider mill, and after six months of decline the stock market moved up. Financial writers jubilantly speculated on "The Coming Advance Past 1000!" Better still, *Forbes* magazine printed a story about minicalculators containing very favorable paragraphs about Bromberg and the impending merger with CCC. The Securities and Exchange Commission cleared the proxy statement in record time, the Bromberg stockholders held their meeting and approved the merger, and the underwriters distributed our amended Prospectus all over the country. There weren't many other issues coming at the same time, the price of CCC's common stock was climbing — not fast but steadily — and there was talk of fixing the conversion price of the Debentures a shade below the market price of the stock into which the Debentures could be converted, thus giving the buyers an instant premium.

I could hear the verdict in the excited voices from New York: Charlie Conroy has made it again, CCC is off to the races!

The big reception hall of the Hyde Place had been arranged as an auditorium. The Curtis String Quartet played Vivaldi by candlelight. They sat on folding chairs beneath the tapestry with huntsmen and dogs and the Château de

Montmort, Professor Rosenthal's $140,000 Gobelin that once belonged to William Randolph Hearst.

The hall was full. By hook or crook MacDiarmid and I had collected a good cross-section of the business community — bankers, brokers, manufacturing people, real estate people, a congressman, a member of our Supreme Court, a famous ophthalmologist, a famous architect, a newspaper publisher, the president and three directors of Manayunk Steel — and of course their wives.

I watched Karin Bromberg glowing in the candlelight, while she watched Graham Anders, who sat in his wheelchair beside his wife, way off at the left side of the hall, smoking a cigarette with his eyes shut, drowning in the music.

Two helicopters had brought the Brombergs and their friends from the airport, and that in itself was another triumph — as much for Conyers & Dean as for Charlie Conroy — because Ames Mahoney had gone into the Court of Common Pleas for Chester County with the argument that the antihelicopter ordinance exceeded the township's constitutional police power; our supervisors couldn't ban helicopters in open country any more than they could ban cars. Pending final decision the judge granted us a temporary injunction against enforcement of the ordinance. The concept that millionaires have constitutional rights tickled the fancy of the news media, so MacDiarmid had not only society reporters to record the initiation of Conroy House, but television cameras as well. That very evening, watchers of the eleven o'clock news would see the helicopters landing in the lower pasture, the horsemen on the ridge, and Karin Bromberg in slacks climbing out of the cabin, platinum hair streaming in the propwash, being welcomed by a grinning Mr. Charles Conroy in Harris tweeds and Tyrolean hat. (Bob

Bromberg and his mother didn't come East, for reasons never clearly explained. If Charlie was peeved he didn't show it.)

The party was supposed to celebrate the final closings, at which the underwriters were to pay for CCC's Debentures and the merger with Bromberg would go into effect. However, at the end of September the market was still going up, so the underwriters wanted to sell the Debentures a week later; that put the party between the day the bonds were sold — that is, the day the underwriters actually went on the hook — and the day they would pay for them.

The actual sale to the underwriters seemed like an anticlimax to me. A couple of elegant young men from First Hudson sat with us in Charlie's office, crossing and uncrossing their legs, reporting that the syndicate was willing to take the Debentures if they paid 8½ percent interest and were convertible into CCC Common Stock at twelve dollars per share — which was half a point below the closing price that afternoon, and meant that every buyer could convert his debentures at a small premium immediately. The bankers were clearly jubilant; most conglomerates were still under a cloud, but a few were picking up renewed investor interest. CCC was one of the lucky ones — mostly due to the Bromberg connection.

Charlie understood all this and didn't seem inclined to haggle. "You satisfied this price will jazz up the deal? It'll be a hot deal?"

"We can't promise you a hot issue, Mr. Conroy, not after the year we've had, but we think the bonds will sell out right away and trade at a premium after the syndicate is closed. That's our best guess."

Charlie looked at me. "I bought that tapestry, the one you saw in San Francisco."

"Sounds like you'll be able to afford it," said I, and the bankers looked puzzled. "Charlie, could I talk to you alone a minute?"

Charlie frowned. The bankers, also frowning, withdrew into the outer office.

"Charlie, I think you ought to call Bernard Bromberg and discuss these terms with him."

His face reddened. "Why the hell should I do that? These are perfectly good terms. What's the matter, you think I shouldn't give them that conversion sweetener?"

"I'm sure the terms are all right. That's not my point. My point is you ought to consult him, you ought to ask him what he thinks. He's going on your board next week, he's likely to wind up your biggest stockholder, you sold him the whole deal on the theory that he's going to be your *partner*, Charlie — and if you alienate him any more you're going to have nothing but trouble."

An uncommitted grunt.

"Honest to God, Charlie! He told me that himself."

Looking out the window, lighting another cigarette: "Maybe you're right."

"I know I'm right. It'll make all the difference. Let me have Nancy place the call."

The call went through quickly, and it was the Irish Lullaby all over again: Hey Bernard, how are ya? Been looking at your August numbers, they're great, really *great.* . . . No, I'm not kidding, our people can hardly believe it. . . . Hey, the boys from First Hudson want to go with the Debentures tomorrow, they're here talking price and I'd like to have your input on their proposal. . . .

"Okay, you were right," admitted Charlie when he hung up. "Now call 'em in again. Where do I sign?"

He didn't have to sign anything that afternoon. We telephoned Tommy Sharp at the printer and read him the exact numbers to fill in on the cover of the final Prospectus, which was then printed and taken down to Washington by one of our youngest lawyers. Next morning each member of the underwriting syndicate sent a representative to First Hudson's office at 60 Wall Street. When all of these men had signed the "Agreement Among Underwriters" the syndicate was legally in existence.

A vice president of First Hudson, representing the syndicate, and Jack Renfrew, representing CCC, prepared to sign the underwriting agreement — but not before Harry Hatch had reviewed the first "comfort letter" delivered by the Messrs. Pennypacker Poole & Co., independent certified public accountants.

As Graham Anders and Tommy Sharp kept explaining to me, these comfort letters are getting to be more and more of a problem. Although the Prospectus has to be prepared and printed, things keep happening to companies, and the underwriters — afraid of getting sued if there is an omission — want more and more assurances that everything is still okay right now, *today* — or at least yesterday. On the other hand, the accountants are also being sued every time somebody thinks they overlooked something, so they are backing away, carefully explaining what checks they made, what checks they *didn't* make, the fact that what they did do wouldn't necessarily reveal anything. . . .

But subject to this explanation, nothing came to our attention in the course of the foregoing procedures which in our judgement would indicate that during the period there was any material adverse change in the consolidated financial position of the Company and its subsidiaries from that set forth in the balance sheet included in the Prospectus, or any material adverse change in the consolidated results of operations as compared with the corresponding period in the preceding year.

Pennington Poole's letter followed the language required by the underwriting agreement and the merger agreement with Bromberg. Harry Hatch was satisfied, so First Hudson signed, Jack Renfrew signed, and Tommy Sharp called me in Philadelphia. I switched to the other line, connecting me to our young lawyer at the pay phone in the reception room at the SEC.

"File," I said, and file he did.

Everything except the interest rate and the conversion price had already been cleared with the SEC staff, so the boy was back on the telephone a few minutes later. "We're effective as of ten-fifteen, Mr. Smith."

I called the conference room at First Hudson. "Congratulations, Ordway!" Harry Hatch sounded genuinely pleased. "This one's been a ball-breaker. Will we see you at the closing?"

"Wouldn't miss it," said I, and called the printer. One truck full of final Prospectuses left Little Italy for Wall Street, another for La Guardia Airport.

I sat in my silent room and looked across at the statue of William Penn. The thing was as good as done.

Was I glad? Was I relieved? I felt only emptiness.

And shame.

Shame?

Well, isn't telling a lie something to be ashamed of? What would have happened if — ? But it *didn't* happen, I didn't really tell a lie, I made an accurate prediction . . . and I saved the deal, I saved CCC, I saved Charlie Conroy.

267

Didn't I?

I hadn't told Graham Anders what happened, and he didn't ask, but I had to talk to somebody, so I talked to Marie.

"All right, you made a mistake," she said. "You gave in to pressure and you did something you shouldn't have done, now you've learned something and you won't do it again."

"How do I know I won't do it again? Do you think I went crazy? Do you think I may have lost my mind for a minute?"

"Ordway, for God's sake! Stop stewing over it, you're not the first person who made a mistake under pressure, and anyway it all came out all right, which means that your luck is still holding out, and that's the most important of all, I think."

So I tried to forget about it, to work up the enormous bill we could submit to CCC after the closing, to move the other matters on my desk, to attend board meetings of the Greater Philadelphia Movement and the Art Museum, to go riding with Ailsa, and to join in MacDiarmid's festival rites.

They were playing Mozart now, or maybe it was Haydn. I can never tell the difference, and I was tired. Not satisfied with one helicopter expedition, Charlie and MacDiarmid had insisted that we fly the Brombergs down to Unionville for a picnic lunch at the hunt races, which happened to be held today. Needless to say I was the one assigned to plan this part, to assure an apoplectic race committee that the horses wouldn't be distracted, to negotiate with the first wife of my cousin Freddie for permission to land in her field on the hill above the racecourse ("My God, Ordway, you're not *serious*? They'll tar and feather me! . . . Oh he would? How much? Hmmm . . .") and to arrange for extra deputies to keep children away from the helicopters.

Fortunately the weather was good so it all worked out pretty well: the flight across the county, slanting over the treetops . . . hills and valleys and whitewashed fences, quarries, barns and houses, swimming pools scattered everywhere like emeralds . . . Charlie shouting "Ordway, show the sights!" . . . Karin leaning close to hear me over the clatter of the engine as I pointed out the Brandywine and Longwood Gardens . . . then the landing, dust and hay blowing up around us, crowds strolling across the fields, tailgate parties, a cluster of horse carriages and restored stagecoaches, people drinking, people in exotic costumes looking at each other . . . in the distance the races themselves, hoofbeats, horses and riders disappearing behind the hillocks, reappearing, floating over the timbers, the ghost of O. Smith, boy steeplechaser, riding along . . .

"Tell me about Mrs. Bromberg," said Marion.

"Well, for one thing she likes to ride. I've asked her to come out with us . . . I mean with Ailsa, tomorrow morning."

"Why didn't her husband come? Or her mother-in-law?"

"I don't know. . . . Her husband's been cool to the deal. Possibly the mother, too, I'm not sure."

"So she sets off with her husband's father, three days in New York, somebody told me — "

"Marion, what are you trying to suggest? You can't be serious! You haven't the *slightest* — And they have an entourage with them, the Silverstones, those other people — "

She shook her head. "Something's odd. I don't know, I just have a feeling. . . . Oh look, there are Freddie and Jill!"

But Marion's casual remark released a suspicion that had been stuck on the muddy bottom of my subconscious and now floated to the top. As we wandered about the racecourse, greeting people, smiling, talking, watching the races, I had more than one opportunity to turn my field glasses the other way for a quick look at some faces.

Karin Bromberg leaves the group crowding the elegant bar of MacDiarmid's caterer and strolls along the line of cars. Her hair is tied back in the same black scarf she had worn beside her swimming pool.

Another group is gathered around the tailgate of Caroline Anders's station wagon — some younger men from Conyers & Dean, their wives, their children. Picnic hampers. Thermos bottles. Graham Anders sits on the tailgate dispensing drinks. Tommy Sharp glances over somebody's shoulder, moves out of the circle, returns with Karin Bromberg, introduces her.

Caroline Boatwright Anders, sipping a martini, expressionlessly watches her husband, who is deep in conversation with Karin Bromberg.

Bernard Bromberg, strolling beside Charlie Conroy, returning from a visit to the bookmakers, suddenly stops smiling.

O. Smith stands on the sunny hillside, looking through beautiful little field glasses (Carl Zeiss — Jena), once the property of Alfred von Waldstein, presented when O. Smith (age 20) got his ensign's commission. O. Smith pretends he is looking at the new group of riders moving toward the post.

"You're putting on quite a show for us," said Justin Silverstone, puffing a little as he came up the hill.

"Bernard and Charlie seem to be having a good time. They've been down there supporting the turf accountants."

"Tell you the truth, Ordway, I'm relieved that everything's ended so well, the Debentures sold . . . and . . . and Conroy in such good shape. Well, you know we were having doubts." His tone changed. He looked worried again. "Say, do you know where Karin has got to? She wandered off — "

"She's right over there, talking to Graham Anders, one of my partners. Haven't you met him? Come on over and meet them, Justin, his wife's name is Caroline. . . ."

Poor Justin.

MacDiarmid wore a deerstalker cap and a tattersall greatcoat reaching almost to his ankles. He looked at the sky, then at his wristwatch. "Wind's rising. Time to decamp, wouldn't you say? Musicians arrive at seven, and everyone still has to change. . . . Did you get much flak from the horse people?"

"Not too bad. . . . Look, I want to say I think you've done a good job — with the house, I mean. I was worried what it would look like, but it looks splendid. Much better than when the Hydes had it."

"So kind of you to say so. Of course it helps when everything is assembled at once, according to a plan, as it were. Most people just accumulate one thing after another, makes for rather a mishmash sometimes. . . ." Brief pause — "I say, old man, should have brought this up before, probably needn't even mention it, but had you thought of sort of a toast during dinner? For Bromberg? and for Conroy? Could do it myself, of course, but it might look pushy, I'm only a hired hand, after all — "

"That's all I am, old man."

"Oh come now! Trusted counselor, neighboring squire — "

"Go find your pilots, MacDiarmid. You know I'll give the toast."

Charlie welcomed his guests in the big library: a roaring fire, leather-bound sets of Shakespeare and Trollope and Sir Walter Scott rising to the ceiling, candelabra on the long refectory tables illuminating silver dishes of caviar, chopped egg, chopped onion, lemons, crystal decanters filled with ice-cold Polish vodka . . .

MacDiarmid and I worked hard, moving people around, bringing people to meet Charlie. One moment when I was alone, I thought about how we used to digest our cases in this room — and looked at Karin Bromberg, who wore a white dress with long sleeves. She was talking with Graham Anders.

Over in the corner, Charlie was delivering a speech on his plans for the house, talking much too loud, almost shouting, about restoring the tennis courts, the swimming pool, the stables. . . .

Marion detached herself from that group and came over. "Are we required to drink straight vodka at this party?"

"Oh no, they'll get you whatever you want. . . ." I signaled a waiter. "MacDiarmid claims you must drink vodka with caviar. . . ."

"I think Charlie Conroy's already drunk too much of something."

"He's just excited, maybe a little ill at ease, he doesn't know half these people and he's never done this sort of thing before."

"But you and Captain MacDiarmid will show him how, won't you?" She moved off to speak with one of her cousins — and I turned to find myself facing the Chairman of the Board of the William Penn Trust Company.

"Charlie seems more excited than usual tonight," he said. "Had you heard this plan about an office building on stilts? Wants to build an office building over Thirtieth Street Station!"

MacDiarmid, now wearing a bemedaled dinner jacket above an Argyll and Sutherland kilt, was lecturing his corner of the room about the investment quality of good antiques: "Regard that cockfighting chair, gentlemen. Genuine article, London *circa* seventeen-sixty, care to wager what that'll bring ten years from now? Perhaps these lawyers could work out a new type of futures contract, antique futures? What about that, Smith?"

I looked at Bernard Bromberg, who was talking to a banker but looking over the banker's shoulder, looking across the room.

Seventy people sit down to dinner. A little ensemble — not the string quartet — plays show tunes. When the champagne has been poured, O. Smith stands up, stops the music, and proposes a toast.

"After you finished, he never stopped talking," said Marion later. "And it wasn't the vodka, it wasn't the champagne, he didn't drink all that much, Ordway, he talked like a man *possessed*, he was *spraying* all over poor Mrs. Bromberg. . . ."

As we moved out of the dining room Charlie grabbed my elbow. "That was a nice speech, Ordway. I liked it a lot."

"My pleasure."

His face was flushed, but I was relieved to hear him speaking quietly. "What's all this about an office building on stilts?"

A sly expression. "Jack Dawson tell you about that? Just

thought I'd plant the seed, you know. Hell, they've been talking about those air rights above the railroad tracks for years, wanted to build the stadium on stilts, wanted to build the Bicentennial thing on stilts, how about a CCC Tower on stilts, fifty-sixty stories, biggest thing in town?"

"Conroy's Tower."

He roared with laughter, so loud that people turned. Then confidentially again, blowing bad breath into my ear: "Talk to you about it next week, after we close with the underwriters. Now I want to hit the head before MacDiarmid's violins begin."

The musicians finished in a crescendo of strings, the great hall rattled with applause, a hand touched my shoulder. MacDiarmid.

"Telephone, old boy. Will you take it in the study?"

They hadn't done much to the musty little room where old Clarence Pickford Hyde used to lock himself away from his family, play solitaire, smoke cigars and figure out how to steal another trolley company. Some filing cabinets, straight chair, table, brass spittoon, telephone.

— Tom Sharp, Ordway. I'm sorry to bother you, but we've got trouble.

— What's the matter?

— Well, the guys from Pennypacker Poole are making their cold comfort review, of course, and they've turned up a problem at Darby Turbine. They want to have a meeting tomorrow.

— Tomorrow's Sunday.

— I know it, but they're supposed to show a draft of their comfort letter to Harry Hatch on Monday at the pre-closing, and there's going to be trouble about it, I gather.

274

— For God's sake, they already delivered the comfort letter on Wednesday, when we signed —

— But they've got to update it, deliver a second letter at closing. The underwriting agreement and the merger agreement both require the update, it's standard procedure, Ordway.

— Well, what have they turned up? What's the matter at Darby now?

— I'm not clear about the details, but it concerns the West Virginia project, you know, the generating plant they're building on the Turkey River.

— I thought that was practically finished. . . . Didn't you go down there to look at it?

— Sure, we looked at it back in July, it is finished, but now apparently there's something wrong with it, the limestone scrubbers are clogging —

— What's clogging?

— Ordway, I don't understand exactly, all I can tell you is P-P called me at home, John Lundquist himself called me and he said they want a meeting tomorrow and he sounded really shook up, Ordway.

— Lundquist sounded shook up?

— That's correct.

— Well, I guess we'd better have a meeting. Where do they want to have it? Their place?

— Our place. Would ten o'clock be all right?

— Yes. Do they want Charlie Conroy? How about the underwriters?

— No, they want to keep this on the technical level first, they're asking Larry Lenz, and Robinson from Darby Turbine and some engineering people are coming in to give us all the facts. I think they want us to get our ducks in a row before we break the news to the underwriters . . . and to Charlie.

When I returned to the front of the house the cars were being driven into the porte-cochère, and people were leaving. Other people were crowding back into the library, where coffee, cognac and liqueur were being served.

I was still innocent. My main concern was that I would have to go into town on Sunday morning, and wouldn't be able to ride with Karin Bromberg.

*　　*　　*

Extract from notes to financial statements, page 65, Prospectus of Conroy Concepts Corporation effective October 8, 1969:

> *Note D — Profits on Long-Term Construction Contracts in Progress.* The Company records profits earned by its construction subsidiary on long-term construction contracts through estimates on the percentage-of-completion basis. The profits so estimated and recorded are subject to the provision of such allowances as may be considered advisable, taking into account the stage of completion of each contract, possible increases in costs not included in the estimates, guaranteed liabilities, unsettled contract adjustments and other factors. The performance of such contracts may extend over periods of several years, and revisions in the contract estimates and allowance requirements during performance and upon final contract settlements have the effect of including in subsequent accounting periods adjustments necessary to reflect the results indicated by the revised estimates and allowances.

21.

The Limestone Scrubbers

Mr. Alex Morrisson, chief engineer of Darby Turbine, had apparently been to church. He wore a blue suit and a white shirt and a gold watch chain over his vest and a Masonic emblem in his lapel, and there was one thing that he wanted made entirely crystal clear right from the outset, and that was that his people were not going to take the blame for this, because this is exactly the kind of thing he'd been warning about, exactly the kind of thing that will happen if you bring in fancy hotshot atomic energy people from General Electric and Westinghouse who don't know a goddamned thing about coal-burning furnaces and give them fancy titles and fancy salaries and put them over top of people who have been building coal furnaces all over the world for forty years, and let them make decisions about how to bid and what to guarantee and not to guarantee, and anybody who isn't wet behind the ears will tell you that at this stage of development you don't promise that a limestone scrubber is going to work no matter how bad you want to get any particular contract, and his people had explained this until they were blue in the face, but no, nobody will listen to what engineering people with forty years in the coal business have to say, they let a kid just out of engineering school call the shots about bidding a coal-burning power plant —

"Simmer down, Alex," said Hewitt Robinson, president of Darby Turbine, formerly a divisional vice president at

Westinghouse. "That kind of talk isn't going to get us anywhere, and we didn't guarantee the scrubbers anyway."

"Tell that to the power company lawyers," said Alex Morrisson.

"Could we start at the beginning?" I asked. "Would somebody tell me what a limestone scrubber is?"

Sunshine was streaming through the windows of Conference Room A, and the place smelled of the coffee Tommy Sharp had concocted in the adjoining kitchenette. John Lundquist and his accountants hadn't said a word yet, but they looked unhappy, even more unhappy than Hewitt Robinson and Jack Renfrew, who wore tweed sport jackets and seemed angry at being summoned to town on Sunday morning to deal with yet another crisis the lawyers had dreamed up. Everybody leaned forward to watch as one of Morrisson's engineers flipped open a fat book of specifications to show me a schematic diagram.

His boss explained:

The electric generating plant on the Turkey River was designed to burn local West Virginia coal, 2½ percent sulphur content; furnace gases consist of sulphur dioxide and fly ash; a full-scale stack gas cleaning system was required by the state environmental control agency and specified by the electric company; Darby agreed to include the newest-type system, utilizing limestone injection into the furnace and wet scrubbers for particulate and sulphur dioxide removal. . . .

The other engineers joined in, and I tried to follow as best I could. First the coal is ground as fine as talcum powder, then it is burned in a mixture of air and powdered limestone. Hot gases from the furnace are forced into enormous tanks, in which they are "scrubbed" by a spray of water and limestone, a "slurry." This mixture of water and gas and limestone is forced up through a bed of crushed marble. The sulphur dioxide and fly ash are turned into other chemicals and washed out the bottom. The scrubbed gases rise through a "demister" — which heats out the water that would create white clouds — and finally up the tall smokestack.

"And now it isn't working?" I asked.

Well, they were having a lot of trouble. The fly ash and the limestone slurry tended to form hard cement-like deposits that clogged the marble beds, clogged the demisters, clogged the water jets, and clogged the inlets to the scrubbers. They were having so much trouble that the electric company had just refused to pay the last installment of the construction contract.

"Can't they operate the plant without the scrubbers?" asked Tommy Sharp.

Alex Morrisson shook his head. "Ever seen that valley? River's a hundred yards wide, then there's a railroad track, a highway, a half mile of bottom land, then mountains straight up on both sides. Unless you get a wind blowing down the river the smoke will lie in there, there's three little factory towns strung along that valley, they had to close a chemical plant because they couldn't get rid of the fumes — "

"Could bring in low-sulphur coal," said one of his men.

"Yeah. From Wyoming or someplace. Know what that would do to their electric rates? They're sitting right on top of the cheapest coal in the country, they'd be nuts to haul in expensive coal — "

"That's not really the point, is it?" John Lundquist looks like an intelligent college student, but he is one of the youngest and most brilliant partners in the worldwide accounting firm of Pennypacker Poole & Co. He has published a book on accounting and flies about the country explaining the latest pronouncements of the Accounting Principles Board to less sophisticated colleagues.

"The point is that the electric company is disputing payment of the contract price, on the ground that they can't operate their plant. If they hook up the limestone scrubbers they clog and choke the furnaces, and if they bypass the scrubbers and put the smoke right up the stack, then the State of West Virginia will close them down — so we've got a dispute over a very substantial amount of money here — we don't even know how much, but the full contract price is about a hundred and seventy million dollars — "

"A hundred and — *what?*" I couldn't believe my ears.

"That's right, and thirty-five million of that represents the sulphur dioxide removal system — which doesn't work — and the unpaid part of the contract is . . . how much?"

"Ten percent," said Larry Lenz, CCC's comptroller. "Roughly seventeen million, of which maybe a million-five is profit — "

"And that's profit Darby's already taken into income," said John Lundquist.

I still didn't understand. "How could they have taken it into income if they didn't get it yet?"

Lundquist folded a copy of CCC's Prospectus back to page sixty-five, and pointed his gold pencil: "Take a look at Note D again. Percentage-of-completion method. Typical in long-term construction contracts." He leaned back, took off his glasses, and settled into what was obviously a familiar lecture. "The trouble with contracts that run over several years is that they cause a conflict between two principles of accounting. One principle says that income is recognized only when the right to payment has become unconditional. That would mean no income on a long-term contract until the work is accepted — none. On the other hand, we also have a principle that says you must give an accurate picture of the results in each accounting period — each year — and that means you should take the profit in the same year you expend the costs, the same year you're doing the work. For example, if it takes you five years to build a plant, you're spending money those five years but if you only take the profit when they accept the plant and finish paying you, in year five, then you've distorted your results in years one through four. Does that make sense?"

I said I guessed it did.

"Of course you can also use what we call the completed-contract method: defer *both* costs and revenues into the year the contract is finished — say year five — but what does that do to your results in years one, two, three and four? You're really working those years, you're really earning money but it doesn't show in your results, so you're distorting again. So the Accounting Principles Board recommends the percentage-of-completion method for long-term construction contracts when you can make reasonable estimates of costs to complete and reasonable estimates of how long it's going to take — which you can, in Darby's case. Usually. So that's the method Darby uses. Perfectly correct, generally accepted accounting principles. Clear so far?"

"Yes." I began to see where he was going. Tommy Sharp, way ahead of me as usual, had turned the pages of the Prospectus to CCC's earnings statement and was making computations with his slide rule.

John Lundquist continued. "Okay, percentage-of-completion method, we tell them that right there in Note D, we tell them in effect we're estimating some profit factor in each year's earnings, we're taking in some earnings in each year even though we haven't finished the job. But what happens now? Now instead of a profit on this Turkey River contract, it looks like we might have a *loss,* because of this fight about the limestone scrubbers — "

"*No way* are we going to have a loss on Turkey River!" Hewitt Robinson interrupted angrily. "Despite Alex, we never guaranteed those scrubbers, and anyway we're going to get them to work, and we'll get paid for them too!"

"Okay, fine," said Lundquist. "If Conyers & Dean will give us a bulletproof opinion that the electric company has to pay you the full contract price, then maybe we're all right. But if not, then we've got to set up reserves for losses, and what does that do to the earnings we've reported in the Prospectus? They'll have to be adjusted."

Numbers filled the air. How big would the reserves have to be? What would the effect on CCC's per share earnings be?

My mind was reeling. "Are you trying to tell me this Prospectus is *wrong?* After six months of work? After two hundred thousand dollars of accounting fees and legal fees and printing costs?"

"No," said Lundquist, looking up from his computations. "The financials weren't wrong as of the time we reported on them, as a matter of fact I don't think the Prospectus was wrong as of last Wednesday, when it became effective — "

" — and you delivered your first comfort letter."

"That's right, but then something happened, you see, a subsequent event that changed the facts. So in the light of these new facts we obviously can't deliver the same letter on Tuesday — at least not in the form required by the underwriters. I can't very well say that nothing has come to my attention that would indicate a material adverse change in consolidated results of operations — unless, as I say, your firm is willing to go on the hook with the opinion that the electric company will have to pay for the scrubbers whether they work or not."

"This is ridiculous," I said. "They've been building this plant for what . . . four or five years? And up to last Wednesday nobody knew there might be trouble about these scrubbers? After four or five years of work something like this is discovered between Thursday and Saturday? Is anybody going to believe that?"

"My God, we climbed all over that plant," said Tommy Sharp. "The underwriters were there, the people from Iselin Bros. were there, nobody said a *word* about this!"

I didn't like the way he sounded. He sounded frightened, and Tommy isn't easily frightened.

"Of course *they* didn't say a word about it." Alex Morrisson was not frightened at all. On the contrary, he sounded pleased. "This was *their* baby, *their* brilliant idea, Mike Barkus practically invented the scrubbers, you know — "

"Who's Mike Barkus?" I asked.

"Mike Barkus is a kid six years out of Carnegie Tech, a kid who's going to show the whole profession how to build coal-fired power plants, a kid who sold this whole ball of wax to people who know all about atomic energy — "

Jack Renfrew cut in. "Ordway, could Hewitt and I see you alone?" He sounded very tired.

The three of us stepped out into the musty corridor.

"Jesus Christ!" said Hewitt Robinson.

"Shoulda gotten rid of him *years* ago," said Jack Renfrew. "Didn't I tell you? Look, Ordway, what we got here, as you can see, is company politics, Darby politics. Alex is a holdover from the old gang, from before Charlie got control, he's got a chip on his shoulder because other people have been put on top of him, and underneath him too."

"That's right," said Hewitt Robinson. "Now this kid Barkus is a good example, a brilliant kid, a real nut on coal, comes from Pittsburgh, claims that coal is going to solve all our problems, he's done a hell of a lot of work on these stack gas cleaning systems, he's a real pioneer in this field and that's how we got the Turkey River contract, because he convinced those people that we could make the thing work, they could burn their own coal in that valley — "

"So you did guarantee the scrubbers?"

"No, we did *not* guarantee them, we said we'd build the plant to specifications — "

"Did our firm prepare the contracts?"

"No, we still had the Openshaw firm, they worked it out with the electric company lawyers in Wheeling."

"But we must have reviewed it in connection with this underwriting."

"Ordway, we've got these agreements all over the world, I don't think you had to read every one of them."

"Well, in any case we'd better look at it right away, and you'll have to bring young Mr. Barkus over from West Virginia — in fact you'd better send the Learjet out for him this afternoon. . . . How much does Charlie know about this?"

They looked at each other.

"Not a damn thing," said Jack Renfrew.

"This hasn't ever come up in discussion?"

They shook their heads. "Ordway, this is just an engineering problem, we assumed the thing would be built according to the specs, that it would work the way they said it would — "

"Even though Morrisson warned you that it wouldn't?"

"Ordway, you don't know Alex Morrisson! He's been crying the blues ever since CCC acquired Darby! Everything's been done wrong, everything's screwed up, nothing's going to work — we just don't pay attention to him, we let him talk. Jack's right, I should have got him out a long time ago, but he knows the utility engineering departments, they like him, he does have his uses, and he has to retire this year anyhow — "

I opened the door and led them back into the conference room.

" — personally no skin off *my* ass," Alex Morrisson was telling the accountants. "Pension's vested, condominium in Lauderdale is paid for, sold my Darby stock to Conroy and bought triple A utilities — "

I had to interrupt him. "Tommy, will you find a copy of the Turkey River contract? We'd better take a look at that right away. . . . Gentlemen, I think we might as well disband for the moment. John, if your people could sit down with Larry and come up with some numbers, some estimate of what kind of reserves you're talking about and what effect they would have on the earnings. . . . I think we've got to set up a meeting with the underwriters tomorrow morning, first thing. They are going to be very unhappy underwriters."

"Hey Dad!" Ailsa came running out of the stable as I drove into the courtyard. "You know that German lady rides like a son-of-a-bitch!"

"Yes," I said. "I know she does."

"Dad, she jumped the waterfall! Took Minnie right over the waterfall, I couldn't stop her, I couldn't even keep up with her, she cantered right down the sand quarry, I think she's *nuts*, Dad!"

"Minnie isn't hurt?"

"No, she cleared all right, but suppose they'd fallen? Into the millrace? Remember the time the Pickerings' pony — "

"I'm sorry, Puss, I should have warned you. She's hard on horses but she knows what she's doing. Did you take her back to the Hyde — I mean to Conroy's?"

"Oh no, Mr. Anders came to pick her up."

"Mr. Anders did? I thought he was in a wheelchair."

"He didn't get out of his car because he can't walk, he told me, but he drives this cool Mercedes, Dad, it's real old and it has doors that open from the top like birds' wings, you know? Are you going to ride now? Can I come with you?"

I went upstairs to change. Marion came out of the bathroom in tennis clothes.

"Is there trouble?" she asked.

"Yup."

"Bad trouble?"

"I think so. That headless monster Darby Turbine again. I may have to go to New York tonight, but first I've got to find Charlie. He doesn't even know about it yet. I'm going to ride over with Ailsa. Want to get some air, I'm feeling jittery."

"Did you know that Mrs. Bromberg — "

"Yes, I'm sorry — "

"Ailsa was absolutely *beside* herself. I've never seen her so upset."

"My fault. I forgot. I should have warned her."

"You knew this woman rides like that?"

"Yeah, I had a ride with her in California."

"Oh did you?"

"Yeah. I did."

"Did you hear that Graham — "

"Ailsa told me."

"Well?"

"Well what?"

"Well, are you supplying girls for Graham Anders now?"

"That's a strange remark. You know he's been doing this

all his life, it's just the way he is. He certainly doesn't need anybody to supply — "

"I'm on my way to Sally's. Suppose Caroline is there?"

"Suppose she is?"

At the door, Marion turned. Her face was flushed. "You're all a bunch of bastards!"

"Hey, wait a minute!" I followed her down the stairs. In the hall she grabbed her cardigan, her purse, her tennis racquet, flung open the door, and marched across the courtyard to her station wagon.

Ailsa was standing in front of the stable, holding both horses, watching us.

Marion was in the car, starting the engine, putting on her sunglasses.

"What's the matter, shug?" I asked.

"You know perfectly well what's the matter. Let go of the door, Ordway, I'm late."

"Listen, we might not have to go to New York tonight, we might get the helicopter to take us over first thing in the morning. They have a pad right at the foot of Wall Street — "

"Okay, I'll see you this evening then." The station wagon moved out of the courtyard. When it was passing the big lilacs the brake lights went on, so I walked up.

She looked at me through her sunglasses. "I'm not Caroline Anders, Ordway. I'm not going to have people feeling sorry for me." The station wagon roared down the driveway in a spray of dust and gravel.

Hoofbeats.

Sunshine.

Wind in my face.

Stirrups under my soles, the mare's flanks rolling between

my legs. On an October afternoon this is the most beautiful country in the world. Ailsa rides like a jockey, head down and tail in the air, keeping exactly level with me, taking the fences on the same step. What difference does it all make? These fields will still be here. Won't they? Can I pay the taxes? Limestone scrubbers in West Virginia. Percentage of completion basis. Have to paddle my own canoe, the Old Man said. Karin driving with Graham, could they do it in that car? Full of cortisone. Euphoria he said. Like being drunk. What will I tell Bernard? Don't I have to see Charlie alone first? I'm still representing Charlie, not Bernard. But what good would it do to keep this from Bernard a few hours? Justin Silverstone will be sensible. Probably go to a motel. Suppose she'd jumped the mare into the millrace? Wants to die. And I know why. Stop that, think about Harry Hatch tomorrow: Conyers & Dean didn't know about the limestone scrubbers? Company counsel didn't know about the limestone scrubbers?

Bernard Bromberg was taking a walk with Justin Silverstone. They stood outside the big ironwork gates of the Hyde Place and saw us coming, galloping all the way down the long easy slope from the ridge and around the orchards.

"That's quite a sight," said Justin Silverstone as we reined in.

"I thought Karin would be with you," said Bernard Bromberg.

"She went driving with Mr. Anders," shouted Ailsa before I could say anything.

I dismounted and handed my reins to Ailsa. "I guess she's just doing some sightseeing, Bernard." His expression revealed nothing. "Is Charlie around?" I asked. "I'm afraid we've got a problem."

They looked at each other. "Apparently Charlie isn't granting audiences today," said Bernard Bromberg. "Frank Ferguson and two directors of Manayunk Steel just drove away, madder than hornets. Seems that last night Charlie asked them to come over and talk about the merger, maybe watch the Redskins, drink some beer. . . . But then he wouldn't come downstairs. Justin and I tried to entertain them as best we could, but they didn't seem very happy about it. Ferguson left word that Charlie knew where to find him if he wanted him."

"Is Charlie sick?" I asked. "He was pretty high last night. . . ."

"We wouldn't know, Ordway. As I say, we haven't seen him." Bernard was angry too. Justin Silverstone said nothing.

The hell with this, I thought, and marched upstairs. The door to the master apartment was shut. I knocked. No answer. I knocked again. When I opened the heavy oak door, I heard the television, Redskins and Dallas Cowboys, but it was dark as I turned through the dressing room into the master bedroom, and the smell was stale beer and cigarette smoke. The curtains were closed and the only light came from the television set.

Charlie slouched in a leather armchair, enormous, dressed in striped pajamas, black silk kimono, slippers. Around him, empty beer cans and overflowing ashtrays.

"Are you all right?" I asked, still standing by the door.

No answer.

I walked in, walked past him, turned off the sound of the television.

Still no comment.

I pulled one of the curtains just a little bit, so that a beam of sunlight pierced the smoky darkness.

"Cut that out," Charlie snarled. "The light hurts my eyes."

He rubbed his hands across his face, then looked up angrily. He hadn't shaved or combed his hair, but he sounded sober.

"Have you got a hangover?" I asked. "What you need is some coffee and some fresh air."

"What I need is peace and quiet. I slept two hours last night. Can't I have some privacy and quiet in my own home?"

"Charlie, we've got a problem with the accountants, they've turned up a serious mess at Darby Turbine — "

I sat down on the unmade bed and told him about the limestone scrubbers.

I suppose I expected an explosion: shouts of rage, galvanic action, telephone calls, threats, decapitations....

There was no reaction at all. He seemed to be listening, but his eyes strayed back to the television screen.

"Charlie, you understand what this means? If P-P doesn't give comfort, Harry Hatch won't let the underwriters close, won't let them pay for the Debentures, and that in turn means we can't merge with Bromberg — "

" — and I can't pay off the banks," said Charlie, his voice like lead, still staring at the silent football game. He understood, all right. I waited.

After a long time he said: "It also means I'm a shitty manager, a guy who doesn't know what's going on in his own companies." He looked at me with an expression I'd never seen before. "It confirms what you and a lot of other people have known for years — Conroy's a big fraud, CCC's a house of cards."

"Now wait a second, Charlie — "

"A fucking house of cards! You know it better than anybody! Bank debt, convertible debentures, stock trading at crazy price-earnings ratios, earnings based on creative accounting . . . What's going to happen if I can't pay off the banks? You know what those loan agreements say!" With that he sank back into the chair and lit a cigarette, his hands shaking.

I'd never seen him like this. I knew he had his ups and downs, but I couldn't believe this was the same man who soared to the skies last night, who was going to buy Manayunk Steel, who was going to build his tower sixty stories over Thirtieth Street Station —

"And you know it better than anybody," he said again, through a cloud of cigarette smoke. "Charlie Conroy, the gardener's son who had to wear patched knickers, who had to walk down to the road to meet the school bus, whose father stank of cheap rye, whose mother cried. And now he's a big shot! I can hear all of you laughing!"

I suddenly thought about the Frenchman who had always gotten him out, diverted him somehow, protected him when such a mood hit. Where was the Frenchman?

I did the best I could.

"Nobody's laughing at you, Charlie. You've built an empire with your own energy, your own courage and brains, you've built yourself an empire out of nothing, but every empire has troubles out along the borders, and it's a long way from the emperor's palace to the places where troubles develop, so you've got communications problems. But when you see the trouble you've got to jump in and deal with it. Now we have this mess down in West Virginia, it's no use crying over it, we've got to decide what to do. We've got a meeting with the underwriters in New York tomorrow. We've sent for the engineers to explain the problem to everybody, but you're going to have to be there, Charlie! They'll want to hear what *you* plan to do about it."

He sat there and stared at the football game.

"I've done what I can, Charlie. I've told Renfrew to send

the Learjet out for the engineers. I've got our best people reviewing the construction contract, to see if they can tell whose responsibility those scrubbers are. I've arranged for the helicopter to take us to New York first thing in the morning. But when we meet with the underwriters they'll be looking at *you!* You're going to have to convince them that you're on top of the situation."

"Never should have bought Darby. That's what changed everything. If I was so damned smart, why did I go into hock to buy Darby?"

"Charlie, you're stuck with Darby! You've got to deal with this particular crisis tomorrow morning, and I've got to tell Bromberg and Silverstone about it, right now before they find out from somebody else. We've got to have them on our side in this, or the whole house of cards really will collapse."

I stood up. "Will you be ready at dawn? I want to see the engineers for an hour or so before the underwriters have a go at them."

No answer.

"Charlie? Would you rather I go over first thing with Tommy Sharp and send the chopper back for you and Bernard? I've got to be there when Harry Hatch examines the engineers."

He stared at the football game, smoking a cigarette.

"Charlie?"

"What difference does it make? Do what you want, just leave me alone."

I got up and left him alone and went downstairs to tell Bernard Bromberg and Justin Silverstone about the limestone scrubbers.

22.

What Would It Do
to the Bottom Line?

First Hudson's conference room was packed. Outside the big windows a breathtaking view of New York harbor, blazing sunshine, a stiff ocean breeze raising sparkling whitecaps on the water; inside, fifty worried men ignoring the view, glumly listening to a tall young engineer preaching his particular gospel.

It was the same working team that assembled in Philadelphia so long ago, plus First Hudson's chairman, First Hudson's syndicate manager, their assistants, two professors of engineering called in to advise First Hudson about this crisis, Hewitt Robinson with a battery of Darby Turbine engineers, and Sandy Simon, flown in from San Francisco on Sunday night to represent the Bromberg interests.

Mike Barkus wore a Zapata moustache, a striped shirt with fat necktie, and a knitted suit with bell-bottom trousers. "Some funny-looking engineer," muttered First Hudson's slicked-down pinstriped chairman, but they listened attentively to his message about how the world was running out of oil, about the cost and danger of atomic fission, about a five-hundred-year supply of coal right here in the United States, about how we would *have* to use our coal to generate power, would *have* to burn it without polluting the air. . . .

This was in 1969. Nobody gave a damn about energy

shortages. The underwriters became impatient. They wanted to hear whether Darby would get paid for the Turkey River plant, and the questions came:

What was the matter with the limestone scrubbers? Could they be fixed? Why hadn't anybody anticipated that this would happen?

Harry Hatch's spectacles glistened as he warmed to his cross-examination: Why hadn't anything been mentioned when the underwriters visited the plant? How many other limestone scrubbers were in operation? Had they been inspected by Darby's engineers? Did they clog too? What was being done about them?

Mike Barkus stood in front of his photographs and his blueprints and held his ground like any true believer. Nothing was mentioned when the underwriters came because nothing was wrong: the scrubbers hadn't even been assembled then. A few other plants were installing scrubbers, and they were having trouble too, all different kinds of trouble depending on the type of plant, the type of coal . . . you always have trouble with new processes. Did we know how much trouble they were having with the nuclear installations?

He was young and he was smart and he believed in his cause, and even the professors of engineering couldn't shake him. The limestone scrubbers were going to work.

"But who is going to pay for making them work?" demanded Harry Hatch. "And how much is it going to cost?"

Mike Barkus had some thoughts about what it might cost, but he guessed the lawyers would decide who had to pay for it. All eyes swiveled to me, and I turned to Tommy Sharp, who had been up all night too. While I talked he distributed the memorandum of law our people had prepared.

I cleared my throat. "Now in the first place, I want to explain that the contract for construction of the Turkey River plant provides that it be interpreted under the law of West Virginia, and of course we can't give a formal opinion on the law of another state — "

"Oh now, wait a minute," said John Lundquist.

" — but we've reviewed all the decisions we could find, in West Virginia and elsewhere, we've prepared this memorandum Tommy is distributing, and we hope to get it backed up by a formal opinion from West Virginia counsel."

"By tomorrow morning?" asked Harry Hatch.

"We're working on it."

Everybody read the memorandum — ten pages of discussion and citations, put together by young lawyers working all Sunday afternoon, revised by Ames Mahoney Sunday evening, retyped Sunday night. . . . The silence was deafening.

Harry Hatch to John Lundquist: "Is this the bulletproof opinion you wanted?"

John Lundquist: "No."

Ordway Smith: "Well, we don't claim it's bulletproof, but it's all we can say in the circumstances."

I knew it sounded lame, but if you can't predict a result you can't predict it.

Another silence. The underwriters looked at each other.

Sandy Simon piped up: "Could somebody give us hard numbers? If reserves have to be set up, what would it do to the bottom line?"

That's what they really wanted to know. Larry Lenz and John Lundquist began to talk. The gold pencils came out and the slide rules. Of course there was no way of knowing exactly what it might cost to put the scrubbers into operating condition, or what would happened to the contract if that couldn't be done, but Mike Barkus's boys had supplied a safe high number and a minimum low number and so we've worked out the adjustments on two levels. . . .

"All right, call it five cents a share for the quarter," Harry Hatch was saying, bent over his pad.

Grunts of agreement around the room.

"Why don't we sticker the Prospectus?" somebody asked. "Postpone the closing one day, print a sticker explaining the problem, show what the adjustment might do to the earnings, paste the explanation on the cover of each Prospectus, let each bondholder make his own decision?"

Harry Hatch turned to look at his underwriters. "Want to sticker?"

Dubious faces. "Doesn't that mean the customers could back out? Wouldn't have to take the bonds they ordered?"

"That's what it means," said Harry Hatch. "Of course in theory they never have to take securities until they get the final Prospectus with their confirmation — "

"In practice people don't back out," said First Hudson's syndicate manager, "not if they want to keep doing business with us."

"But if we wave a sticker under their noses and say, 'Look at this terrible thing that happened, are you sure you don't want to change your mind?' "

"That's different."

"You're goddamned right it's different."

"Maybe we'd better go out and call our people."

Harry Hatch followed them out. I had the feeling he had some solution up his sleeve — everything that can happen must have happened at Iselin Bros. & Devereaux at least once before — and Harry wanted to produce the rabbit that would save the deal, but only at the moment providing the maximum glory for the magician, the moment just before the apocalypse.

Intermission. The meeting fragmented into separate discussions. Secretaries brought sandwiches, and coffee in Styrofoam cups. The engineers bent over their rolled blueprints. I looked out across the harbor, then forced myself to focus on a new debate between Tommy Sharp and Sandy Simon.

"What good would a sticker do you?" asked Tommy, munching. "Even if the underwriters let us sticker their Prospectuses, what about your Bromberg stockholders? They got the same financials in their Proxy Statement. Are you going to send them another Proxy Statement, hold another meeting, have them vote on the merger all over again?"

Sandy lighted his pipe, looking profound. "Mm. We've considered that."

Tommy plowed ahead. "And if you postpone the merger, call another stockholders' meeting, then our Prospectus is wrong again because it contains the Bromberg earnings and it says the Bromberg holders *have* approved the merger!"

Sandy nodded. "Fortunately, you'll recall the merger agreement says that Bromberg's officers can waive certain conditions of closing, if it appears to be in the best interests of Bromberg's stockholders."

That was the first time the word "waive" was heard in the room.

Now Tommy Sharp looked skeptical. "You're going to waive the comfort letter?"

"Not the whole letter, of course, but perhaps we could work out some change in the wording. . . ." At the other end of the table, the accountants stopped talking among themselves. Sandy Simon rose and went over to confer with John Lundquist.

Tommy Sharp leaned toward my left ear: "I don't know if Bromberg realizes it, but he's really in something of a box."

"Why?"

"Well look, when the merger was first announced, before it was announced, Bromberg stock was worth what? Sixteen-seventeen dollars a share, something like that? But now it's traded as if the merger's accomplished, and CCC is up, so right now Bromberg stock is worth about forty. Right?"

"Right."

"So let's say the merger aborts, the merger doesn't take place because the Bromberg control people — that's Bernard and Bob — insist that every technical closing requirement be met, that the comfort letter says word for word what the merger agreement requires . . . so the merger doesn't come off, what happens? Each and every Bromberg stockholder has a loss of twenty-three or twenty-four dollars a share. Who are they going to go after for that loss?"

"Charlie?"

"No, not if Charlie was willing to go ahead with the merger. They're going to go after Bernard and Bob, that's what they're going to do!"

A girl came in. Telephone call for Mr. Sharp. He was back a moment later. Two young lawyers from Conyers & Dean had arrived at Iselin Bros. & Devereaux with the Trust Indentures, our final legal opinions and the other closing papers, and people from First Hudson were already at the bank, counting and packaging the executed Debentures for delivery tomorrow.

"They want to know should they go ahead with the pre-closing," said Tommy. "The Trust Indentures are signed, but it'll take all afternoon to go over the other things with Harry Hatch's people. . . ."

"But nothing is delivered until tomorrow, when the underwriters bring their checks?"

"That's correct."

"Well sure, they'd better get everything ready on the assumption that we'll close on schedule."

Tommy went off to transmit the order.

— Mrs. Westphal's office.

— She there please?

— Who may I say —

— Mr. Smith.

— Mr. Smith? May I tell her —

— Just tell her Mr. Smith.

— One moment please. . . .

— Ordway?

— Hi.

— Hi. Where are you?

— Wall Street. I want to see you.

— Right this minute?

— No, tonight, but that's the problem, we'll be working late, I don't know what time —

— Do you have to go home?

— No, I'm staying over, we have a closing tomorrow. Charlie Conroy's Debentures.

— Well, I don't think there's any problem.

— You mean you're alone?

— That's right.

— Where is —

— London. Where else? Ordway, you sound —

— I'm having problems. . . . This thing with Charlie is beginning to scare me.

— Ordway, you've never been scared in your life!

— I'm scared now.

— No, you're not, you're just upset. Do you think you'll want some dinner?

— I don't know, I just don't know what's going to happen down here. . . .

— All right, I'll have something I can heat up, just give me a call so I can warn the doorman. . . .

I returned just as the second act began. Charlie Conroy, Bernard Bromberg and Justin Silverstone were at the table now, and the underwriters were crowding back into the room.

"All right, is the fire out?" demanded Charlie. He seemed completely recovered.

I turned to Harry Hatch. "Are you going to sticker the Prospectus?"

"No sticker. Market's off six points this afternoon. If we offer people an excuse to get out from under their orders, there may be some doubt if the syndicate will hold together — "

"Not *our* customers," interjected First Hudson's chairman. "No problem with our customers. But we had to form one hell of a big group, and some of the smaller houses can't promise they won't have cancellations in a down market, and of course nobody wants this deal to turn sticky — "

"I think we'd like to hear from the engineers," said Bernard Bromberg.

So Mike Barkus had the floor again, the same story but in more detail, the blueprints, the photographs, the conviction that he knew what he was talking about, that he was right, that the scrubbers would work. It was just a matter of trial and error, adjusting the pH control, changing the acid content in the slurry, speeding up the movement of the slurry through the pipes. This time the engineering professors were nodding in agreement.

Bernard Bromberg leaned forward, listening, completely absorbed.

Charlie Conroy's scowl reflected anger and impatience. "So what's the big problem?" he finally interrupted. "It's a new concept, it's going to take some time to make it work, why are we making such a big deal about it?"

Patiently John Lundquist explained again: percentage-of-completion method, earnings already taken in might have to be backed out, adjustments might be required. . . .

"So what? So we'll make the adjustments! It can't amount to more than a couple of cents a share. . . ."

"But you see, the comfort letter requires us to say . . ."

Back and forth, a Ping-Pong match. The sun moved behind the city and rain clouds blew in from the sea. A tanker came out of the East River. An army transport approached Fort Hamilton. A white seaplane flitted behind the towers, landed in the water, and taxied toward the foot of Wall Street. Surreptitiously, some of the younger brokers began to peek at their wristwatches.

Suddenly Charlie exploded: "All right, let's cut out all this bullshit! What are we going to *do*? I've got sixty-five million in bank notes coming due next week. Are you people trying to tell me you're walking away from this deal on account of some trouble at one power plant in West Virginia? One project out of two dozen we've got going all over the world? On account of a *possible* adjustment of five cents a share? Is that what you're trying to tell me? We're going to

301

write off six months of work and two hundred thousand in expenses and tell the banks, 'Sorry, fellas, our limestone scrubbers got clogged, you'll have to wait a while!'? And what about Bernard's stockholders? They think their stock's worth forty bucks a share because they're merging with CCC tomorrow. What are we going to tell *them*? Now come on, wake up! We're paying you guys the kind of fees we're paying you because you're supposed to be the best lawyers, and the best accountants and the best investment bankers in the country, and I'm telling you you'd better come up with the answer!"

In the silence, Harry Hatch took off his glasses and began to polish them with his handkerchief. His moment had come. "Gentlemen," he said quietly, "let's consider our options."

23.

Conroy's Turkeys

Marie whacked an ice cube with the back of a spoon and dropped the pieces into a glass.

"Doesn't sound like such a bad solution," she said.

"That's what I thought. He may be a little pest but he's a good securities lawyer, and he pulled the rabbit from his sleeve."

"From his hat," said Marie, pouring bourbon over the ice and handing me the glass. "Rabbits come out of hats, tricks come out of sleeves."

"Okay, from his hat. I really thought he'd solved the thing, and so did everybody else. The whole room sort of exhaled, people began to talk, it was a whole different atmosphere.

"John Lundquist sat down and wrote out a new paragraph for his comfort letter, sort of what lawyers call a *caveat,* a warning, a condition — there's been no material adverse change in results of operations *except* that such-and-such adjustment might have to be made for losses on the Turkey River contract. Of course that takes the accountants right off the hook."

"But why should the underwriters take a letter with such a hole in it?" asked Marie, walking back into the living room.

"Well, why indeed? But remember, the suggestion came from their own lawyer. So when everybody was milling around Harry took me aside and said: 'Look, this is really a matter of business judgment for the clients, isn't it? The underwriters have the Debentures sold, they'd lose the commissions on a hundred million dollars and frankly it's been a damn thin year for underwriters. That boy Barkus may look a little far out, but he seems to know what he's talking about, and if he turns out to be wrong . . . Well okay, maybe it'll mean they have to adjust, five cents a share . . . What the hell, Ordway, I've told them it's a business risk, so they authorized me to say that if Conroy will take a chance on it, they will too.'

"I told him I didn't know what would happen if Charlie couldn't pay off the banks.

" 'That's my whole point,' he said. 'There isn't time to revise the whole deal, recirculate another Prospectus, try to sell the Debentures all over again. It'll never fly, Ordway. They'll be damaged goods. You know what they'll call 'em in the Street? They'll call them Conroy's Turkeys!' "

"What was Mr. Bromberg doing all this time?" asked Marie as I stopped to sip the bourbon.

"He went off into another room to hold a council of war. After a while Justin Silverstone came out to get me. Just me. I didn't like that, because after all I'm supposed to be representing Charlie. Should I be talking to Bromberg behind closed doors? But I figured the main thing was to solve the problem, to get the deal done, so I went in there with them.

"They were having an argument. Sandy Simon felt they should go ahead, take the comfort letter with the condition, in other words waive the exact language and take a chance on the possibility that the earnings would have to be adjusted . . . which is sort of odd, because Sandy was brought in originally to kill the merger, Bob Bromberg didn't want the merger, and here is Sandy arguing to go ahead, because as he said it was balancing the *possibility* that the earnings might have to be adjusted against the *certainty* that the Bromberg stockholders would lose twenty-four dollars a share if the merger blows up. How could they in good conscience deprive their stockholders of a certain profit by insisting on the exact wording of the comfort letter?

"Justin Silverstone took the opposite tack: 'Nobody guaranteed our people that the merger would go through. The agreement they approved said that CCC had to meet certain conditions, and now they're *not* meeting those conditions — '

"And then Bernard cut him off. Bernard looked terrible, all of a sudden. He looked old and tired and unhappy — just awful. He looked like he hadn't slept all night. He said he didn't want to go over the same old ground. He just wanted to ask me a question — not as Charlie's lawyer, but as a man they'd come to like and to trust. He said these things keep coming out of the woodwork, things that Charlie ought to know about but doesn't. . . . Now what he wanted to know was this: Is anything *else* going to come out of the woodwork?

"I said 'No' quite firmly. 'I don't know of anything else, Bernard,' and Justin Silverstone said: 'If he did, he couldn't give his opinion. Conyers & Dean have to give us an opinion that they know of no omission from the Prospectus — ' but Bernard cut him off again: No, no, he didn't mean that kind of thing. He was talking about Charlie Conroy *himself.* Observing him last weekend, observing him right here today . . . 'Charlie's moody, *very* moody . . . Is it more than moodiness, Ordway?'

"I told him no, there's nothing wrong with Charlie, he's always been . . . mercurial. Many brilliant people are —

"Bernard shook his head. 'Everybody's worried about the

accountants,' he said. 'I'm not. Accountants tell you what *has* happened — or at least that's what they're supposed to tell you. I'm more concerned about what's *going* to happen. And it's people that make things happen. It's people that create these numbers everybody's hung up on. So I'm not asking you for a legal opinion, Ordway. I'm asking you as a man: Should I go ahead with this deal, should I cast my lot with Charlie Conroy, or should I get out while I can?' And he stared at me, Jesus, with those eyes!"

"Oh, that's not fair," Marie exclaimed. "He shouldn't — "

"That's what Justin Silverstone said. 'Bernard,' he said, 'it's not fair to ask him a question like that,' and Bernard said: 'I'm asking anyway.' Still staring at me."

"What did you say?"

"What could I say? I said that as far as I know there's nothing wrong with Charlie, and that I thought he should go ahead with the deal. And he said okay, they would, and I went out again and told the others."

"And everybody cheered?"

"God no, everybody was worn out. The engineers left, the brokers left, Bromberg and Charlie decided to go uptown for dinner, but the rest of us had to go over to Harry Hatch's office to see how they were coming along with the closing papers."

"More problems?"

"No, they had everything in good shape, a room full of documents in neat piles, closing memorandum checked off, there should be nothing to do tomorrow except get the telegram from the SEC saying no stop order has been issued — that's routine — and the checks from the underwriters. Then we'll tell the people down in Delaware to file the papers merging Bromberg into our CCC subsidiary. . . . The boys did a good job."

"Well, then you're all set," said Marie. "The last crisis overcome, Charlie Conroy rides again. . . . Ordway, you're so tired you can't see straight!"

I was. I sat on the sofa and looked at the silver-framed photograph of Alfred von Waldstein and Thomas Mann sitting on a bench in front of our Old Mill, and felt the whiskey take hold.

"What's the matter?" she asked, as I rubbed my hand across my eyes.

"I'm worried. Something isn't right. The four of us finally had dinner together, Tommy and Justin Silverstone and Sandy Simon — who insisted on eating at the Harvard Club, for God's sake — and we had a perfectly agreeable dinner, but there was . . . I don't know . . . something funny in the air. . . . Sandy was chipper enough, but Justin wasn't and Tommy wasn't. . . ."

"How did you get away? Isn't Tommy spending the night?"

"No, he wanted to go home and come back in the morning, but he asked me to ride down to Penn Station in the cab with him. The kid was dead tired too, he's done a terrific job, but he isn't happy."

"Why not? You've both worked so hard and so long, and now you've finished and Charlie's going to get his money — "

"Well, the point is we have to give an opinion, Conyers & Dean's opinion, to the underwriters and also to the Bromberg stockholders, and the opinion says in effect that everything is okay, that there are no omissions in the Prospectus and in the proxy statement, no failure to state material facts. . . . Of course the opinions are all typed and reproduced and dated tomorrow and sitting there waiting for me to sign for the firm."

"But there's nothing in the Prospectus about the problem at the Turkey River, the limestone scrubbers?"

307

"No, of course not, we didn't hear about that till Saturday night. By that time they had distributed the Prospectus all over the country."

"So Tommy Sharp thinks you shouldn't give the opinion? Wouldn't that kill the whole deal?"

"Sure it would."

"But you said you all decided the scrubbers didn't make that much difference, the engineers will get them to work, and even if they don't it won't make much difference in Charlie's earnings — Isn't that what they decided?"

"Yes."

"Well — "

"I don't know, Marie, it just doesn't seem . . . our *name* is on the Prospectus, it says Conyers & Dean passed on the issue, and people see the name, won't it make them feel we've okayed everything?"

"You have okayed everything."

"Yeah . . . but as Tommy points out, the underwriting agreement and the merger agreement both say that Penny-packer Poole will give a comfort letter, they spell out the wording of the letter, so haven't we in effect promised the people who bought the Debentures, promised the Bromberg stockholders, that P-P is going to give comfort — as they laughingly call it — in these particular words? Well, they're *not* giving it, as Justin Silverstone points out. They're excepting the Turkey River contract."

"And you know it."

"Sure we know it."

"But you're not telling anybody?"

"We *have* told them! We've told the other side, the people representing the Bromberg stockholders and the Debenture buyers, and they've waived the exact terms of the letter. Look, this letter is something *we* had to bring to the closing

— I mean Charlie had to bring it, CCC had to bring it, it was something our side had to produce. Okay, we *didn't* produce it. Now it's up to *them*, the Brombergs, First Hudson, the other underwriters — it's up to them to say okay, no ticket, no laundry. Isn't it?"

"Hmm."

"But they're not saying that. They're saying they've studied the problem, they're satisfied in their business judgment that this argument over the Turkey River contract won't have that much effect on CCC's earnings, on CCC's prospects, and they want to go ahead and close anyway. They've gotten the facts, they've consulted with their lawyers and on the basis of all that they've waived this particular requirement, because it's more important for them to· go ahead. Does that make sense?"

"I suppose so."

"If the underwriters don't go ahead, they lose four million dollars in commissions plus another packet in expenses they've incurred — all of Harry Hatch's fees, for one thing. If the Brombergs don't go ahead, their own stockholders are likely to sue them. And if Charlie doesn't go ahead . . . Well, his loans come due next week. If he defaults he's at the mercy of the banks; they can take the company away from him, they can throw it into receivership . . . they can do anything they want."

"So it seems you should go ahead," said Marie. "Ordway, you're too tired to think about this now, let's get you into bed."

"I've got to think about it now, I've got to decide what to do. How did I get into this? This thing could affect the future of the firm. Why do *I* have to decide something like this?"

"Why don't you ask somebody?"

— Caroline? This is Ordway. I'm sorry to call so late.

— Hello, Ordway.

— Is Graham home?

— Is *Graham* home?

— Yeah. I really need his thoughts on something.

. . .

— Caroline?

— No . . . No, Ordway, I'm sorry. Graham isn't home.

— Any idea where I could reach him?

— No, Ordway . . . No idea.

— Hey Caroline? Are you all right?

— . . .

— Caroline?

— Joke's on you, Ordway.

— I beg your pardon?

— No . . . I guess it's on me. Again.

— Caroline . . . I don't —

— Ordway, he's supposed to be with you. In New York. Helping you close Conroy's Debenture deal, or whatever it is.

— Aw Caroline . . . dearie . . .

— Had to take his car, you see, because he can't walk well enough to use the train. . . .

— Caroline, don't, please!

— Good night, Ordway.

"Who else can I ask? Forrester's dead, Rieger's in London, Lansing Merritt would take over the whole show and get into a fight with everybody and just make everything worse, Ellsworth Boyle would tell me to use my own judgment. . . . I guess I could try to reach Phil Rieger in London, but my God, he doesn't know anything about this deal. . . ."

"Could you talk to somebody at the SEC?"

"No. . . . That would be like running to the police. I mean sure, we talk to them all the time, we get them to interpret their rules and they're very helpful, but we can't talk to them about *this*. If we think this is serious enough to ask them about, then there's your answer: we can't go ahead, we've got a material omission, they'll issue a stop order and that'll be the end of the deal. We can't ask them to make a legal judgment about something that's entirely within our knowledge. That's not their job, that's *our* job. If we go to them, then the cat's out of the bag, they'll issue a stop order. Who am I to call down the SEC on my own client?"

"Ordway, I've never seen you so upset!"

"Of course I'm upset. I don't know what to *do!*"

"Well, you're not going to do anything while you're in this condition. You're going to go in there and have a very hot shower and then you're going to have another drink and maybe a pill, and you're going to sleep."

When I stepped out of the shower another glass full of splintered ice and bourbon was standing on the washstand. I rubbed the steam from the mirror and watched myself drinking, redfaced, woozy from the heat and the alcohol.

The bedroom was pitch dark. "Did you say something about a pill?"

"Hmm. But then I had a better idea."

"Oh . . . Hey listen, I'm not sure this is going to work. . . ."

"You just don't worry about it, Ordway."

"Are you awake?"

"Yeah . . . Wow." My muscles were stiff. I felt as if I had been unconscious for a week.

Her naked arm reached toward the luminous dial. "You've slept for six hours. It's nearly daylight and it's raining. How do you feel?"

"Better." I tried to wrap my arms around her.

"Oh no," she said, extricating herself, climbing quickly out of the bed, zipping herself into a blue quilted housecoat, turning on the light by her mirror, brushing her hair. "You've slept. You're all right. You're going to find the answer to your problem."

I covered my eyes against the light. "Oh Christ, the answer to my problem . . . I wish this day was over. I want to go back to sleep and wake up tomorrow morning. What would happen if I just stay right here until tomorrow morning? Would the world end?"

"Don't be so silly, Ordway. Here, put on this robe and come into the kitchen."

By the time I had gone to the bathroom and splashed cold water on my face my daytime nightmare was in full focus again.

I sat down at the kitchen table, watched her measuring powdered coffee into the cups, watched her take butter and bread and eggs out of the refrigerator, watched her take the whistling kettle off the gas flame and pour water into the cups.

"What the hell am I going to do, Marie?"

"Ordway, I don't know the answer, but I know that you will have to work it out yourself. What about Tommy Sharp? What does he think you should do?"

"He doesn't know either, he just sees the problem. We could be in terrible trouble either way. What we're really doing when we issue the opinion is risking Conyers & Dean for Charlie, we're putting the necks of all our people on the block. . . . But you get so involved. . . . Did I tell you how I actually *lied*? I told them Charlie signed the merger agreement when he hadn't signed it?"

"That's over, Ordway. He signed. Forget about it!"

I can't forget about it.

"Isn't this the same thing? I'm being sort of dragged along into something I deep down don't want to do because I'm afraid that everything will collapse if I don't. But why is it that I'm so reluctant to give the opinion? I'm supposed to be Charlie's lawyer, I'm supposed to look out for his interests, for CCC's interests, those other guys are supposed to look out for their people. If they all want to go ahead, why is it *my* job, why is it C & D's job to say we can't go ahead? Whose side am I on, anyway? Lawyers aren't like accountants. P-P are independent accountants, that's how they hold themselves out, they make independent audits and the public is supposed to rely on their opinion because they're *independent*. That's their whole point. But lawyers aren't independent. Lawyers are just the opposite. Lawyers are *advocates*. Spokesmen. Mouthpieces. Lawyers owe the highest duty to their clients. Don't they? Isn't that what we've been taught?"

Marie didn't say anything. I drank some coffee and looked down into the dreary courtyard — a few lighted windows, fire escapes, rain falling into the grayness.

"Does C & D owe some duty to all the people out there who bought Debentures? Does C & D owe some duty to Bromberg's stockholders? They're all represented by excellent lawyers, by Harry Hatch, by Sandy Simon, by First Hudson, by Bernard Bromberg, and they've all decided that they want to go ahead, they want to close. . . . Where does C & D get off telling them we're not going to give our opinion?"

Marie sat down and poured some hot milk into her coffee.

"Do you remember that place — was it in Pennsylvania? Where people died? Because of the coal gas? What was the name of that place, that valley somewhere?"

"You mean Donora?"

"That's right, Donora. What happened there?"

"My God, you don't think . . ."

"What happened?"

I looked out of the window again, trying to remember. "Donora. Jesus. I don't remember, it was back in the 'forties, wasn't it? They had factories in this valley, and the air got trapped, and people breathed smoke from the factories, I think some people died. . . ."

"What would happen?"

"On the Turkey River? Oh, they'd never let them do that today!"

"That's what I mean, people in those valleys must be pretty conscious of these problems even now, don't you think? Are they going to let the electric company use that plant if they have the slightest doubt — ?"

"No, of course they won't."

"What will happen if they just can't use that plant, and the electric company doesn't have to pay the money — "

"— and it costs Charlie more than five cents a share?"

"Yes. Or . . . I don't know, suppose for some reason they *do* let them use the plant, and there's trouble, people get sick . . . Or they don't get electric power in that valley, they don't get enough power for their industries . . . I mean, they must need this plant or they wouldn't build it. . . . A hundred-and-seventy-million-dollar plant and now they can't use it? Ordway, one way or another there's going to be a scandal, isn't there?"

She stopped to drink some coffee.

"Suppose you go ahead and give your opinion, you close

the deal, everything is fine for a few weeks, a few months, then something else happens to Charlie, to another one of his companies, or the whole stock market collapses again? And the people who bought the Debentures are sorry, the Bromberg people are sorry — won't they look for a scapegoat?"

"Sure they will."

"And then they say, 'Well, if we'd known about this mess in West Virginia, we wouldn't have paid for those Debentures, we wouldn't have merged into CCC — but Conyers & Dean approved everything. . . .' What could they do to you? I mean, to the firm."

"I don't know. . . . Sue us for malpractice, say we violated the securities laws, sic the SEC on us. . . . You can always sue. . . . I mean we had an old professor at the law school who would yell, 'Can you sue? Of course you can sue, you can always sue, you can sue the Bishop of Birmingham for bastardy, but can you prove your case? *Can you win?*' "

"Could they win?" asked Marie.

"I don't know. I never heard of a case like this. . . . I mean, is it my job to look out for *them*? Isn't it my job to look out for Charlie, for CCC?" It was getting lighter now. "My God, a suit like that would cause an uproar! Even if we won, we'd never hear the end of it. And it would take years!"

Thinking about the portraits in the library, the portraits in the hall, Frederick Dean and Judge Conyers and George Graham and even my Old Man. What about the ones who are alive? My brothers.

Partners, associates, wives, secretaries, children, grandchildren, mortgage payments, tuition payments, pensions . . . how many lives will be touched if I do the wrong thing this morning?

I put my head in my hands. "Marie, I don't know what to do!"

"I think you do," she said.

"But he's my *client*. He trusts me. He needs me. Am I going to put the firm ahead of the client?"

"Suppose something else happens tomorrow, something else comes out of the woodwork, as Mr. Bromberg says. . . . How long can you keep on cleaning up Charlie's messes, or sweeping them under the rug?"

"I'm a hired gun. It's my job."

"Well, I wonder," she said. "Is the name of Conyers & Dean going to mean anything if people think that's your job?"

I got up and walked into the living room. Gray morning light came past the curtains. I wandered around, looking at the books and pictures. Down on 79th Street cars were honking now.

"Marie, I just can't do it. Walk into a room full of people, a room full of people assembled for a closing, and tell 'em sorry, I've changed my mind, C & D are chickening out, we won't give our opinion? When Harry Hatch's firm is giving theirs? When Sandy Simon's firm is giving theirs? Two of the biggest firms in the country? All those guys are going out on the limb, and company counsel *won't*? I just can't do it! Can you imagine what Charlie would do? He wouldn't only fire us, he wouldn't only refuse to pay our fee, he might even bring suit against us! Our own client sues us for malpractice. How would that look in the papers?"

I walked over to the table and picked up the framed photograph of Alfred von Waldstein with Thomas Mann. I looked at the faces.

"What would he have done?"

"Thomas Mann?"

"No, your father."

"Well! You know the answer to that. If there's a law it must be obeyed. More Prussian than the Prussians. But he wasn't a lawyer. I think lawyers are not always so clear about what the law is. What would *your* father have done?"

I had to smile. What would the Old Man have done if by some inconceivable circumstance he'd ever been faced by something like this?

"I'm afraid Charlie would have fired him long ago. Or vice versa."

"Ordway, why don't you get dressed? I can't tell you what to do. I'm not a lawyer. The only thing I can tell you is that you're smart enough to know what's right, and strong enough to do it."

I shaved with her husband's razor, took a shower, got dressed. Marie brought me a fried egg and another cup of coffee. I drank the coffee but couldn't look at the egg.

"The rain seems to have stopped," I said. "I think I'll take a walk."

"Ordway?" She stood at the door of the apartment as I rang for the elevator. "Why do you always sell yourself short? You can do anything you want to do, don't you know that?"

"Oh really? Somebody once told me that I wasn't a serious person, that I was a very nice rich boy who knows nothing about life."

She shook her head. "People can change. You've changed more than anybody I know."

"Well, I'm not rich and I'm not a boy, that's for sure."

"You think that's what I meant?"

A bell rang and the elevator opened. I got on. Marie stepped across the hall and grabbed the door. The bell rang again and the door pushed against her hand.

"You think that's what I meant?"

We stared at each other.

"No," I said. "I know what you meant."

"I thought you did. Good luck, and please call right away to tell me what happened." She let go, the door closed, and the elevator descended. It was seven o'clock.

I walked over to Park. It was too early to take a taxi, so I turned down Park and kept walking. Wind from the sea was blowing the rain clouds apart and the sun was shining through. What am I going to do? It's only five cents a share. Five cents a share is not a material amount in relation to CCC's earnings, or so they all say. Harry Hatch thinks it isn't. Sandy Simon thinks it isn't. Law Review, both of them. Ready to sign off on behalf of their clients. I didn't want to stop walking because that would mean I would have to decide so I walked on and on, right through the echoing hall of Grand Central, already abustle with commuters, then back up the ramp to Park. It's not my job to prevent their clients from waiving a condition my client promised to perform. That's their job. Isn't it? My job is to help my client do what he wants to do. What he *has* to do, really. What choice does Charlie have? They are supposed to look out for their clients and I'm supposed to look out for mine. I'm worried about C & D. What will happen to C & D if word gets around that we're chicken, that we were afraid to stick our neck out in a situation where other people were not, that we abandoned a client in mortal danger? Is that going to bring in business? Isn't that a greater threat than the remote possibility that a disaffected Debenture holder will sue us over five cents a share he wasn't warned about? The neighborhoods changed. Seedy stores, seedy bars, loft buildings. Below Fourteenth Street I marched on and on through a no-man's-land where I'd never been, lost in the East Village, secure only in the knowledge that Broadway eventually meets Wall, down and down and down on Broadway, buses and taxis and trucks, more people now pouring from the subway exits, thousands of people who never heard of Conroy's Debentures, who never would hear of them no matter what O. Smith does this morning, the only sensible thing is to sign the fucking thing and pray. Isn't it? Why did they leave me alone to decide this? Graham Anders. Karin. First thing Tommy Sharp said when he saw her. Doesn't mean anything, he does it all the time, but what about her? Wants to die. And I know why. Forget it! Forget that stuff, it's none of your business, make up your goddamned mind! City Hall Park, World Trade Center towers looming up over everything, and then familiar names again: Liberty Street, Cedar Street, and just before Trinity Church, the downtown branch of Brooks Brothers.

It was nine o'clock.

"May I help you, sir?"

"I just walked all the way down from Seventy-ninth Street."

"I beg your pardon?"

Cut that out. If he thinks you're crazy it might slow things up. "I want a blue button-down shirt, seventeen thirty-six, a white T-shirt, white underpants, black socks size thirteen. I want to put them on and have you send my stuff home. I have an account here."

"Certainly, sir. Right this way."

As I followed him back toward the changing cubicles I suddenly remembered why Marie's remark sounded so familiar: it was the same thing Graham Anders told me, that afternoon in his hospital room, that afternoon the girl was sitting on his bed, that afternoon he told me it's what you think of yourself that counts.

That instant I felt everything clicking into place. By the time I was dressed again I had made up my mind. I left the store, crossed Broadway and walked over to Chase Manhattan Plaza.

24.

Cold Comfort

I mainly remember the faces. In the huge conference room of Iselin Bros. & Devereaux, young lawyers frowning over closing documents; the Frenchman, for once without sunglasses, squinting his ugly little eyes, signing things; Tommy Sharp looking at me across the room, looking at me and not at the closing papers; a squadron of brokers filing in, talking, shaking hands, smiling; Charlie Conroy also shaking hands, also smiling, a white carnation in his lapel — where had they found him a carnation in Wall Street? Bernard Bromberg, Justin Silverstone, Sandy Simon, all carrying their suitcases for the flight home — where was Karin? Harry Hatch, all subdued triumph behind vest and gold-rimmed spectacles . . .

"Harry, could I borrow an office somewhere? I've got to talk with Charlie."

"Sure thing. Come on back and use my room."

Charlie's smile vanished. "Now what?" but he followed me down the hall.

Harry Hatch is a clean-desk man: no papers, no junk, leather swivel chair, leather sofa, telephone, diplomas, chaste photograph of smiling wife and solemn children, the partners in dinner jackets around tables at the Union Club. . . . His secretary withdrew and closed the door.

At first he didn't understand. "What do you mean you can't give an opinion? We all agreed it was okay, we'll make the scrubbers work and if it costs us money we'll adjust the earnings. . . . They've all agreed it's okay!"

"They're kidding themselves, Charlie. It's not okay. We've either got to put on a sticker to tell people about the problem, or we can't take their money."

"They *won't* put on a sticker, you heard them explain that yesterday!"

"Then we can't close."

The color left his face. "You gotta be kidding."

"You really think I'd be kidding about something like this? This is the hardest thing I've ever done in my life, Charlie, but I've got to do it. There's going to be holy hell to pay about this Turkey River thing. You know there is! A hundred-and-seventy-million-dollar project *and they can't use it*? What's going to happen when that gets into the papers? Where are they going to get their power? Are they going to close down those factories? Is Darby going to get the blame for that? We could all wind up in front of some committee, on television — "

"Ordway, what the hell has gotten into you? You heard the engineers, they spent all day explaining, they're going to use the plant, it's just a question of working out some bugs in a new process — "

"Charlie, I hope to God the scrubbers will work, but that isn't the point. The point is we've got to tell people we've got a problem. This is the kind of thing an investor would want to be told, isn't it? Wouldn't you want to be told? We've somehow talked ourselves into the position that it's not a big problem, it's not what they call material — well, that's bullshit, it *is* material, and both of us know it!"

He stared at me for a long moment. His face changed.

"You're chicken!"

"Aw Charlie!"

"We run into a few problems and the Messrs. Conyers & Dean develop cold feet. Oh, they don't mind collecting two or three hundred grand in fees every year, even from the gardener's son — it's all money, after all — but when we get down to the nitty-gritty, when the client really has his balls in the wringer, then the Messrs. Conyers & Dean suddenly develop very high ethics — "

"That's unfair, Charlie! You know we've overcome one hurdle after another, we've moved heaven and earth for you — "

"For Christ's sake, Harry Hatch thinks it's okay. Are you smarter than he is? One of the biggest law firms in the world?"

"I think he's wrong. This thing is going to come back to haunt us all — "

"Sandy Simon thinks it's okay, one of the biggest firms on the Coast. Are you so much smarter than they are, Ordway? Would you really call yourself a top-notch lawyer? Or would you call yourself a guy who's had every goddamned thing in life handed to him on a silver platter." He was shouting now, his face red. I was thankful the door was shut, but even so —

"Now wait a minute — "

"Every goddamned *thing!* While I had to work my ass to the bone morning noon and night since I was sixteen years old and I built a four-hundred-million-dollar company out of nothing. Out of nothing! A sick old sheet and tube company eighteen months away from bankruptcy, and I built it all up by myself, and you're supposed to be my lawyer! Aren't you supposed to be my lawyer?"

"Yes, I am your lawyer."

"You're my lawyer? A lawyer is supposed to help when his client gets in trouble, isn't he? Here we run into a little flak and it isn't the other guys' lawyers that shoot me down, *it's my own lawyer!*"

There was no use arguing with him. He was frantic. I knew it would be bad but I didn't think it would be this bad. I looked down at the carpet while he struggled to control himself, breathing heavily.

"House of cards," he said, more quietly, his voice shaking. "Banks going to move in — "

"We'll work out something with the banks — "

"We'll work out *shit!*" It came quietly now, through clenched teeth. "You and I are through, Ordway!"

"I'm sorry."

"Are you? Really? Now that everything is going to hit the fan? Or are you just as glad to get those fine gentlemen at Conyers & Dean out of the line of fire?"

"No, I'm as sorry as I've ever been about anything in my life, Charlie. We could really help you, but you've got to play it our way."

"Yeah. Play it your way. You know where I'd be today if I always played it your way? You wouldn't even *know* me, Ordway!" He was speaking more quietly now, but his eyes were still wild and he couldn't catch his breath. "I'm going out there now . . . and I'm going to tell them . . . I'm going to tell them what the great firm of Conyers & Dean has done to me . . . what my own lawyer . . . has done to me — "

"Wait a minute, Charlie." I stood up and blocked his way.

We stared into each other's eyes. He was sweating. I thought he was going to hit me. "If you go out there in this state, you'll really blow everything. Just look at yourself. What are they going to think when they see you? The only way to handle this — after you've calmed down — is to tell them it's *your* decision: *you've* decided to withdraw the issue — on advice of counsel, of course — because of the Turkey River contract, because you may have to restate your earnings and you want the investment community to know that before you put out the Debentures. Honest to God, Charlie, it's the only way!"

A curtain fell over his eyes. "I need legal advice," he muttered, turning away from me, opening the door. "Young lady, would you go find your boss and ask him if he could see me alone for a few minutes?"

As long as I live I won't forget the horrified looks on the faces of the youngest men from Conyers & Dean — the ones who had prepared the closing papers — nor the gleam of surprise in the eyes of Thomas Sharp, Esq., as Charlie Conroy calmly read the announcement Harry Hatch had written out for him. Every eye in the room focused on me. The Frenchman had his sunglasses on again, but it seemed to me that I could see his eyes right through them.

One of the brokers, *sotto voce:* "That's the ballgame. We're in the red for sixty-nine. Bye-bye bonus."

"Bye-bye Conroy," whispered his neighbor.

Harry Hatch's first reaction had been an icy stare: "I take it you know something we don't?"

"No, you have all the facts we have, Harry. I'm just drawing a different conclusion."

For a moment he continued to stare at me, genuinely puzzled. If he knew how, he would have shrugged. Then he swung into action. Young lawyers from Iselin Bros. & Devereaux were suddenly all over the place, very competently moving in, taking charge, calling the branch chief at the SEC, calling the New York Stock Exchange, calling Dow Jones, calling a financial writer on the New York *Times*. Listening to their smooth self-assured explanations of Charlie's statesmanlike decision ("Right . . . Right . . . Under the circumstances we all felt that it was the only proper course. . . ."), you would think it was based on their advice.

I stood in one corner, very much alone, watching Tommy and the others collect the useless closing papers into their briefcases. Bernard Bromberg shouldered his way through the crowd and stood in front of me. He looked better than he had yesterday. There was a small enigmatic smile on his face.

"Had second thoughts, didn't you?"

I nodded.

"Want to hear something strange?" He glanced over his shoulder and moved closer. "I'm relieved. Can you imagine that? Four months of work, four months of negotiations, four months wasted time, fifty-sixty-seventy thousand dollars of expenses down the tube, a paper loss of twenty-four dollars a share, stockholders who will be climbing the walls . . . and I'm *relieved*? What do you make of that?"

"That's not hard to figure out," I said.

"It's not, huh?"

"You didn't really want to sell."

He put his hands into his pockets and stood beside me, facing the room. He said nothing.

"You really want to be your own boss," I said feeling light-headed, feeling numb, feeling that I was saying something I wouldn't say under normal circumstances. "And maybe you really want to give your son a chance to show what he can do."

326

It caught him off guard. He stared at me. Was he angry? I couldn't tell.

"My fine-feathered friend," he said very slowly. "You certainly turned out to be full of surprises." He put out his hand. "I'll say goodbye now, Justin and I are going to round up our people and catch our plane. We'll leave Sandy behind to clean up. It's been quite an experience, Ordway. Maybe our paths will cross again."

The room was emptying. Justin Silverstone shook hands, Sandy Simon shook hands. The First Hudson people shook hands, but they were embarrassed, shaking hands with a dead man.

Tommy Sharp said: "All the papers are packed, we can leave any time."

"No time like the present," I said. "Where's Harry?"

Harry was closeted with Charlie Conroy and the Frenchman, it turned out. His young lawyers were embarrassed too. Piles of CCC Prospectuses overflowed the wastebaskets. We said goodbye, and I led my team of briefcase-laden lawyers out of the room.

We were alone in the elevator. The two youngest men looked straight ahead, stunned.

"I'm sorry, fellows," I said. "You've all done a splendid job on this deal, and I appreciate it. I'm sorry it turned into such a mess."

"Ordway," said Tommy Sharp, "I'd like to say . . . I'd like you to know . . . that I've never been so impressed in my life. I want you to know that."

The other two exchanged glances.

"Object lesson," I said. "How to lose your biggest client."

Tommy Sharp shook his head. "Had to be done. But I

327

else would have done it. I'm never going to for-
...s.

"Thanks. That's very nice of you. I guess I'm not going to forget it either."

Tommy smiled. "The subway's in the basement here. May I assume we're not heading for the helicopter pad?"

"Basement, please." The numbness was wearing off now, the bad pain was just beginning, but for a moment I felt a little better.